✦ ROBERT F. JONES ✦

THE RUN
TO
GITCHE GUMEE

A NOVEL

THE LYONS PRESS

Guilford, Connecticut
An imprint of The Globe Pequot Press

Copyright © 2001 by Robert F. Jones

ALL RIGHTS RESERVED. No part of this book may be reproduced or transmitted in any form by any means, electronic or mechanical, including photocopying and recording, or by any information storage or retrieval system, except as may be expressly permitted by the 1976 Copyright Act or in writing from the publisher. Requests for permission should be addressed to The Globe Pequot Press, P.O. Box 480, Guilford, CT 06437.

The Lyons Press is an imprint of The Globe Pequot Press.

Printed in United States of America
Designed by A Good Thing Inc.

10 9 8 7 6 5 4 3 2 1

Library of Congress Cataloguing-in-Publication data is available on file.

ISBN 1-58574-406-9

For Benno, who paddles his own canoe . . .

North Haven Memorial Library
North Haven, Conn. 06473

THE RUN

TO

GITCHE GUMEE

And here face down beneath the sun

And here upon earth's noonward height

To feel the always coming on

The always rising of the night. . . .

—**Archibald MacLeish**

⟡ PART I ⟡
DOWNSTREAM BEBOP
(Autumn: 1950)

ON THE WATER

From the height of land where the river rises, you can sometimes see the far, faint, steelblue glint of big water in the distance. Lake Superior lies fifty or sixty miles to the north, but more like a hundred if you meant to reach it, as we did, by canoe along the twists and turns of the Firesteel River. The country between the height of land and the big lake was wild and tough, much as its first explorers found it three hundred years earlier. The only thing missing, or so we thought, were the savages who once lived here.

It was a clear, crisp morning in the middle of September. We stood beside a black, rust-blotched iron trestle spanning the headwaters of the river. The logging truck that had brought us this far clattered across the loose floorboards of the bridge and disappeared to the west, toward Solon Springs and a load of white cedar. The canoe, a heavy, eighteen-foot Old Town framed in cedar and covered with dark green canvas, much patched after years of abuse, rested in the grass at the edge of the dirt road. She was a fat old pig, slow and hard to maneuver in white water, but she was our pig and we loved her.

Beside the canoe stood our dunnage, a waist-high, lopsided pile of sleeping bags, fry pans, cook pots, and water pails; orange crates filled with cans and bottles and vials of items as various as Hormel chili, Old Woodsman's brand fly dope, Chef Boyardee spaghetti and meatballs, Quaker Oats, Dinty Moore beef stew, Brisling sardines, bread-and-butter pickles, Ritz crackers, strawberry jam, mayonnaise, anchovies, a mason jar full of brown sugar, two tins of Carnation evaporated milk, a large box of waxed, sulphur-tipped kitchen matches, two boxes of Aunt Jemima's pancake mix, a quart of Skippy's peanut butter, a smoke-blackened coffee pot within which nested a tangle of war surplus aluminum knives, forks, and spoons that tinkled discordantly whenever the load was jostled; three loaves of already squashed Wonder Bread; a stained black canvas tarpaulin that smelled of woodsmoke; two pairs of swim fins and face masks, a spear gun powered with surgical tubing; a leather-sheathed cruising ax that needed sharpening; a roll of fine-meshed mosquito netting; two cased 12-gauge shotguns, Harry's a double-barreled Winchester Model 21, mine a battered Remington Model 29A pump action prone to jamming; and a pair of disassembled two-section flyrods stowed in light, much dented, metal tubes: an elegant, amber-finished nine-foot Payne of split Tonkin bamboo (guess whose) and an eight-and-a-half-foot hardware-store Heddon, all cracked varnish and rusty snake guides, that, when assembled and placed beside the Payne, looked about as graceful as a telephone pole. A case of waxed paper shotgun shells, two canvas reel cases, and several neatly labeled Hardy flyboxes topped off the load. We'd tied all the flies ourselves and we knew they worked. And even if they didn't, they were pretty.

"My God, Hairball," I said, "we don't need half this shit. We'll only be six days on the river. With all this gear we'll be shipping water even on the calm stretches."

"L-luxury, Benjamin," Harry said. "You never know when you'll need a dose of it. Believe me, when you get to K-Korea you'll look back on this journey with delight."

I took some comfort from those words. They were an admission of doubt. Harry stuttered only when he wasn't sure of himself.

On top of the pile perched Harry's black leather saxophone case, scuffed and battered from many trips we'd made together. Harry had discovered Lester Young and Charlie Parker a year or two ago, and he now played the alto sax. He'd always been good at music, even in grade school, and now he was a full-fledged bopper. Or that's how I saw it anyway. On outings like this, Harry riffed on his "ax," as he called it, with me ticking out the beat on empty tin cans or riverside rocks, pushing it up to the big bang on hollow logs in camp at night. Or even in the canoe, tapping time on the thwarts as we drifted in unpromising trout water. But Harry is always above the beat, wailing away with the water.

His sax is fluent where his tongue isn't.

I pulled the Coast and Geodetic Survey map from the pocket of my fatigue jacket and spread the stiff, recalcitrant sheet against the iron beam of the bridge abutment.

On the topo map, the headwaters of the Firesteel resembled a spider web, broad at the top, its strands flimsy and tentative at first, then thickening as the rivulets gained strength from one another, the webbed skein narrowing toward the bottom until it spun itself into a single liana-like strand, the main stem of the river snaking its way toward the lake.

"Okay," I said, placing a finger on the map, "we're here." I looked up from the map, to the north. "Hey, have a gander, you can see Lake Superior! Gitche Gumee, by God. The shining Big-Sea-Water."

Harry adjusted his glasses and peered where my eyes were pointing. He squinted. "Bullshit," he said. "I don't see anything but t-treetops. If your gumee really gitches that bad, I think I've got a can of baby powder in one of those boxes somewhere."

"No, really, if you look real hard you can just make it out—that brighter blue. Hell, I can even see whitecaps."

"Old Eagle Eye," Harry said. "Any action in the wigwam of Nokomis?" He leered and waggled his eyebrows, Groucho fashion.

I looked back down at the map again. Smart ass. Hiawatha was long gone from these parts. "This first stretch of the run seems kind of twisty," I said. "What they call meanders. A lot of muskeg and tamarack, I suppose, slow water. All this country hereabouts is fed by limestone seeps, the roots of mountains scrubbed flat by the glacier. The guy I talked to at that tackle shop in Tomahawk said the upper section of the Firesteel is like an enormous English spring creek, all marl and sand on the bottom, packed full of watercress and big, juicy brook trout."

"Good eating, them specs," Harry said. "And not too choosy when it comes to f-flies."

So why did he have to bring along those canned sardines? Then I remembered. Back in grade school, I'd known him to eat sandwiches made of peanut butter, strawberry jam, and sardines. Sometimes he'd even add a dollop of mayo.

"Well," I said, "we'd better start humping this stuff or we'll never get on the river."

Harry Taggart and I had been friends since kindergarten, growing up together in Heldendorf, a small farming and logging town in central Wisconsin. His dad owned the sawmill in town. My dad was the yard foreman. We both played football, ran track, and swam on Heldendorf High's state championship swim squad, Harry the butterfly, I in the freestyle sprints. During those high school summers we'd worked as lifeguards together at the town's Olympic-sized public swimming pool. But our real love was the wild country, or at least what remained of it. Since we were little kids we'd been prowling the woods and swamps and lakes and streams that surrounded the town, hunting, trapping, fishing, and just generally fucking around in boats. When the war in Korea broke out that June, just after high school graduation, I'd enlisted in the Marine Corps. The great regret of my young life so far was that I'd missed World War II. Here was my chance to redeem that lost opportunity. To get a taste of fame and glory.

So far it was hardly that. I'd completed boot camp at Parris Island during the summer, a ten-week nightmare of aching muscles, muck, bugs, leeches, stifling heat, and soul-crunching humiliation that made football, even in the mud and blood of a Wisconsin winter, look like a game of patty-cake. I was due to ship out from the West Coast at the end of September, when my transit leave was up. In Pusan I'd join the 1st Marine Division. Harry was draft exempt. He'd just started his first year of premed at Marquette University. Though we sensed it only vaguely at the time, this farewell fling on the state's last wild river would mark the watershed between boyhood and maturity for both of us. An alembic of sorts.

Only that morning, deadheading north with the canoe in a logging truck owned by Harry's father, we'd heard on the radio of MacArthur's surprise Inchon landing. The newscaster called it a masterstroke. With one brilliant move, Dugout Doug had outflanked the gook army that had pinned our boys in the Pusan perimeter since early summer. The commies were in full retreat. I remember worrying, as we listened to that broadcast, that the war might be over before I got there. I had nothing to fear. Not that anything scared me in those days. I was, as they say, too dumb to choke.

By straight-up noon we had the Old Town launched and loaded. She rode a bit low in the water, but there was still plenty of freeboard for the rapids downriver. We'd tucked the waterproof tarp over the crates, which occupied the center of the canoe. I paddled stern, with Harry, who was lighter, in the bow. The river ran cold and clear, the color of liquefied amber, and I could see a mosaic of small stones and pea gravel shimmering on the bottom through five feet of silent, fast-moving water. The aspens were just beginning to turn, the oval, pale green leaves yellowing at their roughtoothed edges. Here and there a swamp maple blazed bright as blood against the cloudless blue sky of midday. Ahead, where the Firesteel widened and slowed as it entered the swamp, white cedars grew thick and dark green from the shallow water. In the bow Harry was rigging his flyrod.

"What do you think, an Adams?"

"Might as well," I said. "Try a Number Ten if you've got one—big fly, big trout. I'll use a Royal Coachman. Brookies go ape for them."

The swamp was a necklace of deep, blue-floored spring pools strung on a narrow, cedar-flanked flowage. Elodea fringed the pools. The skeletons of drowned pines stood tall and barkless, bone white against the low, dark alders and cedars that dominated the bog. A family of mergansers sculled downstream ahead of us, the chicks drab but almost full grown, and a great blue heron took flight from the reeds, squawking like a rusty hinge. In places we had to duck low to avoid cedar boughs, but then the channel widened into a broad, quiet, sunlit pool. Here and there hummocks of pale cattail and spiky marshgrass rose roundtopped from the water like the heads of submerged giants. The current barely moved in here, the breeze was dead, dragonflies clicked like knitting needles above the water and mated in midair. No black flies, though. The frosts of early fall must have killed them.

Harry worked out twenty feet of flyline, thirty feet, and dropped the Adams near the right-hand edge of the pool. I backed water with my paddle, stirring up a cloud of pale blue marl from the bottom. We watched the fly turn as it danced on the surface, twirling slow and delicate, its hackles tracing silver runes on the water's meniscus.

A dark blue shadow moved out from waterweed. Fast at first, then slower as it neared the fly. I could see the pale wormlike squiggles across its broad black back, the red and bluegray and yellow spots scattered along its flanks, and the larger red spots haloed in a brighter blue. The large spots looked the size of dimes.

A foot and a half if he's an inch, I thought. No. Twenty inches. Maybe three pounds.

The brook trout hovered beneath the Adams, hesitant and suspicious. Then two more shadows darted out of the weed, smaller fish, and with that the big trout surged upward, engulfing the fly. I could see the take, just a quick white flash. Harry's rod bowed as he set the hook. He turned and grinned back at me.

"Bingo!" he said.

The ratchet of his reel sang, and he snapped back to full attention, caught up in the fight. The big fish bucked at the sting of the hook, rolling with a heavy splash, and I could see the broad, dark orange lozenge shapes of his pectoral fins, edged in ivory, the belly going brick red where it flanked the white along the trout's bottom. Already into his spawning colors. He dove back toward the safety of the weeds.

"Turn him!"

"I'm t-trying!"

Just short of the weeds the brookie tipped sideways and veered off downstream. Harry raised his rod tip and palmed the whirring spool.

"Christ, don't bust him off!"

"It's a f-f-four X tippet. No fear."

He turned the fish at the far end of the pool and began to regain line. By now the bottom of the pool was clouded with stirred marl. I cleared the long-handled landing net from under the tarp. In the milky swirls I could see the dark, panic-stricken shapes of lesser trout darting in and out of the clouds like pursuit planes in a newsreel dogfight. Harry brought the big trout to the side of the canoe, and I leaned forward and netted it. It lay on its side in the mesh, gills heaving. The hook was lodged tight in the hinge of its mouth. Its dark eyes looked big as quarters.

"That's a hell of a fish."

"Biggest brookie I've ever seen," Harry said. "M-much less caught. Do we kill it or let it go?"

"Your call."

"The big ones don't eat that good."

"I bet he goes better than four pounds. Closer to five." I leaned over and spread my hand wide, measuring the trout in spans. "Call it nine inches from the end of my thumb to the tip of the little finger. Damn near three hand spans. Say twenty-four inches." I shook my head in disbelief. "Make a damn nice mount."

"We don't have any ice. By the time we get to the take-out he'll smell pretty ripe." Harry reached down, wet his hands, and worked the fly loose. He lifted the trout clear of the net by its belly and held it upright in the water, head upstream, working it back and forth in the minimal current.

"*In nomine Patris, et Filii, et Spiritus Sancti*," he intoned in a deep voice. "*Ego te absolvo.* Or s-something like that."

The gill action slowed, the big eyes began to roll. Where am I? The fish shook its head, as if shrugging off a nightmare or a hard blow, then burst from Harry's loose grip and lunged back to cover, splashing us both as it dove with a flip of its broad, square tail.

Harry looked up, grinning. "Okay," he said. "This pool is finished for now. What say we absquatulate?"

That brookie fish, taken on the first cast of the trip, proved to be the biggest either of us caught that day. In the next pool downstream Harry did the paddling while I fished, taking three smaller brook trout, ten or twelve inches, which we knocked on the head for supper. In the next pool below, Harry caught a fifteen-incher that we added to the wicker creel that trailed in the water from the rear thwart. From then on we pinched down the barbs on our flies and released everything we caught. Thirty-four brook trout in all that first day. As the afternoon wore along, we fished less and paddled more, hoping to clear the swamp by nightfall. The shadows were lengthening and with them came clouds of mosquitoes, big black ones. We slathered ourselves in Old Woodsman's fly dope and traveled on in an acrid, not-unpleasant cloud that smelled of creosote. "Ah, the traditional aroma of the North Woods," Harry sighed, turning his face skyward as he paddled. "Fresh air, pine needles, babbling brooks, cold stove pipes, and sweaty skivvies. Don't you love it, old bean?"

"You missed your calling, Hairball," I told him. "You ought to be an ad man."

Now the channel broadened. Ahead through the breaks in the cedar jungle we could see sunlight on what looked like open meadows. The skeletons of a few fire-charred white pines stood scattered in a field of bluestem. Blowdowns littered the field like corpses. Wind worked across the grass from the northwest. We entered the last of the spring pools, a deep, broad reach of windowglass clarity, and paused. A pile of big cedar logs lay crosshatched on the bottom, half sunk in the blue marl. I pulled out the topo map and studied it.

"The tackle shop guy in Tomahawk said there's old burn just below the swamp," I told him. "We can pull out there, plenty of dry firewood from the deadfalls, and that breeze should keep the mosquitoes down." I looked at my watch. "Ten of six. Plenty of time to pitch camp. What do you say to a swim? This water's too good to pass up."

"Let's do it." Harry grabbed a pair of fins and his face mask. "I wonder what's hiding out down there in the cedar logs?"

"We'll see soon enough."

I tied off the canoe to a cedar stump and stripped to my red nylon Heldendorf racing trunks. Harry was already in the water, adjusting his fins and spitting on the glass of his face mask, spreading it in a thin film to prevent fogging. He rinsed the mask lightly in the water and slipped it on. I eased over the side, careful not to capsize the canoe, and joined him.

"Move quiet," I said. "We don't want to spook anything down there."

The pool was maybe twenty feet. We dove without splashing and finned our way down, clearing our ears en route. I could see feathers of sand squirting from vents in the marl bottom, the springs at work, feeding the Firesteel. We ghosted down toward the logs.

They don't grow cedars like that anymore. Some of them looked to be a yard through at their bases. Thirty, forty feet long. All neatly sawed and limbed, felled by the crosscut crews back in Paul Bunyan times. They must have broken loose from a logging raft during the spring breakup half a century ago or more, hung up here in the swamp, then got waterlogged over the years and sunk. Nowadays loggers take them before they mature. If you could retrieve these logs, snag them the hell out of here and dry them out, you'd make a tidy penny. Maybe after Korea. . . .

Harry pointed ahead, down toward the bottom. A pod of medium-sized brook trout gathered around the biggest spring vent, circling it as if hypnotized. They paid us no heed. I nodded to indicate that I saw them. Harry shook his head and pointed again, into a blueblack shadow cast by the thickest cedar log. I looked closer. Then I saw it, a long, dark, torpedo-shaped form, almost motionless except for the barely perceptible sideways sweep of its tail. Harry swam closer. The fish looked to be a yard long, maybe more. With the magnification provided by the face mask, they always seem bigger than they turn out to be. I glanced over at Harry and raised my eyebrows. Wow! Then gestured toward the surface.

"Either that's the biggest brook trout in history," he said when we'd caught our breath, "or it's M-Moby Sturgeon."

"I'd vote for sturgeon."

"But I didn't see any bony plates or whiskers and the tail seemed symmetrical. I looked pretty close."

"You're not wearing your glasses, Hairb."

"At that range I don't need 'em. I was only about six feet from him. Christ, Ben, he makes that brookie I caught in the first pool look like a minnow." Harry swam back to the canoe. "I'm g-gonna take the spear gun and have another look."

"Could be a giant brown," I said. "One of those cannibals you read about. The guy in Tomahawk told me the stretch below the swamp is brown trout water. You don't want to spear a trophy German brown. Not when we could take it on a fly."

"I'm only bringing the spear for p-protection," Harry said. "See you in a m-minute or two."

"Go get 'em, Ahab," I said.

Peering from the surface through the mask, I watched him finning slow and easy down toward the log. He was approaching it against the current, in the fish's blind spot. When he got to the log, he ducked to the very bottom on the side away from the shadow. He pulled himself forward along the rotting bark. Big chunks of it pulled loose in his hand and spun away lazily in the stream. Clots of bark and waterbugs spiraled toward the surface. When he was opposite the darker shadow of the fish, he pulled himself up and peered over the top. Suddenly the shadow moved into the sunlight—a long, dark-flashing flick of muscle and mocha brown flecked with a galaxy of black spots, butter yellow along the vast bulge of its belly—the biggest brown trout I'd ever seen. Its jaws were hooked, its amber eye huge.

Gone in an instant, upstream. . . .

Harry burst through the surface a moment later and yanked off his mask. His eyes were sparking. "You were right! A giant brown! My God, did you ever see a t-trout like that?"

"Never. He's got to go twenty pounds or better. A cannibal all right, and this pool's his cafeteria. Let's come back tonight when the moon rises and have a shot at him."

Harry bobbed his head up and down, grinning. "You're on!"

2

THE CANNIBAL-KILLER

W e made camp on a gravel bar a few hundred yards below the swamp, under a cutbank that would protect us from the night wind. There was plenty of time until dark. While I collected water-smoothed stones for a fire ring, Harry took the ax and wandered back into the meadow of deadfalls to gather wood. I pulled the tarp off the canoe and rigged a lean-to with a couple of dead, fire-hardened pine poles to serve as end poles, trimming them to size with my handy-dandy K-Bar knife, weighting the windward edge with heavy rocks. Then hauled the sleeping bags, gun cases, and orange crates up to the shelter. I gathered sticks for kindling, pulled over a big, barkless log of beached driftwood and placed it upwind of the makeshift firepit for us to sit on. Then I went up into the field to help Harry with the firewood. I could hear him thudding away, cussing, before I got to the top of the bank.

"This ax is dull," he said when I came up. He had a sizable pile of pine branches stacked beside the blowdown already. They looked less chopped to length than chewed.

"There's a new invention on the market," I said. "It's called a file. In combination with a whetstone, it works miracles on dull steel. You might think of getting one. Maybe even both."

"I've got a file somewhere in that pile of crap I brought along, but I never remember to use it."

"This is firewood enough anyway," I said. "Let's haul it back to camp."

Halfway to the river Harry veered a bit to the right and called me over. "Take a look at this," he said. "I spotted it earlier coming up."

In a low, wet swale was a fresh pawprint, broad at the toes, narrow at heel. As long at least as my own foot, size eleven. Three inches out from the toetips were the indentations of its claws, thick around as a No. 2 pencil.

"Black bear," he said. "And there's a big shit pile over there aways, full of seed hulls." He pointed with his chin toward a thicket of blackberry bushes.

"Looks pretty recent," I said. "He's a big guy. Or gal. Fattening up for winter. Fuck. I just hauled the food boxes up from the canoe." I looked around. The only trees near our campsite were a few spindly aspens a hundred yards or so downstream. "No trees tall or strong enough to cache it in, either."

"Maybe the fire will keep him away, and we've got the guns if it comes to that."

"Bird shot will only piss the bastard off."

"I brought along a box of slugs, just in case," he said.

"Christ," I said.

"Maybe he's moved on," Harry said.

"Let's hope so."

There was a bit of a nip to the air now with the sun low on the pine-spiked horizon. Long cool shadows stretched across the meadows, and the wind had the taste of ice. I got the fire going. Harry rummaged around in his duffel bag and I heard the clank of glass on metal. "Ta-*da*!" he said, turning toward me with a triumphant grin. He held up a bottle of Johnny Walker Black Label and a couple of tin cups. "I liberated this from my dad's liquor cabinet. For medicinal purposes only, of course. But as a member of the profession, albeit somewhat junior, I hereby officially diagnose us as suffering from incipient hypothermia, dehydration, scrofula, and, uh, d-d-dengue fever, the specific for which is Squire Black's Peerless Elixir, such as that contained in this phial. The recommended dosage, the American Medical Association assures me, is half a cup, diluted to taste with cold, crystalline branch water. Repeat frequently if necessary."

"Not too frequently, one hopes," I said. "Not with that bear on the prowl, and a cannibal brown waiting for us."

We dined that night on fried brook trout and onions, boiled potatoes with plenty of salt and black pepper, and a watercress salad fresh from the Firesteel, slathered with Hellman's Miracle Whip for dressing. We shared a river-chilled can of sliced peaches for dessert. They slid down smooth in their syrup. There was, after all, something to be said for luxury. I hadn't eaten near that good at Parris Island.

We sat beside the fire after dinner, me sipping black coffee and Harry noodling around on his saxophone, while we waited for the moonrise. It occurred to me that I hadn't thought once of Korea since we got on the river. I wasn't scared, but I sure was nervous about it. Despite all the gung-ho crap they fed us at boot camp, I wasn't ready yet to die for the Crotch, as the old World War II Marine vets called it. Our DI at Parris Island was a lifer from Louisiana, Staff Sergeant Beauregard Stingley, an old China hand. He'd taken a face full of Japanese grenade fragments on Peleliu and his skin was pitted like the moon. He wore a wicked little cookie duster of a mustache, jet black, and his eyes were cold as a shark's. The foulest-mouthed man in America. "You were born from the crotch, and you'll die for the Crotch," he told us every day. "You'll die for your buddies, and they'll die for you. That's the way it works. You'll charge machine guns and throw yourselves on grenades and be blown to fuckin' bits. But your buddies will collect every last little motherfuckin' chunk they can find of your sorry butt so they can bury it with you. I've peeled jarhead tongues and eyeballs from the hot coral of Bloody Nose Ridge, and untangled miles of ripe jungle green guts from the mangroves at the mouth of the Tenaru, and you'll do the same or worse in Korea. Get used to the idea, you candyass pogues. It's your motherfuckin' future. The loyalty of the Crotch."

Bloody Nose Ridge, I learned later, was the Jap strongpoint called Umurbrogol on Peleliu that was supposed to be an easy walkover but turned the campaign into ten weeks of hell. That's where S.Sgt. Beauregard Stingley, then a PFC, caught his kisser-load of steel. The Tenaru River was on Guadalcanal. Tough old Sergeant Stingley's dead and gone now, fifty years later, but I still dream about those tongues of his.

The main post-prandial question confronting our two-man debating society was what to throw at the monster brown. We sorted through our flyboxes by the flickering light of the campfire, looking for something enticing. Dries wouldn't work, not even our largest, nor would nymphs. Nothing buggy. This guy liked sushi, and he liked it alive and twitching.

"What we really need here is a streamer," I said.

"None of those brookies we saw in the pool were very big," Harry said. "He's probably scarfed down all the good-sized ones." He opened a flybox and pulled out a fistful of long-shanked ties—old patterns like the Gray Ghost, Yellow Butcher, and Parmachene Belle; an assortment of Muddler Minnows in various sizes; darters both gold and silver; a couple of gaudy Mickey Finns.

"The Mickey Finn's a good attractor, all right," I said. "And the Parmachene Belle imitates the pectoral fin of a brookie. But we need something big and meaty for this guy. A great hairy muddler, maybe a Number 2, bigger than anything we've got in here, or better yet a long, shaggy bucktail—something in red and white and green and a touch of yellow, like a small brook trout."

"Wait a minute." Harry went back to the canoe and rummaged around in the bow. He came back with a tackle box full of bait-casting hardware: silver spoons, Bass-O-Renos, Dardevles, Pikey Minnows, and such like. "I figured we might troll one of these things from that telephone pole of yours if we came to some long, dull stretches, you know, downriver aways. But I think there's a big bucktail in here somewheres. My dad uses it for northerns and muskies." He clanked around in there a bit, then said, "*Voilà!*"

He showed me a long, bushy hunk of deerhair dyed in all the aforementioned colors. It was perfect. We cannibalized the lure, discarding the heavy 4/O hook, and then stripped a beat-up White Marabou down to its No. 4 Mustad-Viking longshank. In lieu of a fly vise, I held the hook in the firelight with a pair of needlenose pliers while Harry, who already had a surgeon's deft hand with knots, tied it to my directions—weighting the hook first with a thin strip of hammered lead, then wrapping the shank to the bend in leftover oval silvery tinsel, winging the fly in long strands of white and red bucktail topped with green peacock herl from our bag of spare feathers, and touching it off with cheeks of jungle cock flecked in yellow. After he'd whip-finished the tie, we daubed on a hefty drop of black lacquer for a head.

"Okay," I said as we waited for the lacquer to dry, "now what do we do about the bear? We can't just leave this food lying around camp. He'll smell it a mile off. But if we put it back in the canoe, it'll be a bitch paddling upstream to the pool. Remember that stretch of rapids just when we left the swamp?"

"I think he's gone," Harry said. "Skedaddled. Moved on to greener pastures. He'd about cleaned out that blackberry patch, from what I could see, and they travel far and fast in the fall. He's probably clear over to Antigo by now."

"Well, if you say so. Most of that chow is yours, anyway. I was figuring on us living off the land on this trip. Let's just take a light load in the canoe, the necessaries—matches, the coffee, salt and pepper, maybe that tin of lard to grease the skillet."

"And a loaf of Wonder Bread, along with the peanut butter and strawberry jam. I might get hungry around midnight."

The moon, waning toward its last quarter, sneaked over the horizon at about ten o'clock. Coyotes hailed it in the distance, their yelps and yips and yodels coming faint to us as the country turned cold silver, peened flat in the moonlight. We paddled back upriver by its dim glow. The canoe rode high in the water now and we made good time. There was a snag sticking up in the midstream shallows just below the rapids, shuddering in the current. We tied the canoe off to it, dropping the mushroom anchor as an extra precaution, and waded wet to the far bank, carrying our flyrods and a flashlight. I led the way with the light. Harry carried the makings of his midnight snack in a brown paper bag. The water was cold, below fifty I reckoned.

The going in the swamp was tricky. The gravel of the riverbottom quickly gave way to marl and black muck. It sucked at our sneakers and sometimes with a misstep we sank to knee depth. I eased over to the bank of the channel and tried to walk the tops of drowned sawlogs but they were slick with algae. To do it right you needed the balance of a gibbon. Mosquitoes were out in force by now, and we'd forgotten the Old Woodsman's. Harry fell twice. With the second splash he cursed out loud. "Fuck! I think I got the Wonder Bread wet."

"Pipe down," I whispered. "Cannibal browns have sharp ears."

We slogged to the edge of the big pool, where we found the footing slippery but a bit firmer, then hunkered down to watch and listen. The moonlight glinted on the dead calm water and the pool's bottom seemed to glow with a faint, dancing incandescence. The sunken cedar logs looked like submarines down there. We could see a few small shadows still circling at the spring vents but no sign of the big brown. But he could be in the shadows of the logs, which were blacker by now than Sergeant Stingley's mustache. And twice as ominous.

Back at camp we'd flipped for first cast and Harry'd won. He had the new-tied bucktail clinch-knotted on a 2X tippet, taking extra care in lubricating the turns with saliva and drawing it tight with the pliers. We'd named our invention "The Firesteel Cannibal-Killer," christening it with a splash of Johnny Walker.

"Give it a shot," I whispered. "Lay it out parallel to the log where we saw him, and let it sink good and deep."

"I know, I know. What do you think I am, a baby?"

"No. Babies eat pablum, not peanut butter and jelly. And watch your backcast in here. You don't wanna get hung up and lose our best fly."

"Fuck you, d-d-daddy-o," he said.

He rolled the heavy streamer clear of the water, then loaded the rod up with two flat backcasts and threw a long, tight, forty-foot loop. The line snaked out straight and the Cannibal-Killer dropped to the surface with a hollow plop. We could see the fly sinking fast and squirrelly through the translucence. Just short of the log he checked its descent and began stripping in. Short, erratic strips at first, then a long one, then three more short. The streamer looked nearly a foot long down there, pulsing back in toward us magnified by water and moonlight, the deerhair undulating and swelling, then thinning again, like the pumping of a fish's gills.

"Looks good enough to eat," I said.

Two of the bigger brookies agreed. They darted up from their holding pattern near the vent toward the Cannibal-Killer, slowing as they approached it, then tailed it along the log for a ways before losing interest. Harry brought the fly in. No sign of Mr. Big.

"Give it half a dozen more casts, from different angles."

He nodded.

Harry worked the streamer every which way we could think of, varying his retrieves with each cast, fast and slow and in between, deep and shallow, short pulls and long, twitchy ones, even changing the direction of the Cannibal-Killer's route from time to time by swinging his rod tip right or left, up and down. Nothing doing.

"There's nobody home," he said at last.

"He could be up in the channel or one of the other pools. You want to go have a look-see?"

"It's your turn to throw," he said, handing me the rod. "Have at it. I'm gonna make myself a midnight snack. This flycasting is hard work. Gives a man an appetite." He opened the loaf of Wonder Bread and began slathering on the goop with his hunting knife.

I circled the big pool alone, wading waist- and sometimes tit-deep through marl and icewater, holding the rod high over my head with the Cannibal-Killer secured in the Payne's keeper-ring. Mosquitoes browsed on my neck and face, batting around with frantic zings in my nostrils and earholes. Tough going. I stopped often to look and listen, careful to make as little noise and disturbance as possible when I moved, especially as I entered the upstream feeder channel. It was dark in there, kind of spooky. The marl was like quicksand, and with every forward step I worried that I might hit a sinkhole. Harry would have a hell of a time hauling me out. Just by themselves, peanut butter and jelly had a soporific effect on him, like a cup of hot cocoa and two sleeping pills before nap time. I suspected he'd smuggled a tin of sardines along—he didn't like my kidding him about that childhood addiction—and I knew that the combination of fish oil, peanut oil, and sugared strawberries worked on him like a left hook from Sugar Ray Robinson. But I'd waded plenty of swamps before, especially on the long night marches with full field pack at Parris Island, where the sunken sawlogs had a way of turning into alligators when you stepped on them. "Gators like pogue-meat," Sergeant Stingley said. "Nice and sweet and tender. It's like candy to them. If one of 'em rears up and roars at you, just stick your rifle down his throat and squeeze the trigger. Give him a lead headache. That'll cool him off."

A short way up the channel I heard splashing ahead. It was loud in the silence of the swamp, magnified by the darkness, it seemed. My first thought was ducks—those mergansers we spooked earlier. But the splashes sounded bigger than anything a preening duck would make, and not near as regular. I eased my way forward, bent low beneath a cedar bough, then straightened up slow and easy. The narrow, kinky waterway ahead of me was partially lit by moonlight, stronger now than an hour earlier when the moon was low on the horizon. Something was working the right-hand edge of the channel. Quick silver flurries threw water wide on the rippling flowage. It pattered like falling birdshot. Then I saw a huge shiny back break the surface—otter, I thought. But it was followed by the rise of a broad, finned, forked tail.

The cannibal brown.

He was only about fifty feet away. I looked up and behind me to see if I had clearance for my backcast, but the cedars were too close. If I could only move ahead about twenty feet, I'd have a chance at him. He was preoccupied, busy rooting some hapless fish or bullfrog out of the brush roots. Maybe he wouldn't notice me. Crouching low, I snuck forward, the rod angled flat to the water. Like aquatic deer-stalking, I thought. No quick moves, no noise, move slow but steady. Then I was close enough. I unhooked the streamer from its ring and stripped off thirty feet of flyline, hold-ing the big loops loose in my left hand. I'd only have time for one quick backcast. Again I checked overhead and behind me. Okay, this is it.

I picked up ten feet of line and leader, snapped it out low behind me, the Payne loading up quick and heavy with the crisp, sure, elastic flexion of bamboo, then zipped the cast out tight to the water. The Cannibal-Killer splashed down with an attention-get-ting splat, ten feet ahead of my target and just a short way out toward the center of the channel. Right where I wanted it. Keep it shallow, I thought, so he can see it against the moonlight. I started stripping, a long, leisurely, lah-de-dah pull at first, brookie out for a midnight stroll, then picking up the pace as if the stroller sensed or saw its nemesis back there in the shadows and was scurrying to escape. Perhaps my own anxiety communicated itself up the rod and line, broadcasting a signal of panic, because in an instant the big brown turned from its hunt in the brush pile, flashed toward midstream with a visible bow wave, and slammed the streamer. Hard. The rod shuddered and I pulled back with my line hand. The No. 4 Mustad bit home.

I raised the rod tip with a whoop.

The channel exploded as the cannibal brown soared out full length, throwing water every which way—long and thick and dark and writhing like an irate anaconda. The hook of his kyped jaws ugly in the moonlight. Then he took off upchannel to the scream of the reel. I couldn't hold him, couldn't turn him, anymore than I could have held back the Midnight Special at full steam. Line whizzed off the spool as I sloshed after him up the waterway, the electric feel of him coming down the rod and up my arm like an ampule of adrenaline straight to the heart. I could hear Harry splashing behind me now, blowing hard. He'd come fast at my whoop.

We staggered and splashed ahead, me cranking in line when I could but losing more in the next step, slipping and skidding over drowned logs, feet snagged in soggy snarls of rotting brush, then breaking free, and at last we were at the rim of the next pool. The bottom sloped off and I stopped, burying the heels of my tennis shoes into the muck.

The cannibal brown sounded.

Thank God.

In the moonlight I could see the glint of bare metal at the heart of the spool. Only a few wraps of backing left.

I could feel him shaking his head, deep in the pool. He was mightily pissed.

Harry slogged up beside me, wet to the top of his crewcut. I raised the rod tip and dropped it, trying to pump the fish. He only shook his head harder. I tapped the rod butt with the heel of my hand. No go.

"I can't move him," I said. "He's down there and he won't budge." The Payne was bowed in a perfect, quivering arc. "You want to feel him?"

"Gimme."

I handed the rod to Harry and he shifted angles on the hook, moving the rod tip steeply to the left, then the right. Sometimes you can tip a fish on its side that way, confuse it, addle it, and then it gives up. The danger with this tactic, of course, is that you'll enlarge the hole in the fish's lip and the hook might pull free. We'd learned over the years to turn fish on their backs before trying to remove the hook. A trout or bass or even a big northern pike goes almost comatose when you show its belly to the sky.

But this guy wouldn't tip over.

"How was your sandwich?"

"Delicious."

I could smell sardines on his breath. "Up to your old kindergarten tricks again, I see. Or whiff. What's wrong with just plain peanut butter and jelly? It's an American classic. Only a geek would add fish."

"It's the new taste sensation," he said. "Ambrosia. They serve it in all the best restaurants from Palm Beach to New York. Hemingway himself invented it, back when he was a poor, struggling young pederast in Paris. If you weren't such a stodgy, unimaginative troll, you'd try it yourself. And lay *offa* me, why don't you?"

At that moment the cannibal brown said to hell with it. He took off upstream again. "Oh, fuck!" Harry yelped. The reel screamed. He leaned back against the surge, the rod bowed even steeper, the tip bounced once, twice—then snapped up straight.

I could swear I heard the hook pull loose, a hundred and ninety feet away.

"Shit house mouse," Harry intoned.

When we got back to camp, we saw that the bear—as it were—had eaten our homework.

3

"SERVIVERS WILL BE
PERSSACUTED!"

To give us a taste of what awaited our sorry butts in Korea, Sergeant Stingley one day marched the platoon out into the boonies and had us hunker down in a sandbagged bunker. The bunker was hopping with sand fleas. All the woods and swampgrass in the vicinity had been chewed up and pulped, pounded flat by machine-gun fire. An abandoned sharecropper's shack still stood about two hundred yards from us, all rotting boards and swaybacked roof, the windows fanged with shards of glass. Sergeant Stingley carried an SCR-563, what the doggies call a walkie-talkie. He called in the map coordinates of the shack to a mortar pit half a mile away. Way off through the swamp we heard a whump, then a long moment of silence broken only by the whine of mosquitoes, then a whuffling high in the sky that rose in pitch to a loud throaty whistle as it descended. The sharecropper's shack disappeared in an ear-splitting gout of orange and black. The ground shook. Wood splinters and clods of hard-baked clay bounced off our helmets. "That's just a small fuckin' hint of what a 81mm mortar round can fuckin' do," Stingley said. "We've got one now that's fuckin' 4.2 inches in fuckin' diameter."

When the dirt settled and the cordite fumes cleared, the shack looked like what was left that night of our camp on the Firesteel. The bear had left by the time we crunched ashore on the gravel bar. Our fire had died down, but when we got it blazing again, we saw what was left of our gear scattered all over the place. The bear had smashed most of the orange crates to splinters, eaten all of Harry's Wonder Bread, including the wax-paper wrappers, chewed up the cans of chili and spaghetti and spit out the mangled metal, covered the sleeping bags with a snowfall of Quaker Oats, holed the evaporated milk tins and sucked them dry, emptied

Aunt Jemima on the tarp and licked up most of the pancake mix. He must have absconded with the jar of brown sugar. Harry searched through the debris with the flashlight but couldn't find it anywhere. He did find his horn though, still safe and snug in its case. He whooped with joy, took it out, and blew a quick riff around "Yankee Doodle."

Then his eyes went all squirrelly. He glared at me.

"Where are the guns?" he shouted. "I can't find the guns!" His eyes all white at the edges, round in the dance of the firelight.

"Don't get your knickers in a twist," I said. "They're under the bug netting in the bottom of the canoe, under the ammo box. I knew this might happen and I didn't want 'em busted up or the barrels dinged. We'll need some firepower to keep us in meat the rest of the way downriver."

"Fuck downriver," Harry said. He stepped back to the canoe and retrieved his Model 21. He sorted through the shell boxes and came up with a couple of rifled slugs. "I want revenge, right now. That big fucking b-bully made off with my sardines."

"Don't be an asshole. He's at least half a mile away by now, and even if you did catch up with him, you couldn't be sure of hitting him in the dark. Not fatally at least, not with only two rounds in your tubes."

"G-g-goddamit," he said. He sat down heavily on the driftwood log by the fire and I thought he was going to cry. "I was looking forward to oatmeal and brown sugar for breakfast."

"And sardines for dessert, no doubt."

I was examining the sleeping bags for damage. Only a few claw rips, some kapok poking out, easily mended with the USMC sewing kit, what they call a "housewife," I'd brought along in my fieldpack. "It's okay," I told him. "I'll get up early and catch us a few trout for breakfast."

After checking the perimeter to make sure the bear was really gone, we spread the sleeping bags on the warm, dry sand near the fire. Harry settled in while I kept the first watch. Our loaded shotguns lay beside us. I made a pot of coffee and poured me a cup. Before Parris Island, I'd always put lots of cream and sugar in it, but Sergeant Stingley caught me drinking a cup of sweet, white java in the mess hall one day and chewed me out royally for all kinds of a pogue. "What's that fuckin' slop you're drinking, Slate Head? Looks like cum mixed with fuckin' dishwater. Has that got fuckin' milk in it? What's the fuckin' problem, you miss your mommy's titty?" The other guys in the platoon had a good laugh. Now I drank it black, and actually preferred it that way. Wonder why.

It was nice sitting there slumped against the log in my fartsack, owls hooting in the dark across the river, stars scattered like powdered sugar overhead. Now and then a shooting star whizzed across the sky, like a tracer round from God's machine guns, and once a night heron squawked as it flapped upriver, wondering at the flames along the shore. *Quok?* I got to thinking about Lorraine. She was my steady in high school, a dark-haired girl with big tits. My first. I remembered every detail: the threadbare upholstery in the front seat of my dad's old Plymouth, parked along the Pigeon River one fall night after a movie, her straddling me as I sat with her skirt hiked up over her hips and her skivvie shorts dangling from the gearshift. A night very much like this one, except that the car radio was humming, turned down low, and the windows were all steamed up. Teresa Brewer, I think it was—"Till I Waltz Again with You." Or maybe that was later. But still, it sure was some waltz. I was so grateful that I pledged undying love. Fidelity forevermore. Then Korea exploded. Other passions prevailed. When I joined the Marines, I broke it off with her. It didn't seem fair, either to Lorraine or to me. I'd be gone for four years. My *fidelis* from then on would have to be *semper* all right, but to the real Crotch, not hers, sweet as it was. And yet . . . And yet right now, and many a night at Parris Island, God knows, I missed her. Missed her bad.

Well, there's always tomorrow. Nothing is irrevocable, I thought. Nothing is forever. A guy can always change his mind. If this trip came off according to our time schedule, I'd still have

three or four days before I had to shove off for Camp Pendleton.
Maybe, if I still felt this way when we got back to town, I'd give
Lorraine a call.

When the Big Dipshit had clocked four hours around
Polaris, I kicked Harry awake. Poured him a cup of joe, handed
over the pump gun, and hit the rack. I slept like a poleaxed
Hereford.

A cold, dank ground fog shrouded the country when we awoke,
but it burned off fast as the sun gained strength. While Harry
searched the bear's trail for more of his gear and goodies, I waded
the undercut banks clear up to the swamp, throwing nymphs—a
pheasant tail at first, then a gold-ribbed hare's ear that worked its
usual glittery magic in the early morning light. All Harry could
find in his treasure hunt were a handful of spoons and forks, a bottle of ketchup, and the jar of Miracle Whip, with toothmarks the
size of .30-caliber bulletholes through the lid. We shoved off after
a breakfast of fried brook trout, black coffee, and two dry slices of
toasted Wonder Bread from Harry's remaining loaf.

For fifteen miles below the spring pools the Firesteel runs
clear and cold over beds of glacial till, through country scalped flat
by loggers half a century earlier: old white pine country now
sprouting thickets of popple and alder, tamarack and yellow jackpine, studded with giant stumps that hunker amid the second
growth like hobnails on the soles of Paul Bunyan's boots.
Mountains of slash decay in the woods. Deer fled at our approach,
waving tall white flags of alarm. Twice we passed the ruins of old
logging camps, the shacks and sheds still standing, furred in lavender lichen.

The water was strong, smooth, broken in spots by easy riffles.
Good running. For the first hour I paddled and steered from the
stern while Harry threw wet flies close to the bank—cast, big
upstream mend, strip, strip, strip, then pick up the line and cast
again. When he got bored, he'd break out his ax and improvise tone
poems around whatever pop tune came into his head—"Stardust,"

"Blueberry Hill," like that—while I tapped out a 4/4 beat on the canoe thwart ahead of me, throwing in changes every now and then with an aluminum fork for a drumstick and two empty tin cans for my cymbals.

Every hour we switched places in the canoe. The fishing was fast at first, medium-sized browns up to fifteen inches, and a few rainbows that glittered like stainless-steel exclamation points as they cleared the water. For a while an osprey followed us, ghosting along on crooked wings, waiting for the canoe's sudden shadow to flush trout from their lies, then stooping to hook them with its long yellow talons. Then it flew ahead to its huge, messy nest of twigs and branches with the fish still writhing in its grasp. We could see the nest in the distance, perched at the top of a dead spruce near the riverbank, and as we swept past we saw the gawky gray heads of three near-grown hatchlings clamoring to be fed. It must have been a late nesting, her first clutch wiped out in some unrecorded domestic catastrophe. Maybe a weasel or pine marten raid. Or crows dropping by for a visit while Mom was out at the fish market. Nature is full of heart-warming stories like that.

Toward noon we spotted smoke ahead, not a wildfire with its greasy yellow-gray sprawl shot full of frantic sparks, but a single white plume as if from a stovepipe or campsite. Around the next bend we saw another decrepit old logging camp. It stood on the eastern bank. A weathered, crudely lettered sign at the landing said, "No Tresspasing, this meens You! Servivers will be Perssacuted!" A lopsided skull and crossbones underscored the message. Harry read it and frowned. "Why do people always put quotation marks on signs like that? And what's with all the exclamation points? Like at the diner in Heldendorf. 'Ma Metzger's Good Eats!' I doubt anyone ever actually said it."

The smoke rose from what looked to be a bunkhouse. There were other signs of habitation: a kitchen garden out back—corn, pumpkins, some fat tomatoes ripening—and a clothesline hung with wash. Faded lumberjack shirts, underwear, canvas pants, and—a bit offputting—a string of mammoth pink brassieres that would have fit Elsie, the Borden cow.

"Let's see if they'll sell us some fresh groceries," Harry said.

"Looks like they don't want company."

"I've got money, though, the long green. These folks are probably pretty hard up. Some corn on the cob would go good with supper." It was time for a break anyway so we pulled ashore and walked on up to the long, low bunkhouse built of peeled pine logs. The sign had made me uneasy, though. Some of these North Woods loners can be pretty nasty. They protect their privacy. We couldn't very well walk up to the house armed, but I strapped the sheathed K-Bar to my calf, under my khakis, just to be safe. The skinned carcass of an out-of-season deer hung next to the woodpile in the shade of the porch, fresh-killed but already glazing toward black in the last real heat of summer. A few slabs were missing from the backstraps and haunches.

"Anybody home?" Harry yelled as we neared the place. No answer. He looked at me and raised his eyebrows. I shrugged and pushed the door. It swung open with a muted squeal. We peeked inside, into darkness hot as a steam room. Someone was seated in a rocker facing a red hot woodstove, under a tattered shawl. The person's back was toward us. White hair to the shoulders. A deaf old lady?

Then a creaky voice whined, "Is that you, Curly?"

I cleared my throat, and the chair spun around. But it was a guy, an old man with a scraggly white beard. His face was a mass of scar tissue. He had no eyes. Where they'd been were deep black tunnels, like the mouths of bottomless mineshafts. The scar tissue seemed to writhe as the outside light hit it.

But he was only trying to smile in welcome. "Come in, come in," he piped in his high, scratchy voice. "We don't get much company down here on the Firesteel anymore. I'm Lawrence Hackbarth." He grinned, strong white teeth flashing in a ruined mouth, and stood up from the crude, homemade rocking chair. He shuffled toward us, swinging a heavy knobbed cane ahead of him.

Lawrence Hackbarth was very tall, six-six at least. A faded, elbow-patched, but neatly ironed and starched red flannel shirt was tucked trimly into the flat-bellied waistband of his khaki trousers. On his long, narrow feet he wore fluffy pink bedroom slippers. They were way too small. "Don't be put off by my pan," he said. "I'm really quite friendly. The injury transpired whilst blowing a log jam on the river, that was back in the winter of '22. A mishap with blasting caps. We're three old bindlestiffs living here, Wobblies all of us, even the Injun gal, holdovers from the olden days when this camp was still in business. It shut down in '23. Yiss, yiss, we're spooky old geezers, mean as hell, bushwhacky, two grungy old stumblebums from way back when and a Chippewa woman named Florinda Wakerobin. We grow our own giggleweed, distill enough corn liquor and potato schnapps to keep our innards rust free, and generally live off the land." He reached out with the cane and tapped our shins as if to fix us in place, and none too gently, I might add. "And who, pray tell, might you gentlemen be?"

I told him. We shook hands. His was twice the size of mine, hard and rough as Carborundum. "We saw your garden out back," Harry said. "A bear raided our camp last night while we were out fishing, and we wondered if you might be able to sell us some supplies. We don't need much, maybe a few potatoes and some corn. A c-c-can of sardines if you've got them. I can pay you whatever you ask."

"We don't have much use for money around here," Hackbarth said. "We're against it on principle, radicals, you know, heh-heh, and besides, the nearest store is forty miles east by shank's mare. But you're welcome to whatever we can spare. Flo is our storekeeper. No canned goods on hand, though, Mr. Taggart. Soon's my companions get back, I'll send the Injun gal down to the root cellar. We got plenty of corn and spuds, that I'm sure of. And deer meat up the ying-yang. Yiss, yiss. Curly's a crack shot, served with the Leathernecks in the first war. The AEF—Château Thierry, Belleau Wood, the St. Mihiel salient?"

I started to smell a rat, just a faint prickly whiff of one. Was Lawrence Hackbarth stalling? Waiting for Curly to get back? Curly—an old jarhead, I thought. Fifth Marines. None tougher. Judging by Sergeant Stingley and other members of the Old Breed I'd run afoul of so far, the older these salty types got, the meaner they became. Curly—despite his innocuous name—could prove to be bad news of the worst sort. He might make Stingley himself look like a pogue.

"When will your partners be back?" I asked the old man. "We've got to push on downriver, I'm afraid, make another ten miles before nightfall if we're going to meet our ride on time. If you could maybe just point us toward the root cellar, we'll grab a few spuds and be on our way. Thanking you very kindly, of course."

"We're back right now," came a deep voice behind me. Turning to the door, I saw the muzzle of a neatly oiled Springfield '03 aimed straight at my chest.

Curly stepped into the room, a short, dark, thick-legged guy with heavy shoulders that nearly grazed the doorjambs. His name-sake hairdo puffed out like two giant Brillo pads on either side of a slick, suntanned avenue of scalp. His tiny eyes were ice blue. Behind him came an even shorter, broader figure, a woman of indeterminate age. She had a long, heavy-barreled pistol in her hand, an old cap-and-ball Colt Dragoon by the look of it. It was trained on Harry's groin. Both of them wore greasy buckskin hunting shirts, homemade, that hung halfway to their knees. Moccasins on their feet.

"Let's get some light on the subject," Curly said. "Chop-chop, Flo." The Indian woman went over to a table in the shadows, and we heard the scratch of a kitchen match. Yellow light from a kerosene lamp flooded the long, low-ceilinged room: a kitchen and cookstove at one end and a rank of neatly made bunks at the other. Leaning against one of the beds were a Thompson submachine gun, the Al Capone model with a drum and knurled grip on the fore end, and a BAR—Browning Automatic Rifle, the finest weapon in the Marine Corps arsenal. Both pieces gleamed with fresh gun oil.

Lawrence Hackbarth flinched at the sudden glare, fumbled in his shirt pocket, and put on a pair of smoked, wire-framed glasses. "Goddamit, Flo, dim it down, dim it down! You know it hurts what's left of my optic nerves."

"Ah, you old pussy, stop your whinin'," Curly said. "Octopus nerves, my ass. So what have we here? A couple a fuckin' collitch boys, looks like. Candyass tourists."

"I'm a Marine," I said.

He looked me up and down. "They must be gettin' pretty desperate," he said. "I've wrung better-lookin' pieces of shit out of my deck-swab on latrine duty. So whadda they teach you in boot camp these days, how to roll blind geezers for pogey-bait?"

"All we wanted was to buy some v-vegetables," Harry said. "A few potatoes, maybe some corn. I've got plenty of m-money."

Curly's eyes lit up. "Let's see it."

Harry pulled out his wallet, still damp from last night's wading, and pulled out a fat wad of bills. Curly took them, thumbed through the stack, gave up counting when the bills stuck together, and pocketed it.

"I thought you guys were radicals," I said. "Wobblies or something. That you didn't believe in money."

"That's just Doc talkin'. Ol' Larry, he used to pal around with Big Bill Heywood and them guys. Me and Flo, we're capitalists from way back." He poked me in the ribs with the barrel of the Springfield. "You wanna see the root cellar, you said. Let me show you the way." He swung the rifle on Harry. "You too, you puny little puh-puh-puh-pogue."

Flo waddled into the kitchen and stooped to grab a recessed iron ring in the floorboards. She opened the trapdoor and looked up at us with slitted black eyes that glittered like basalt. She giggled and winked. A gust of cool air puffed up in our faces—mole fur, potato rot, damp dirt. Worn wooden stairs led down into darkness.

"March!" Curly said.

We felt our way down the rickety staircase and the trapdoor slammed shut.

"The b-b-boom of doom," Harry said. "Oh shit, oh dear."

4

THE FLAMBEAU BOYS

Someone pulled a heavy object over the trapdoor, maybe the icebox, and we heard them go into the main room. Their voices came to us through the floorboards. A bottle clinked, then glasses, followed by the glug-glug of something being poured.

"Go easy on that corn," Doc said. "You know how you get when you chug it too fast."

"I'll be the judge of that," Curly said. "Now what're we gonna do with these snoops? I say shoot 'em and haul 'em out in the woods for the brush wolves. Like we did with those fuckin'-tramps who poked their noses in here two years ago."

"Isn't that a bit crude?" Doc said. "Anyway, the Slater kid says they've got a pickup scheduled downriver aways. When they don't show up, all hell will break loose. Next thing we know there'll be state troopers in motorboats, buzzing all up and down the Firesteel. No, I've got a better idea. We'll drown 'em nice and quiet, then you and Flo take their bodies downstream a few miles, below Kingfisher Rapids, say, and sink 'em in the Blue Hole. Bust up the canoe like it hit a rock. Just another river accident."

"Do we have to kill them?" It was a woman's voice, a surprisingly sweet one, the first words heard from Flo. "They're such nice-looking boys. And polite, too."

"That's your pussy talking," Curly said. "Don't me and Doc prong you enough, you need more?" He uncorked the bottle and poured another drink. Three glugs this time. "Women," he said.

"We could keep them down in the cellar a few hours, then say it was all just a joke, an object lesson. We hope they'll spread the word around that our No Trespassing sign means business."

"Too dangerous," Doc said. "If they report us, the law will want full descriptions. And I'm sure there are plenty of wanted posters still hanging in every town hall and post office north of Neenah. Pour me another one, Curly. And stoke up the fire, please. I'm freezing." He sighed. "I knew this would happen one day. Five years we've been safe and sound here, six, come next April. The perfect hideout. Ah, well, all good things must come to an end."

"Not if I can help it," Curly said. "When I finish this drink, I'm goin' down to their canoe and see if there's anything we can use. Then, come dark, I'll take the boys for a swim."

"Larry, Flo, and Curly," I said. "Sound familiar?"

"The Three Stooges?" Harry answered from the darkness. Mister Cool. "Except the haircuts are wr-wrong, and in one instance the gender. Moe and Flo sound close enough, though. . . . I've got it. We've entered an alternative universe, and these are their evil twins?" He read a lot of science fiction.

"No, the Flambeau Boys. They used to operate in these parts during the depression and all through the war." In those days I read a lot of crime stuff. "The leader was a tall, skinny, well-spoken gent name of Lawrence Haugenbusch. They called him Doc. Hailed from Lac du Flambeau. He used to run with Dillinger and Pretty Boy Floyd, that crowd. When Dillinger was killed, Doc set up his own outfit. Pretty minor league. They stuck up taverns, IGAs, filling stations, but now and then a bank or two. Mainly they operated up here, all across the northern tier from Fargo and the Twin Cities clear over to the Soo. They had an Indian as their wheel man—nobody agrees on the name. Short, wide, and deadpanned is the best description. Whoever it was, he or she was a lead-footed son of a bitch sure enough. No one could stay on the road with them, not even the G-men. The muscle was an ex-Marine named Cobbett or Corbett, Frank Corbett, I think it was. He carried a drum-fed Tommy gun. Big mop of bushy black hair. They called him . . . ."

"Don't tell me—Curly!"

"You got it. First time out of the box."

"I thought the FBI nabbed them," Harry said. "Down by Green Bay or Oshkosh or someplace like that."

"Oshkosh, and it's only a rumor. Wishful thinking. The Flambeau Boys were blowing the vault in a bank and one of them fucked up. They had three or four customers and a teller in the vault with them as hostages when the nitroglycerin blew prematurely. All the cops found when the smoke cleared was a mess of body parts. Nobody ever sorted them out. Cunts and cocks and teeth and assholes, all stuck to the ceiling." Christ, I was starting to sound like Sergeant Stingley. "Anyway, Doc and his pals could have escaped in the turmoil."

"So you think this is them?"

"It all adds up. Doc, Curly, and an Indian. Haugenbusch, Hackbarth. Close enough. Now here they are, tucked away in the back of beyond and armed to the teeth. Doc's eyes were probably blown out by that nitro explosion."

"You've been reading too much Mickey Spillane."

"Well, you tell me then. Why the fuck are they holding us prisoner? Why are they planning to kill us?"

By now our eyes had adjusted to the gloom of the cellar. Slivers of light filtered down through cracks in the floor. I got up from a lumpy burlap bag of potatoes to check the place out. It was walled with big riverbank boulders neatly laid, no cement to hold them together, with a dirt floor. Except for a space at the foot of the stairwell the cellar, about ten feet square, was jampacked with sacks of cabbages, spuds, turnips, and carrots. A low ceiling, not high enough for me to stand fully upright. In the northeast corner was an alcove. I crawled over the sacks for a closer look. It was a cellar access. For a moment I had hope. But when I wiggled up into the space and pushed upward, the sloping door wouldn't budge. Locked from the outside. But the stones that lined it felt loose.

"Look for something to pry these stones with," I whispered, "like an old broom handle. I've got my K-Bar, but it's not long enough to give me any leverage. Maybe we can get out of here after all."

I started pushing and pulling at the rocks, wiggling them from side to side, up and down, like worrying a loose tooth in its socket. Dirt and chunks of rotting cement sifted into my hair. Harry crawled over the potato sacks and handed me a stick. "Found this under the stairs," he said.

I slid the stick into a crevice in the wall and began prying. "Stand by and take these rocks when I hand them to you. Put 'em down nice and easy on the bags. Don't let 'em clack together. If we can hear them, they can hear us." It took a few minutes but then the first rock came loose and I passed it back to Harry.

After that they came fast, like removing the first olive in the jar frees up the rest. In short order we had a hole that seemed big enough to squeeze through. I cleaned it out, on up to the roots of the buffalo grass that grew tall and thick around the bunkhouse.

"What are they doing upstairs?" I asked Harry. He slid back into the dark, but returned in a very long minute.

"I could only hear Doc and Flo," he said. "Curly must still be outside, looting our canoe."

"Then we'd better make a break for it now. Doc can't see and the Indian woman might not blow the whistle even if she does spot us." I pushed the stick up through the sod, followed it with my hand, and began pulling down big clots of dirt and grassroots. Harry pushed up beside me and bore me a hand. Damp dirt cascaded on our faces.

"Ugh," he said.

"What?"

"Got a w-worm in my mouth." He spat and shuddered.

"Swallow it. We haven't had lunch yet."

Then there was light. It hurt our eyes at first, but we wiggled on out of the hole, Harry first, and crouched low against the side of the building. We were on the meadow side of the bunkhouse, next to the woodpile. I pulled out the K-Bar and then looked around for another weapon. A splitting maul stood leaning against the far end of the stack. "Come on."

We bellycrawled down the length of the woodpile, and I grabbed the maul and handed it to Harry. Then, motioning him to stay put, I snaked on over to the corner of the building. Peeked around. Curly was sitting in the sun beside our canoe, his back rested against it, raising a bottle to his lips. My pump-gun rested across his lap, an open box of shells beside it. Another canoe, an aluminum Grumman, was hauled up beside ours. The one he and Flo had arrived in. Curly glanced upriver, sat up straight, placed the bottle down next to him, nesting it carefully in the gravel. He mounted the gun as a knot of ducks swept past. I could hear the whistle of wind through their primaries. Blue-wing teal, judging by their dark bellies and the chalky patches on the leading edge of their wings. He swung with them, smooth and fast, and shot. One shell. Three birds splashed down near the shore.

"What's that?" Doc's voice came from inside the bunkhouse.

"Curly's shooting hors d'oeuvres," Flo said.

"Is he pie-eyed yet?"

"You couldn't tell it from here."

"That boy always could shoot, drunk or sober."

I guess he could. So Curly, armed and accurate, stood between us and freedom. Then I remembered the Thompson and the BAR in the bunkhouse. I crawled back to Harry.

"Listen," I whispered, "I need a diversion. Something to get Flo out of the place for a minute while I duck in and grab those automatic weapons." I pointed to the splitting maul. "Take this and go down to the far end. Keep low so she can't see you through the windows. When I give you the signal, start banging it against the wall, not so loud that Curly can hear it and come running, but enough to bring her out in a hurry." He nodded. "We've got to move fast when the shit hits the fan. Curly can't hurt us with the shotgun, not at this range, but once I've got that BAR in my hands I can waste him at leisure."

"Okay, S-Sarge." He grinned. "Gosh, it feels just like a war movie." Like I said, Mister Cool. But he swallowed hard just the same.

"Get hopping."

Harry scuttled in a stoop down to the far corner and looked up. I nodded. He started tapping on the bottom log.

"Now what?" Doc said from inside. "Sounds like those kids are up to some mischief. Trying to bust loose I guess. Go out there and cool 'em, Flo. Take that hogleg with you. Put a couple shots through the wall if you have to."

I heard Flo's footsteps clumping out the door. Waited a couple of seconds for her to get clear, then sprinted around the back corner, the front corner, and piled into the bunkhouse through the open doorway. Doc sat on one of the bunks, with the Thompson and a cleaning rag in his lap. He looked up with his wasted face. "Back so soon?"

I was on him in an instant, wrenched the tommy gun loose, then grabbed up the BAR.

"What the fuck . . . "

I ran for the door. From their weight, I could tell both pieces were loaded. Around the far corner came Flo, followed by Harry. He was carrying her pistol. He grinned. "It's okay," he yelled, gesturing with it. "She's on our side. She wants to come with us."

Blam! A load of spent bird-shot rattled against the wall of the bunkhouse and kicked up dust around my feet. Curly had spotted us. He was running up from the river, a hundred yards away, red-faced and firing as he came. His Brillo-pad hairdo bounced as he ran. I tossed Harry the Thompson—"Hold on to this!"—and raised the BAR to my shoulder. The piece weighs twenty pounds, but it's accurate out to 600 yards. I flicked off the safety, laid the leaf-sight square on Curly's chest, then dropped it a tad and tripped off a four-round burst at his feet. I couldn't bring myself to kill the fucker. I wasn't enough of a Marine yet. He skidded to a halt and let the pumpgun fall.

"Doc's still inside," I told Harry. "See what he's up to."

At that moment Doc came groping his way out the door, a big, blocky Colt automatic in his hand. He winced in the sunlight, his face screwed up even tighter and uglier than usual. He pointed the .45 in our general direction and blasted away. Harry raised the Thompson, but he hadn't racked a round into the chamber yet. He damn near snapped off the trigger trying to squeeze it. Flo grabbed her Dragoon from where he'd stuck it through his belt, walked up to Doc straight through the gunfire, jabbed two fingers deep into his eyeholes, then reversed the hogleg to hold it by the barrel and bopped him square on the bean. *Thwock!* He dropped like a sack of cement.

Harry laughed. "Just like in the movies," he said again.

I turned back to Curly, but during the fracas he'd turned again and was sprinting for cover, a thicket of bankside aspens a hundred yards upstream. He reached it before I could raise the BAR.

"Point-blank range and none of us even got nicked," Harry said, prodding Doc's inert body with his toe. "He wasn't much of a marksman."

Doc groaned and stirred, his fingers twitching. I picked up the pistol.

"Plenty good for a blind man, though," I said. "He didn't have to hit us. He bought enough time for Curly to give us the slip." My mind was racing. We had to clear out of here, but first I wanted to check for more ammo—both the Colt and the Thompson took .45 pistol rounds; the BAR fired full-length .30-06s—and find out what had brought about Flo's change of allegiance. She was already inside the kitchen, packing food and personal gear into a wooden crate. I gave Harry the BAR, showed him how it operated, and told him to keep watch on the aspen grove. Also on Doc. Shoot or at least shout if he saw Curly. I set the selector switch on single-fire—I didn't want him emptying the rest of the 20-round magazine on a single frantic burst—and went into the kitchen.

"So you changed sides," I said to Flo.

"Five years with these bimbos," she said, not looking up, "and still they treat me like the help. A housemaid is all I am to them. I cook for them, clean for them, make their beds, lug water, gut game, muck out the privy, haul firewood, even do windows, and every month or two they're gracious enough to throw me a ten-second fuck. Like it or not, I have no say in the matter. Somehow I've lost my enthusiasm for the job."

"Didn't you used to drive their getaway car?"

"No, that was my son, Morton. His Chippewa name was Moonbeam. He loved engines from little on, raced motorcycles on the dirt tracks up here, a Flying Merkel he rebuilt himself. He dreamed of becoming the first Indian to run at Indy, but the only driving job he ever landed was with these galoots. Then he caught a slug on a stickup in St. Cloud, Minnesota—that was the winter of forty-four. A thirty-eight in the belly. They brought him to me on the Bad River rez up here. I'm a medicine woman—not the black magic kind, the herbal and sweat lodge variety. But it was no use. Septicemia, and penicillin in short supply because of the war. The black market price was sky high. We needed more money and a real sawbones, one who wouldn't rat them out to the cops. That's why they pulled the bank job in Oshkosh where Doc got his eyes blown out. I only drove for them that once. I had to. Morton died anyway. Just a month short of his twenty-first birthday. . . ." Here she sighed and closed her eyes. She looked up again. "So we all moved up here," she continued, deadpan, "to the late, lamented headquarters camp of the Firesteel Logging Company."

Could I—*should* I believe her? It could all be a setup. What's Doc up to? Or maybe Curly? She looked up at me, inscrutable, then kept on packing.

"You'll want more rounds for the Thompson and Doc's Colt," she said, "and aught sixes for the Browning. There's a full bandolier for the BAR under that bunk where the guns were, and a carton or two of forty-fives in the chiffonier by my bed. Then we'd better make tracks. Doc we can leave here. But Curly, he's dangerous."

The sun was a hand's breadth above the horizon when we loaded the canoe. Harry was still covering the aspen grove. With the

Thompson, I stitched five quick holes through the bottom of the Grumman. Curly could always patch them, of course, but it would take him awhile, and we needed all the river room we could get. Flo took the paddles from the aluminum canoe and stowed them under our thwarts. We waded out and boarded the Old Town. Flo took the stern thwart, I sat amidships, facing backwards with the BAR, and Harry shoved us off, then swung aboard and paddled bow. We left Doc hogtied on one of the bunks. He was conscious, silent, staring bottomless black deathrays at us as we backed out of the cabin. Then in his high, squeaky voice he said, "I'll see you later, boys. You can count on it."

I realize that we should have shot him then and there, but we were good boys in those days. The Ten Commandments still meant something to us. I learned better up on the Chosin Reservoir in North Korea, then later on the MLR. But I'm getting ahead of myself. . . .

As we swept around the first bend below the logging camp, I saw Curly emerge from the aspens. He looked at us disappearing downriver and sprinted up toward the bunkhouse, hell-bent for leather—to find out what had happened to Doc, or just for his rifle? I'd pulled the bolt from his Springfield, smashed the stock with the splitting maul, and taken all his bullets—'06s like those the BAR ate—but I was sure he had more bullets stashed away someplace, Flo had indicated as much, and maybe even a spare bolt or two. He'd mend the busted stock one way or another. Old Marines are like that with their weapons. As Stingley said, "Treat her right and your rifle will be truer to you than any cunt in Christendom." Curly and Doc would be after us soon enough.

I swung around facing forward, grabbed one of the extra paddles and dug into the water. It resisted, sullen and dark and deep but flowing the way we wanted to go. Then it was swept away, behind us. "Pick it up, pogues," I said in my best Sergeant Stingley voice. "We gotta make holes in the water. Big fuckin' whirly ones, and plenty of 'em."

5

TWODOGGONE LAKE

My first instinct was to paddle all night, and all the next day too if we could hold up that long—clear to Lake Superior if possible. But that soon proved too dangerous. With night falling fast, we entered a chain of increasingly steep sluices and rapids, the river whipping left, then right, then left again, the sound of it rising from hiss through grumble to ominous growl. The second-growth forest of jackpine and spruce grew tight to the banks, and its lengthening shadows swallowed the river in darkness. All we could see up ahead were the seething white eruptions where water smashed against rock.

"Chippewa people call this the Bonebreaker," Flo shouted to me above the roar of the rapids. "It's tough to run even with the sun shining."

"You know the river better than we do," I yelled back. "What do you suggest?"

"Let's pull over and line down the rest of the way. It's not much farther. Maybe a mile or two."

"Okay." I leaned forward and nudged Harry's back with the tip of my paddle, gestured toward the right bank. Flo dug her paddle in deep on the right side and held it to turn the bow shoreward while Harry and I paddled hard. We swept in fast between two white-fanged boulders and then we were into the slack water, close to the bank. Harry jumped out, hip deep, and held the canoe.

"We've got to line it down the rest of the way," I told him. "If we dump the canoe in this whitewater, we're finished."

"Good enough," he said. "That was getting kind of scary."

Flo went ashore with her hatchet and cut a small spruce, limbed it and whacked off the top. "You two take the bow and stern lines. I'll use this pole to help brake her and fend off if the current sets us onto any sharp rocks." She clambered back in and stood amidships. I tied the stern line to the towing ring aft while Harry knotted another to the bow thwart. We let out line. The Old Town struggled against us like a harpooned whale, bulled this way and that by the braided currents and eddies. Slowly we inched our way downstream, knee deep, thigh deep, sometimes wet nearly to the navel, dragging our heels in the gravel of the riverbottom to slow the canoe's descent. I don't know how long it took us to clear the rapids, but it felt like all night. My arms were being ripped from their sockets. Twice we spooked large animals from the shore—deer most likely, come down to drink.

Then, as we rounded a particularly nasty bend, Harry stepped into a pothole and dropped his line. The full weight of the canoe came to bear on my arms. I couldn't hold it, felt the burn of rough manila as it slipped inch by inch through my palms. Flo glanced back at me, shipped her pushpole and scampered aft to the stern thwart, unbelievably agile for a woman of her bulk. She grabbed up a paddle.

"Let it go," she yelled. "I can run this next patch."

I dropped the line, grateful, and she swept off into the roaring, black and white darkness.

We waded down through the shallows, splashing, stumbling, falling, skinning our shins on sunken rocks. The moon was just rising through the trees to our right. At each turn I expected to see the canoe ahead of us, wrapped around the boulders with its back broken. But then the roar of the river eased to a mutter, a whisper, and stopped. We'd reached the end of the fast water. Below it widened into a long, slow pool on which floated the canoe. Flo saw us and raised her paddle. It glinted in the moonlight, a welcome sight.

A smaller stream entered the Firesteel just below the rapids. Flo said it drained a lake about a mile to the west. "The first white man to explore the Firesteel country called this tributary Stony Creek. That was in the 1680s. The lake is called Twodoggone."

"Strange name."

"Strange man. Daniel Greysolon, the Sieur du Lhut. That's spelled L-H-U-T. Your people got the letters screwed around, thus the great city of Duluth, Minnesota. Du Lhut had a pair of war dogs with him, mastiffs. He sicced them on any Indian who dared to get uppity with him. After his Chippewa paddlers portaged him up to the lake, they were paddling across it when the dogs spotted a swimming moose. They jumped overboard and capsized the canoe with all the furs he'd taken from the Indians so far. Sank without a trace. The dogs caught up with the moose all right, but it drowned them. The Chippewas were delighted of course. They named the lake Two Dog Gone. It stuck."

"What's the lake like nowadays?" Harry asked.

"It's privately owned," Flo said. "Some rich moke from Milwaukee, a banker. President of Heartland National, in fact. Morison Stoat. No roads in to the place, he flies up here in a float plane—a big red and black DeHavilland Beaver. Stoat's got a fishing lodge on the lake, a huge place that looks like a Tinker Toy castle, electricity from diesel generators, summer kitchen, servants quarters, boathouses, knotty pine paneling in the toilets, a flagpole that reaches halfway to the moon, speedboats, water skis, the works. His caretakers shoot at anyone who dares to trespass on his water. There's big muskies in Twodoggone and he saves them for his big customers."

Harry's eyes lit up. "My dad banks at Heartland," he said. "I've never landed a muskie. Let's go up there and see what it's like. We're looking to shake Doc and Curly anyway and they'll never think of following us up the Stony. We can let them shoot on past, wear themselves out on a wild goose chase, then when they've dragged ass back upriver in a day or two, we'll just continue on down to Lake Superior."

"We'll probably miss our lift in your dad's truck."

"So what? One of us can hike into town and hire another. I've got plenty of . . ."

His face fell. Curly still had his wad of cash.

"Your money?" Flo said. "Don't worry. Before we shoved off I grabbed what was left of Doc's loot from the cookie jar in the kitchen. I'll loan you enough to get back home. I agree it's a good idea to throw them off the scent. We can hide the canoe up the Stony—it's a hell of a portage—and hike up to the lake in the morning."

We hid the canoe in an alder brake about a quarter of a mile up the feeder stream and made a quick camp above it in the pines. No fire, too risky. While Flo and I cached the supplies in a rocky cave she knew from previous visits, Harry slapped together some peanut butter and jelly sandwiches with his last stale slices of Wonder Bread. That was our supper, washed down with tin cups of icy creek water that tasted faintly of iodine. Then we grabbed some shut-eye. The ground was ten percent sand, the balance made up of rocks and roots and half-buried pine cones. When I finally managed to doze off, I dreamt of eyeless men and roaring water. In the morning, covered with mosquito bites, we rolled our sleeping bags, picked up the weapons, flyrods, and some eats from Flo's supply, then hoofed it to Twodoggone Lake, chewing deer jerky on the way.

The sun was directly behind us when we got there, a long, narrow reach of brass-colored water with rocky shores. Ospreys rowed the air above the lake, three of them this time, rakish birds with fierce yellow eyes that dove like fighter planes to strafe the water and hook up wriggling panfish. Like most of the lakes up here in those days, Twodoggone was home to at least one family of loons. We could hear them before we saw them. They were weird, beautifully marked, low-swimming birds that dove deep and swam far, then reemerged to turn the lake eerie with their cowboy yodeling and wobbly laughter. To me that sound was the essence of Up North.

The loons were congregated at the north end near a big lodge built of squared and varnished white-pine logs. It stood in a large clearing, surrounded by a close-cropped, bluegreen lawn. A long white dock projected into the lake from the bottom of the lawn, with a white boathouse squatting solid beside it. Stoat's float plane bobbed at its moorings off the end of the pier, a bulky no-nonsense Beaver as Flo had said, and a big float boat, mounted on long pontoons and powered by a massive outboard motor on its stern, was anchored in the shallows. A pair of rowboats were pulled up on a narrow, sandy beach shaped like a fingernail clipping. From this distance they looked like Adirondack guide boats.

As we watched, the boathouse doors opened and a long, sleek speedboat emerged—a low, mahogany-hulled Gar Wood with a reverse sheer to its cambered bow. A fast, rich boat with a throaty purr that sounded of money. A few minutes later it was trolling a pair of suntanned young ladies in bikinis behind it on water skis, blasting along at full speed. The Gar Wood ran the lake like it owned it. With a bone in its teeth it rocked the shores with thunder and the rowdy waves raised by its wake. The boat swept toward us with a roar from its old World War I Liberty engine. We ducked down in the brush as it passed. Waves slapped the rocks. We could hear the girls squealing.

"Looks like Stoat's got the family up for the weekend," Flo said. "The blonde girl's his daughter, Cora. I don't recognize the other one."

"You seem to know the family pretty well," I said.

"You mean for an Indian? No mystery about it. I used to work for Stoat's wife, Eunice. Talk about neurasthenic. I was her herbalist. Dogbane root for heartache, blueberry buds for madness. Barks, roots, and flowers. Tonics, lotions, pastes of pulped roots to ease those imaginary twinges in her joints and nether parts. She spiked the tonics with gin, and they seemed to work."

"Do Doc and Curly know about this place?"

"No. That was before they showed up in my life. I didn't want to tell them about the Stoats because Curly would sure as hell want to burglarize the lodge, maybe even kidnap Cora and hold her for ransom."

"What's Cora like?" Harry asked.

"Ditzy but kind of sweet. At least when I knew her. Now she's going to some girl's school back east, Bryn Mawr or one of those places. But we always got on well. Old Stoat's another matter."

"Would he give us a hard time if we showed up at his door?" Harry asked. "Told him we were fishing the Firesteel, dumped our canoe, lost all our supplies, and wanted to borrow, say, a cup of . . . rice?"

"Or a can of sardines," I added.

Flo chuckled. "He might give you the bum's rush, but not if Eunice is there. She never wanted me to leave."

"Let's do it."

"Why?"

"Maybe we can spend the night in the lodge. I'd sure sleep better without worrying about Curly or Doc cutting my throat in mid-snore. With a houseful of people they're not likely to break in."

Flo shrugged and looked at me. I nodded agreement. "Okay," she said, "I'll flag down the boat."

The Gar Wood was still whizzing around the lake. Flo walked out on a rocky point and stood there with her arm raised, like someone hailing a cab. The blonde girl spotted her and signaled to the boatman. The Gar Wood circled in toward the promontory, then slowed and wallowed to a stop, its engine idling. The two girls sank in the water, ski tips up.

"Florinda?" the blonde girl yelled. "Is that you?" When Flo nodded, she kicked off her skis and swam ashore. Harry and I stayed back in the bankside shrubbery.

"She's got a good stroke," Harry said. I could see sparks of love in his eyes. Or anyway lust.

The girl and Flo talked for a bit, then Flo waved us out of hiding. We must have looked pretty shabby by now, rumpled and sunburnt and lumpy with bug bites, but Harry brushed back his buzz cut anyway, tucked in his shirt, and put on his shyboy smile.

"I'm Cora," she said, smiling and offering her hand. "Any friends of Florinda's are friends of mine." The other girl swam over and Cora introduced her as Wanda Nachtisch, a Bryn Mawr class-mate from Pennsylvania. She was a cute, shy brunette with short hair and China-doll eyes, which she batted at us. Then blushed.

We rode in the Gar Wood uplake to the lodge. The sleeping bags, BAR, and Tommy gun were hidden in the brush along with our other gear, and we carried only the flyrods. Harry also had his horn, of course. The boat ride back was too noisy for talk, but as we approached the dock, we saw a man emerge from the screened porch at the front of the lodge to stand at the top of the lawn with a drink in his hand.

Morison Stoat was a short, narrow-chested gent. He was wearing plaid shorts and a fancy white shirt, all pleats and embroi-dery, what they called a guayabera shirt. Pale, skinny legs stuck out of the bottoms of his Bermudas like bent pipe cleaners, and he car-ried one of those double-walled plastic glasses that have gaudy trout flies embedded in them. A tight, hard potbelly poked through his shirt despite the Cuban couturier's best efforts. He had a ruddy face, even in winter I was sure, with white, wavy hair and the thinnest wisp of hair on his upper lip that could pass for a mus-tache. His nose was long, and I suppose you could call it patrician despite the webwork of ruptured capillaries that crawled over it like so many wireworms. In a region where most people drank brandy or rye with beer chasers, he looked like the sort that sipped scotch whisky neat, no ice—Black Label, if you please. I could hear music from a Victrola echoing opera out over the water. The boat-man tied the Gar Wood to the dock. It bumped to the slow onshore chop against neat, white fenders. Stoat came down the lawn to greet us.

"Daddy, you remember Florinda Wakerobin, don't you?"

He looked Flo up and down. His eyes were bulbous and watery, a delicate blue, like Cora's, but with a faint trace of yellow in the whites. Thinner, fainter cousins of the wireworms on his nose laced his eyeballs. Still, they were shrewd eyes, I realized, chilly, giving away nothing, but quick to read weakness. A gun-fighter's eyes, or a poker player's.

"Ah, yes," he drawled in a tony back-east accent, "the Shawnee shamanette. Or should I say the Winnebago witchdoctor? I never can remember all those tribal names. But I don't suppose it makes much difference. All you redskins look alike anyway. What are you peddling today, my dear? Eye of newt spritzers or essence of eagle's urine?" He smiled at his own wit, then turned to Harry and me. "And what have we here, your halfbreed sons? They're certainly dark enough, I'd say."

Harry laughed. "We've been on the river," he said, smiling and putting out his hand. "I'm Harry Taggart from Heldendorf, and this is my friend Ben Slater. He's on leave from the Marine Corps. It's a pleasure to meet you, Mr. Stoat. My father, Jake Taggart, owns Heldendorf Lumber. He's a c-customer of yours."

"Yes," he said. "A good one." Stoat shook Harry's hand with reluctance but pretended mine wasn't there.

Harry gave him the sob story about losing our supplies in the whitewater and asked if we could maybe buy some replacements from his larder. Stoat frowned, coughed, and seemed about to speak, but then we heard a screen door slam. A thin, pale woman with marcelled blue hair, wearing a florid sunsuit and wedgies, teetered her way down the lawn to join us. She was grinning from ear to ear.

"Florinda!" she ululated. "You're back!"

Stoat muttered something under his breath, but I could see we were home free.

6

A LOON HUNT

I nside the screened porch, as Harry and I passed it on the way to the back door, I could see the glint of tines on the big-racked deer heads mounted there. A full-length muskellunge, four feet long at least, hung over the door leading into the parlor, glass eye glaring fire and its mouth wide open. "I want one just like that, daddy-o," Harry said.

Stoat, under his wife's gaze, had told us to go around to the kitchen and take what we needed by way of supplies. No need to pay for them, but in return we could help him with a chore he had waiting out on the lake. Before launching into a recitation of her current physical woes, Mrs. Stoat had insisted that Flo and "the boys" spend the day at Twodoggone, and the night as well—"We have oodles of room."

In the kitchen, a stout black cook named Evangeline escorted us to the cool, cavernous, well-stocked pantry, indicated a stack of empty cardboard boxes in one corner, and said, "Help yourselves. He got 'bout everthang in here, and more on call by radio if we run short." Harry took her at her word and started loading up. I didn't want to watch. It would only lead to petty arguments, me on the side of less, he wanting more-more-more. Once again, when we got back down to the Firesteel, the canoe would be wallowing gunwhale deep in unnecessary goodies.

What sort of "chore" did Stoat have in mind? It wouldn't be pleasant, that's for sure. The Stoats of this world give nothing away for free.

He was waiting for us in front of the porch when we staggered back with two heavy cartons of canned goods. He smiled grimly. He had a pair of shotguns with him, one tucked under each arm. "Put the boxes inside for now," he said, then led us down to the

dock. The Gar Wood bobbed there in the sunlight. I looked down
into the speedboat. Red leather seats, gleaming brightwork, rich,
clear-lacquered mahogany strakes. The mooring lines were coiled
to perfection fore and aft. Out on the lake a loon was sounding off.
Ha-oooo. Ha-ooo-oo-oo . . .

"Damn those birds," Stoat said. "They keep me up all night
when the moon is out, and when it isn't, they wake me at the crack
of dawn with that dratted laughter of theirs." He said it more like
"drotted loffter." He handed us each a shotgun. They were Belgian
Browning A-5s, top grade, with ventilated ribs.

"I'm not a man to be loffed at, day or night. I'll drive, you
boys ride up on the forward deck with the shotguns." He stepped
into the cockpit, popped a locker beside the wheel, reached in and
handed us a box of 12-gauge Federals, no. 4s.

"What are we supposed to be shooting at?" Harry asked.

"The loons, of course."

Long silence as Harry digested the notion.

"B-but aren't they protected?" he asked. "I think it's illegal to
shoot them."

"Cripes O'Grady," Stoat said, shaking his head. "They're
ruining my sleep, I tell you, annoying me day and night. They're
pests."

"It's s-s-still illegal."

"You ingrateful little weasel, what're you going to do? Turn
me in to the game warden? I *own* him. Just as I own this whole
damn lake, this lodge, this priceless one-of-a-kind speedboat. I
own that plane, and a whole lot more. I own half the county and
then some. Now are you going to fulfill your end of the bargain, or
just waste my time with more of your pitiful palaver?" He stared
iced steel at Harry, then composed himself. "Don't disgrace your
father, m'lad."

"Get in the boat," I told Harry. He looked at me, aghast. I
winked and gave him a little nod. I had a plan.

Stoat lit off the engine and cast the mooring lines free. We
hunkered on the cambered deck, up on the broad bow with the

shotguns propped between our sneakers. "He said we had to shoot at the loons," I said under the purr of the motor. "That doesn't mean we have to hit 'em."

We started loading the Brownings. They were unplugged, illegal for waterfowl, and took ten rounds apiece, plus an extra shell in the chambers.

There were two families of loons working the lake, I saw, one flock of five, another of four. The young were already in adult plumage, iridescent dark green heads, long, sharp-tipped black bills, black-and-white checkerboard collars, but their markings looked brighter than those of the parents, and they seemed— well—*livelier*, more prone to what looked like play, racing at one another and splashing a lot with flurrying wings. Avian teenagers teasing each other.

Stoat two-blocked the throttle and the Gar Wood bounced up on the step, heading for the larger group at flank speed. The birds had been circling in midwater, diving now and then, but now they gathered together as we approached and swam faster, away from us, toward the false protection of a weedbed. The boat bounced and splatted, throwing a long bow wave. "The guns are full choked," Stoat shouted as we came within eighty yards. He backed off on the throttle and the Gar Wood settled down. "Commence firing!"

I stood, raised the Browning to my shoulder, and shot—ten yards behind the closest loon. Beside me Harry fired twice. I saw the shot patterns slash the water, long and ragged and white, and the dark green heads disappeared. Stoat spun the wheel and hit the throttle again. The Gar Wood jumped from a burble to a roar, heading to where the shot hit. We circled the spot, staring down into the water. Stoat's voice came loud and querulous, "You missed the bahstahds!"

"We were t-t-too far away," Harry said. "You t-told us to shoot too soon. Maybe you can get us in c-closer next time?"

Stoat's face went redder than ever.

Two hundred yards away, to port and starboard, loon heads and necks began popping from the water like so many checkered corks. They were beyond the weedbed now. We started to circle it. They dove again.

Stoat looked for the other family. They were rafted a quarter mile away, watching the boat. He began idling in their direction, quartering as we went, never heading straight at them. "Don't look at them," he told us. "They're clever little fuckahs. I'm going to try and circle them, get between them and that drotted weedbed."

It took a good ten minutes, but he did. This time Stoat idled in on the birds slow and easy, zigzagging all the way. The loons seemed to have lost their caution. He brought us in closer, closer. When they were only forty yards off, abeam of the Gar Wood, he whispered, "Kill the bahstahds!"

"Watch this," I hissed to Harry. As I swung around to aim at the flock, I pretended to trip on a bow cleat and lurched like a drunk, the shotgun swinging one handed in a wild arc toward the stern of the boat. Stoat's eyes popped wide and he ducked behind the console. I dropped the muzzle and hit the trigger, squeezing twice, three times, fast. Three random holes the size of a baby's fist appeared in the mahogany hull of the Gar Wood, just below the waterline. The lake bubbled in.

"Oops!" I said. "I think we have a problem here."

The boat started to settle, fast. Already the water was ankle deep. "Plug those holes!" Stoat yelled. "Start bailing!"

"With what?"

"Anything—your shirts, that minnow bucket!" Harry and I stripped off our shirts and stuffed them into the shot holes, but the water immediately forced the cloth out again. I squatted down and tried to hold it in place. Harry dumped the pail of shiners over the side and started bailing. Then the hull strakes split where the shots had holed them. No way to stop the water now.

"We'd better abandon ship," I said.

Stoat was white lipped, his bloodshot eyes wide open and bulging like a marmoset's. It was at least four hundred yards to the nearest shore. He opened the locker where he kept the shells and pawed around frantically inside. "Where are those drotted life jackets?"

Nowhere to be found, apparently.

"I think I saw Miss Nachtisch putting them in the boathouse," I said.

"But I can't swim."

"D-d-don't worry, Mr. Stoat," Harry said. "We're both life-guards, licensed and d-duly certified by the Red C-C-Cross. We'll g-g-et you ashore safe and sound."

The Gar Wood was settling by the stern now, pulled down by the weight of the Liberty engine. Harry and I dove over the side, then surfaced facing Stoat. "Jump," I yelled. "We'll grab you the moment you hit the water."

He splashed down, rigid as a post. Before he could sink I grasped his wrist and spun him around with his back toward me, then clamped on a firm cross-chest carry with my other arm. I set out for the near shore in a strong, easy sidestroke. He writhed like a panic-stricken python. "Relax," I said. "Don't struggle. The more you fight, the harder you make it for both of us." But he couldn't loosen his rigid muscles. "Look up at the sky," I told him. "Take deep breaths, pretend you're lying down for a nap, composing yourself for a nice rest, counting your money."

That caught his attention. I could feel Stoat will himself limp.

Behind me I watched the Gar Wood take her final plunge, stern first, the blue and white admiral's flag flapping a last farewell from the short mast on her bow. Big glassy bubbles seethed to the surface as she sank, then died away. She was down there now, full fathom five, along with the bones of the Frenchman's mastiffs.

Harry and I had to trade off twice on the swim to shore. A crowd was gathered on the narrow, rocky beach when we reached the shallows, housemaids, the cook, and the boatman, along with a tall moke in a leather jacket, a Smilin' Jack crush cap, and a cook-ie-duster mustache, clearly the Beaver's pilot. Cora and Wanda stood at the front of the group with Flo, comforting Mrs. Stoat. As we touched bottom at last and struggled to our feet, she broke away from Flo and dashed into the water. Stoat shook me off and stood upright, sodden but furious.

"Morison, are you all right?"

"Yes, Eunice, quite. But I'll be even better when I see these young vandals behind bars. Dobbs," he yelled up to the pilot, "get on the plane radio and contact the sheriff's office. I want to report a felony. Piracy. Have them send a squad car right away."

"Right on it, Mr. Stoat." The pilot grinned at us nastily and legged it for the dock.

"Daddy!" Cora gasped. "You can't! They saved your life." Wanda too looked horrified. Mrs. Stoat bobbed her head in agreement with her daughter.

"These boys are heroes, Morison," she said. "You can't swim a stroke, and they carried you halfway across the lake."

"Only after they sank my boat," he answered. "They purposely shot holes in the hull and foundered her. A sixty thousand dollar treasure! Irreplaceable!"

"That was an accident," I said. "I tripped on a cleat and the gun went off in my hand."

"Balderdash," Stoat said. "We'll see what my good friend the sheriff says."

He waded ashore and set off for the lodge, dripping but dignified.

The boatman was waiting for us to climb the bank. He was a big guy with tattoos on his forearms and a flattened nose, scar tissue over his eyes. He looked like an ex-pug. "You guys come with me now. I'm gonna lock you punks in the storeroom till the law gets here."

"We could turn around and swim for it," I muttered to Harry.

"No good," he said. "Stoat knows my dad. Remember?"

We marched back to the lodge.

"I hope they at least give us lunch," Harry said.

An hour later, Dobbs fetched us from the storeroom, where Harry had made serious inroads on a box of marshmallow cookies.

The pilot marched us into the dining room. Stoat, seated at the table with a plate of soup and a club sandwich before him, had changed to another outfit: a navy blue blazer over a Harry Truman Hawaiian shirt, and ice-cream trousers. The sheriff, it seemed, was away from his office on other business. He wouldn't be back until Monday. This was Saturday.

We offered to dive on the boat and try to salvage her. Dobbs and the boatman, whose name it seemed was Sailor McMahon, laughed, but Mrs. Stoat sided with us. "They could use the float boat," she said. "It has a power winch on it."

"And we've got that portable air compressor out in the garage," Cora added. "You know, the one we use to inflate car tires and the beach balls. They could rig deflated air mattresses along the Gar Wood's rails, fill them with the compressor, and with the help of the winch crank her up to the surface again."

"L-l-et us at least give it a shot, Mr. Stoat," Harry said. "We're very g-good in the water, either under it or on the t-top."

"As you well know, my dear," said Mrs. Stoat.

Reluctantly, Stoat agreed.

"We haven't eaten since breakfast," Harry said. "C-can we have m-maybe a sandwich or something before we start?"

"No," Stoat snapped. "You'd have to wait an hour before going into the water again, and time's a-wasting."

Cora and Wanda rustled up fins, face masks, and an armload of sagging air mattresses while Harry and I lugged the compressor down to the dock. Sailor McMahon had unmoored the float boat and brought it alongside. We all piled aboard and motored out onto the lake. The only one missing was Flo, who was out in the woods collecting what she called "simples"—weeds, bitter berries, and other shrubbery from which to concoct Mrs. Stoat's lotions and potions.

Harry and the girls unplugged the air mattresses and deflated them. Stoat and his wife sat in lawn chairs on the afterdeck, which was carpeted in sisal dyed royal blue. The great man had donned a commodore's hat, all glittering with gold braid. He had a big green Havana stogie lit, an Upmann corona *puro*, and was sipping a gin and tonic from one of his dry-fly glasses. Dobbs sat to one side in another chair. Cora had told me he was an ex-captain in the USAAF. He'd flown P-38 Lightnings in the Pacific with Dick Bong, the baby-faced killer from nearby Poplar, Wisconsin, who'd been the top U.S. air ace of World War II with forty kills. Captain Dobbs, she said, had downed a dozen Nips. "He would have got more, he says, but the war ended too soon." In those days girls were still impressed with martial deeds.

I had a pretty good fix on where the Gar Wood went down, triangulating the position between the weedbeds and the flagpole at the lodge. The lake water was a clear dark green and you could see the bottom at least twenty feet down. After some slow cruising over the area, I spotted the bow sticking up from the weedgrowth down there, the admiral's flag hanging limp from the jackstaff.

"There she is!" I yelled back to McMahon. "Hold it right here and I'll drop the hook." He backed the 125-horse Evinrude, and I uncleated the bow anchor, careful not to let the Danforth Hi-Tensile, which weighed fifty pounds, plummet straight down through the hull of the Gar Wood and cause even more damage.

"I'll go down first and see how it looks," I said. "I'm the one who sank her in the first place." Harry found a smaller, ten-pound mushroom anchor in the stern and bent it to a coil of light manila, securing the bitter end to another bow cleat. This was an old Polynesian pearl diver's trick we'd read about and adapted to our spear fishing expeditions in the lakes around home. You grabbed the anchor line with a hand and your toes at the surface, alongside the boat, then your partner released it and the anchor dragged you to the bottom lickety-split, saving the time and energy you'd otherwise waste in swimming down. I went over the side, pulled on mask and fins, and hyperventilated a bit, charging my blood and lungs with oxygen, then gave Harry the high sign. He unbent the line from the cleat and down I went.

It was twilight on the bottom, a dark green dusk with the waterweeds waving spookily in all directions. Blue gills and rock bass finned out of the murk and goggled at me through the face plate, curious. In the distance I thought I saw a pickerel cruising the edge of the gloom. Looking for lunch, as always. The Gar Wood lay keel down in the weeds, her propellor shaft deep in the muck. The shotguns still lay inside the hull. I picked them up—amazing how light they felt underwater—and kicked my way back to the anchor line. I tucked the guns under one arm, then gave two sharp tugs on the line, our signal that I wanted to be pulled up. Harry hauled away.

When my head broke the surface, I saw Cora and Wanda staring down at me from the railing of the float boat, their eyes as wide as those of the bluegills. Treading water, I handed them the shotguns. "Don't touch the triggers," I warned. "One of them at least is still ready to fire and there's a round in the chamber." Captain Dobbs came forward and took the Brownings.

"How does it look?" Stoat asked.

"We can do it," I told him. "I think we'd better raise her on the level, though, not from the bow—otherwise, that big engine might tear out the transom as she comes up. We'll secure the air mattresses at intervals along the coamings and inflate 'em for added buoyancy. Then we can rig a cradle of heavy line under the hull, tying it off amidships, and attach the winch hook to it."

"Go to it," he said. "Just remember, though, if there's any further damage to my boat I'm charging you for it."

It took us a dozen round-trips to the bottom, with Cora and Wanda tending the dive line, before we had the cradle rigged, the winch hook secured, and the stern mattresses lashed in place. Another dozen dives to fill them from the compressor. We saved time by sipping air from the hose whenever we ran short, but still it was exacting work. You had to be careful with the air hose. Suck on it incautiously and it would blow you up like an overcooked sausage. The water was cold—seventy degrees or so at the surface but much colder on the spring-fed bottom—and we were shivering as we neared completion. Harry's lips looked dark purple and my arms were covered in goosebumps. It felt like my balls had shriveled to the size of peas.

On our last dive we noticed that the panfish, which up to now had been observing our every move with great interest, as if they were taking lessons in knot tying, had suddenly winked out of sight. We looked around for them. Then Harry poked me in the ribs, pointing off into the deeper darkness.

Circling out there, about thirty feet away, was the biggest fish I'd ever seen. It looked as long as a shark, with ruddy brown fins and spike-lined jaws like a barracuda's. Its long, thick, pale green body was covered with wavy vertical stripes, dark ones, in contrast to the pale lozenges that mark a northern pike. This was the fish the Chippewas called *mas kinonge*—the ugly fish. Muskellunge. The Tiger of the North. And a keeper if ever I saw one.

7

COLLEGE GIRLS

Cora and Wanda were sitting at the edge of the float boat's deck, gabbing and dandling their feet in the water while they waited. Harry spotted the flicker of their red-painted toenails as we ascended from the final dive. He looked over at me, winked through the mask, and peeled off from the dive line. He swam up out of their line of sight. I paused on the line to watch. Hiding in the shadow of the hull, he reached out and tickled one of the girls' chubby feet, then quickly grabbed the other by the ankle. We could hear the high-pitched screams underwater.

When we pulled ourselves out of the water, laughing, the girls were waiting for us with furled, wet towels. "Take that, you brute," Wanda said, snapping hers at my butt.

"Hey," I yelled, "it wasn't me! *There's* your Monster of the Deep." I pointed at Harry. They immediately turned on him and drove him, dancing, yelping, and spinning, up against the bow rail.

"Enough of that nonsense," Stoat bellowed. "You're acting like kindergartners. Cora, I'm ashamed of you. You too, Miss Nachtisch. You're supposed to be learning proper, ladylike deportment at college. I'm not spending a small fortune just to see my daughter carrying on like a silly, lower-class guttersnipe, and I'm sure Dr. Nachtisch feels the same." Captain Dobbs stood beside him, scowling with military rectitude.

"Oh, Morison," Mrs. Stoat said. "Don't be such a party pooper. You were young too once, if you can remember that far back."

"But never downright silly, my dear," Stoat said.

"The cradle's rigged and ready, sir," I said. "I think we can try to lift her now."

We all gathered at the forward rail, staring down through the water, as Sailor McMahon worked the winch controls. The falls tautened as he engaged the electric motor, the shivs turned in the blocks, squealing, and I saw the Gar Wood shudder down there. The buried drive shaft pulled free from the muck, and I caught the gleam of the brass prop as it came clear. The boat rose slowly but even keeled from the bottom. The cradle was holding.

Mrs. Stoat clapped, and the girls joined her.

Sailor brought the speedboat close to the surface, then set the brake on the motor. "We don't want to lift her clear of the water," he told Stoat. "Once her full weight came to bear, the brake or the motor bushings might burn out. Let's let the water support her some until we get into the shallows. Then it should be easy to back the boat trailer into the water and crank her up on the skids."

"Very well," Stoat said. "You're the old salt, after all."

We had to motor back to the lodge quite slowly, of course, and the sun was well down in the west by the time we got the Gar Wood out of the water. Stoat had some leftover teak in his workshop—he'd had the porch planked in it—so Harry and I turned to with the circular saw and the lathe, shaping a length to replace the mahogany strake perforated by my shotgun blasts. While Harry fine-tuned the teak, I field-stripped the Brownings, swabbed out their tubes with solvent and gun oil, and lubricated all the moving parts. Then I put them back together again. By sundown, we had the speedboat's hull repaired and caulked, damn near as good as new. Sailor had drained the gas lines and dried out the electrics on the Liberty engine, replaced the wet plugs as well. We refueled and launched the speedboat. When we lit off the engine, it coughed, sputtered, then roared back to life, none the worse for its four-hour immersion. Sailor took us out for a quick spin, and as we pulled back in to the pier, Stoat came down from the lodge, drink in hand as usual.

I jumped up on the dock and snapped to attention, threw him my most squared-away Parris Island salute. "All repairs effected, sir," I said. "Ship shape and Bristol fashion."

He nodded and almost smiled. "Well, Mr. Slater, I must say I'm impressed. I think you and Mr. Taggart have won yourselves a reprieve from the long arm of the law."

"As we say in the Crot . . . er, the Corps, sir, 'Can Do.' We did."

Sailor McMahon, flemishing the mooring lines, looked up and blew a muted raspberry. There's no love lost between jarheads and swabbies.

"I think you've earned yourselves a bite of supper," Stoat said. "Come on up to the lodge. Evangeline has a barbeque waiting. Baby backribs and sweet corn, I believe."

The barbeque pit was behind the lodge, and Evangeline stood before the dancing flames in a crisp white apron and chef's toque, turning huge slabs of meat that sizzled with gleaming red sauce. Flo, now clad in a maid's uniform, was helping her. A massive black kettle seethed on one side of the grill. Cora and Wanda stood beside it, shucking cobs of fresh-picked corn. Captain Dobbs was with them, flyboy hat cocked back to show his curly hair, drink in hand, chatting the girls up. With his free hand he was demonstrating intricate aerial maneuvers. He frowned as we walked up. "What are you punks doing here?" he said.

"Now, now, Francis," Mrs. Stoat said, walking over from a redwood picnic table laden with bowls of German-style potato salad and cole slaw. "Let's have none of that. These boys have redeemed their reputations." She was sipping from a highball glass filled with one of Flo's concoctions. It was redolent of gin. Weeds bobbed on the surface. Some were stuck to her teeth.

Stoat was recharging his dry-fly glass with scotch and ice cubes. "That's right, Captain Dobbs," he said. "Please confine your dogfights to the sky from now on. These chaps are here at my invitation." He turned to us. "Help yourselves to drinks, boys. There's lemonade in that pitcher and plenty of Cokes in the cooler."

Harry went over to the drinks cart and poured us each a tall glass of Coca-Cola. After glancing around to ensure that no one but me was looking, he topped them up with two hefty slugs of Jack Daniels, then added ice from the silver bucket. But Cora must have seen him. She sauntered over, swallowing a smile, and murmured *sotto voce*, "Naughty naughty. *Scandaleuxe. Très méchant, mon cher*. Now pour me one just like yours. And another for Wanda."

Wild college girls, I thought. They're living up to the locker-room legend. Maybe, if we played it cool, a little "free love" awaited us. She was friendly enough, as was the wickedly wonderful Wanda. And after all, as every thoughtful high school boy knew, there's only a single letter's difference between "genial" and "genital."

The ribs were already off the grill. Evangeline retrieved the last steaming ears of corn from the kettle, piled them on a plate, and announced, "Ladies and gents, dinner is served."

Flo went around the table with heaped platters, serving us like a well-trained menial. "What is this?" I whispered to her as she came around to me. "Have you signed on with the plutocracy?"

"She's paying me very well," Flo said in my ear. "And tomorrow, when they close the lodge for the winter, I'm flying back down to Milwaukee with them. A full-time job, well away from the clutches of Doc and Curly. And anyway," as she straightened back up with the platter, "it's none of your business, schoolboy."

After dinner, finished off with fresh, hot blueberry pie à la mode and black coffee (surreptitiously spiked with Asbach Uralt brandy), the girls put a stack of records on the phonograph and we danced with them on the screened porch, under the dim light of Japanese lanterns. Harry accompanied the platters on his sax from time to time, blowing Birdlike runs around the melody line. I realized, not for the first time, that music and an armful of warm girl is the best dessert of all. Captain Dobbs walked by outside, carrying a tool kit down to the Beaver for some preflight repairs. I'd heard him telling Stoat at dinner that there was something wrong with the altimeter. He gave us the fish eye as he went past.

"That stuck-up creep," Wanda said. "He's got his eye on Cora. Warm for her form, as they say. And her daddy's loot, too, I'm sure. All he can talk about is how great he was in the war, flaming Zekes and Zeroes right and left, as if we cared, and making out with army nurses." She frowned and gruffed her voice a bit. "He ain't got no savoir faire."

I looked over at Harry and Cora, dancing belly to belly to the strains of Frankie Yankovic's "Blue Skirt Waltz." You couldn't have slipped a Gillette Blue Blade between them. His eyes were rolling. "Does Harry have it?" I asked.

Wanda laughed. "He's kind of cute, though. I like that little stutter of his, you know, when he isn't really sure of himself?"

"Am I too . . . er, cocky?" I asked. "Like Captain Francis Dobbs?"

She looked down at the bulge in my khakis, then pressed her belly against it. "No," she giggled. "Cockier!"

The record ended and the needle skittered in the groove. Harry walked over while Cora went to the phonograph. "S-s-say, C-Cora's got an idea. I was telling her about that muskie we saw this afternoon, and she suggests we sneak out there in one of the rowboats with our flyrods. The old man's already in bed, and Flo's giving Mrs. Stoat a mud bath in the steam room, so there's no one to stop us."

"What about Dobbs and the Sailor?"

"S-Sailor's hanging around waiting for Flo to get f-free. Cora thinks he's s-sweet on her. And as you can see from here, the flyboy is butt-up in the cockpit of his B-Beaver."

"I'm game," I said.

Cora blew out two of the lanterns and stacked another pile of platters, classical this time, to play while we were gone. Whoever passed the porch in the next hour or so might figure we were sitting there in the dark, listening to the music. Then we snuck down to the beach through the shadows. We chose the bigger of the Adirondack boats. I rowed while the others sat bow and stern. It was dead calm on the lake. The light cedar hull moved fast through the water, despite the load. From the Beaver came only the sounds of tool clatter and muttered curses. Soon we were clear of the light halo spread from the lodge. The moon was not yet up and the lake glimmered black in the starlight. I aimed for the weedbed nearest to where we'd salvaged the Gar Wood. Harry tied the Cannibal-Killer on his flyrod ahead of a six-inch wire leader. I hoped the light, flexible wire was strong enough to withstand those razor sharp teeth we'd seen in the muskie's duckbilled mouth.

"This is the p-place," Harry said. He stood up in the bow. "How's about let's do like we did with that big b-brown. I'll cast first—say a dozen throws—then you take over."

"Okay."

"It's dark out here," Wanda said. "Spooky—and chilly, too." She shivered.

"You should have brought a sweater like I did," Cora said. I took off my OD wool shirt, and draped it over Wanda's shoulders. Then I moved back and sat beside her on the narrow stern thwart. I wrapped my arm around her.

"A true gentleman," Cora said.

Harry worked out flyline and dropped the Cannibal-Killer just short of the weedbed, which we could see faintly in the starlight.

"Let it sink about twenty counts," I said.

"I know, I know. I was down there too, remember?" He waited, then started stripping in, mixing it up as was our wont with big piscivores. Wanda looked up, at me, tucked warm under my arm, those big wide eyes, and what could I do? I kissed her. Forgive me, Lorraine. . . . She tasted tart and sweet, of lemonade with just a hint of bourbon. I felt her hand on my thigh, then it moved up. The ambient air temperature soared.

"Cocky?" she whispered. She was wearing a light cotton summer skirt, mid-calf length as was the style that year, and I slipped my hand under it, up over her knee to her thigh. Smooth as warm silk. Then skating higher, the skin even smoother, almost hot now. Humid. She eased her legs apart, inviting me onward. A touch of delicate fur . . . . No skivvies!

Ah yes, college girls! They come prepared.

We slipped off the thwart, down into total darkness. One thing led to another. The Fly Trap, Sergeant Stingley called it. Baited with honey.

High overhead I could hear the wings of night birds passing. But no, it was only Harry's flyline, false casting again and again.

To hell with Sergeant Stingley. For that matter, to hell with fishing.

I don't know how long Harry kept at it, but when I next raised my head, the only sound I heard from up forward was that of serious smooching. Cora had brought a blanket along, and they were down there beneath it. The moon was just edging over the pines to the east. Wanda sat up, straightening and smoothing her skirt, rehooking her bra, so I tucked myself in and buttoned my trousers.

We'd drifted a bit during our little time-out, and now the boat lay much closer to the weeds. Kneeling amidships—we were rocking too erratically (or should I say erotically?) to risk standing—I picked up the flyrod and I cast down the length of the weedbed. Pike and muskies like to lie in ambush, hidden by weed or sunken logs, which they closely resemble, then dart out to nail any finny passersby that catch their fancy. I retrieved the Cannibal-Killer at a leisurely pace, trying to see myself through the muskie's eyes as a fat, naive alderman of the weedbed, out for a midnight stroll in the new risen moonlight—a silvery creek chub, say, or an outsized dace—ambling along with not a care in the world, maybe even burbling a piscine version of the Colonel Bogey March. The nearly full moon, yellow as a round of Wisconsin cheddar, was high enough now to throw slanting beams through the water. As the fly came into the boat, I saw a shadow cruising behind it, ghosting along like an underwater freight train. It moved up close, until its long snout just tickled the trailing edges of the bucktail, then matched its pace to my retrieve. The Cannibal-Killer swam home toward the rod tip.

Was I imagining this? I slowed the fly when it was still about ten feet out, then stopped stripping altogether. The Cannibal-Killer sank, and the shadow sank with it. I stripped again, fast, a long, hard pull. The shadow rose with the pulsations of the deer hair. Now the fly was right alongside. I held it there in the water, six inches down, then started working it around from the rod tip in a broad, dodgy figure eight. But the shadow had had enough. It sank slowly, back into the dark.

"My God, what was that?" Wanda was standing at my shoulder.

"I think it was him," I said.

"The muskie?"

"What else in this lake could be that big?" I sat down on the thwart, and she eased down beside me. My heart was pounding.

"Maybe I wasn't stripping it fast enough," I said.

"Will he come again?"

"Maybe. With these guys you never know till they hook up. Or don't."

Harry's head poked out of the blanket. "What happened?"

"I had a follow."

"Was it him?"

I nodded.

"Get back out there," he said. "G-goddamit, you have all the luck." Then Cora's hand emerged and pulled him back down. "Let me know what happens." His voice came muffled through Hudson's Bay wool.

I waited a few minutes to allow the muskie to get back to his lie. Then, taking great pains to ensure that the oarlocks didn't squeak, I rowed us out a short distance, to change the angle of my cast and retrieve. Once again the flyline whistled through the air, weaving gleaming white loops in the moonlight, and the C.K. plopped down, far up the weedbed. This time I stripped in much faster, crouching down close to the gunwhale and keeping the rod tip low. Wanda knelt beside me, watching the line snake back in. Then I saw a vee appear on the water, beyond the visible end of the line. A big damned bow wave! He was coming for it, and he meant business. I speeded up my retrieve, almost spastic now, as if the fat alderman had just realized he'd strayed into a bad part of town. Then, *whammo!*—twenty feet out the muskie took. In my head, a flashing x-ray image of the alderman's spine shattering like a matchstick. A great boiling swirl at the top of the water, and the impact jarred the rod clear down to its cork handle. I struck without raising the rod tip, yanking straight back with my line hand, once, twice, three times for good measure, trying to bury the hook past its barb. They have hard mouths, muskies.

The loops of stripped-in line, coiled loosely at my feet, disappeared in a flash, and the drag skirled loud in the darkness.

"Zowie!" Wanda yipped.

Harry popped out again. "Shit Marengo!" he yelled. "You've got him!"

"Or vice versa," I said. Line spun off the reel in a blur and the sound of the drag sang out over the water, loud enough it seemed to wake roosting birds along the shore. I raised the rod tip, then tipped it sideways to try and turn the fish before he reached the sanctuary of the weeds. If he got in there and tangled the leader with gunk, it would be adios. The tippet behind the wire leader was a hefty 1X—but that gave less than ten pounds of breaking strength. This guy, by the feel of him, went at least twice that weight, maybe as much as thirty pounds.

But the maneuver turned the trick. The muskie ran parallel to the weeds for a bit, then sheered off toward deeper water, toward the middle of Twodoggone Lake. If he didn't head down to the bottom and wrap the leader around a sunken sawlog, maybe I had a chance.

Harry was up now and standing beside me. I caught a glimpse of Cora in the moonlight, sitting up from the blanket with her breasts exposed. She looked miffed then glanced down at her chest and went back undercover.

It was then that lights went on in the lodge, on the far side of the lake. "Uh-oh," Harry said. "Looks like we may have disturbed someone's beauty rest."

"Oh, shit," Wanda said. "If old man Stoat catches us out here. . . ."

"Our asses are like unto the grasses." Cora was up again, fully dressed this time. "Not only does he disapprove of what he calls 'daughterly hanky-panky,' he goes positively apoplectic if anyone other than business clients messes with his precious muskies. He lets Sailor and Francis take pot shots at poachers."

"Keep an eye on the lodge," I told the girls. "Maybe he just got up to take a leak."

Cora sniffed. "My daddy doesn't do anything so plebian as 'take a leak,' as you call it. He micturates."

College boys.

The muskie was down on the bottom now, lying doggo. I tried to pump and reel on him, but all I did was stress the drag some more. He wouldn't even shake his head. I tried Harry's trick of jarring the rod butt with the heel of my hand. No response. "Maybe he's wrapped around something," I said.

We heard a loud, hollow roar from the lodge. The Gar Wood lighting off? Sounded like it. Maybe the vibes of the engine did the trick, but suddenly the muskie moved. He was off the bottom and running again, back toward the weedbed. I had to reel fast to take up the slack as he closed with the skiff. I kept my eye on his wake. No, he was headed our way on a collision course!

"Oh, fuck," Harry said. "Now it's Moby Muskie. If he rams us, we'll sink like stone. That'll be the second boat on the bottom since we got here."

But the muskie dove under the skiff and kept on going, spinning me around and tangling my legs in the process.

"Here they come," Wanda said.

I looked over my shoulder and saw the speedboat roaring our way, a spotlight scanning the water ahead of it in wide sweeps.

"Break the fucker off," Harry said.

I did. Then we rowed like hell for the near shore.

8

COYOTE NOWHERE

We bade swift but heartfelt adieus to Cora and Wanda, promising to write. Then we ran for the woods. Once we'd found cover, we flopped down and peered back through the brush toward the lake. The Gar Wood pulled up close to where the girls sat in the skiff. Stoat was at the wheel. Sailor and Captain Dobbs stood on the bow with shotguns. We couldn't make out their voices clearly over the rumble of the engine, but Cora kept shrugging her shoulders and shaking her head. Wanda pointed into the woods, well away from where she'd seen us run. Dobbs raised his weapon and fired three 12-gauge rounds into the shrubbery. We could hear the heavy loads rip through leaves and rattle off tree trunks. Stoat eased the Gar Wood alongside the skiff and Dobbs leaned over to pull the girls into the speedboat. You could tell from the stiffness of his posture and the muscle he exerted to pull them aboard that he was very angry.

"Goddamn that brute," Harry muttered. "He can't treat my girl that way." He rolled over and crawled quickly toward a nearby honeysuckle. I recognized it as the one where we'd cached the gear that morning. He came back with the Thompson cradled in his forearms. Before I could do anything to stop him, he had the gun to his shoulder and squeezed off a rattling burst—aimed high over their heads.

"Christ, you asshole!" I said. "The muzzle flash will give away our position!"

Sure enough, both shotguns blazed away in our direction. Leaves and twigs rained down on our heads. I heard pellets ping on steel, Harry yelped, and a sting like that of a yellowjacket numbed my right hand.

"Make like a sand crab!" I said, and we scuttled back deeper into the woods while they were reloading. We hid there, dead quiet, for what felt like an hour while Sailor and the flyboy pound-ed the shoreline cover for us. Finally they gave up and the Gar Wood headed back across the lake with the skiff in tow.

"Are you hurt?" I asked Harry.

"T-two dings," he said. "One on the forehead, another on my wrist. I think some shot hit the drum of the T-tommy gun, too."

"I've got one in the hand. We'll have to dig them out when it gets light enough to see."

We went back to the honeysuckle, retrieved the rest of our gear including the BAR, and made our way down the outlet stream, back toward the canoe.

"I wonder what's going to happen to the girls?" Harry said.

"They'll be okay. Cora's got her daddy wrapped around her little finger, and Wanda plays the innocent maiden like Shirley Temple."

"She didn't sound so innocent back there in the skiff with you."

"I never kiss and tell. And you're one to talk. You seemed to be making out all right yourself under that blanket."

We both laughed. It was an adventure, all right.

Daylight came on swiftly, cloudless again, and we made good time through the woods, heading downhill. Back at our campsite beside the Stony, Harry built a small, hot, smokeless fire while I fetched the supplies Flo and I had hidden in the cave. He was heat-ing the tip of his jackknife in the flames when I got back. A pan of water steamed on the fire. "Let's see your mitt," he said.

The shotgun pellet bulged blueblack under the skin on the top of my hand. Harry worked the redhot tip of the Schrade blade into the hole, worked it around, and the pellet popped free.

"Ouch! Go easy!"

"'R-r-ruff,' said the dog as he wiped his ass with sandpaper." Harry chuckled. "Don't be a wimp."

He squeezed the puncture wound to get out the dirty blood and rinsed it with hot water from the pan. I picked up the pellet with my free hand. "Looks like a Number 2," I said. "Goose shot."

"Ah, yes," Harry said. "They knew what they were gunning for. We were saps to piss Stoat off that way, after we'd finally got in his good graces. Now he'll probably report us to the sheriff after all."

He found the first aid kit in our baggage, daubed iodine over the wound with a Q-tip, then peeled a Band-Aid to slap on it. He reheated the knife blade, gritted his teeth, and dug out the shot in his wrist.

"You'll have to do my f-f-forehead," he said. "I don't have a m-mirror."

I examined the shiny blue knot above his eyebrow. It was the size of an acorn. "I think the pellet must have bounced off," I said. "I don't see anything inside there. Just the lump where it hit. Not even any blood showing."

"Thank G-God I've got a hard head."

We brewed up a pot of Flo's coffee and ate some more of her jerky for breakfast. Harry pissed and moaned about the two boxes of goodies we'd left behind at stoat's place. Then we dragged the canoe out from its hiding place, reloaded it, and pushed off down the brook.

"I wonder if we've given Doc and Curly enough time," I said as we neared the Firesteel. "Could they have come through, gotten tired of looking for us, and gone back upriver already?"

"Maybe they never came after us," Harry said. "After all, we outgun them. They might have decided to cut their losses, clear out before we could turn them in to the cops."

"Curly's a Marine," I said. "One of the Old Breed. They don't quit easy."

Still, we stopped at the juncture of the two streams and hid the canoe again in the bankside brush. Then we snuck out to the edge of the Firesteel and looked carefully, upriver and down. Nothing in sight but a tall, gaunt heron, fishing for his breakfast. The roar of the Bonebreaker was muted here, but the ground shook to its violence. We were about to put the canoe in the water when a different noise hit my ears.

"What's that?"

Harry listened. "A m-m-motor?"

It got louder quickly, and then both our heads snapped around, looking downstream. The Beaver! The big, bulb-nosed red and black float plane came banking around a bend at treetop level and raced toward us, heading upriver. The right hand door was off.

"Hit the deck!"

We ate dirt as it bellowed overhead, disappearing fast in the direction of Doc and Curly's camp.

"Oh, shit," Harry said. "Now we've got two different sets of bad asses after us. Sailor was sitting in there with a deer rifle between his knees. It had a scope."

Well, we couldn't very well stay where we were. Even if Flo didn't tell him, Stoat would soon realize that we'd left the canoe on Stony Creek, and his pal the sheriff might arrive any minute with a posse. Doc and Curly could be upstream or down. It was good enough flying weather for Dobbs to keep up his aerial hunt all day. The only thing left to do, we decided, was continue downstream with extreme caution, sticking as close to the Firesteel's wooded banks as we could manage. The Old Town was painted green, thank God, and the riverside canopy would give us some cover from the air. But we'd have to be careful rounding each bend in the river, in case we met Doc and Curly coming back upstream.

We shoved off. Harry had the Tommy gun leaning beside him in the bow, muzzle up. I laid the BAR, locked and loaded, on the duffle in front of me while I paddled in the stern. We didn't even bother with the flyrods, which were repacked in their tubes with the dunnage.

Twice as we paddled that morning the Beaver flew overhead. But we heard it coming and had plenty of time to take cover. Finally it headed downriver toward the north, maybe to Duluth or Superior where they'd probably gas up for their return to Milwaukee. I'd overheard Dobbs tell Stoat last night that the fuel storage tank at the lodge had sprung a leak and there was water in the avgas.

Toward noon we came to another small feeder stream, this one entering the Firesteel from the right. We pulled into it and lay up under some willows while we ate more jerky. This diet was getting old fast. We were both dog tired, not having slept since the night before last, and then uneasily. Harry proposed that we catch some shut-eye after lunch, trading off with the watch. We flipped for it, and he won. "Wake me up in an hour, then you can snooze," he said. He unrolled his sleeping bag on the riverbank, under the boughs of a willow, and soon was sawing logs.

I jointed the Payne and rigged it with a lighter leader. Some trout were rising in a shady pool upstream and I figured on catching a few for supper. No more jerky for me, not for a while if I could help it. I saw caddis flies dapping on the water so I tied on a no. 14 Henryville Special, then eased into the creek and waded upstream, knee-deep under the shadow of the cutbank. The bottom was pea gravel, good footing.

The firefight with Sailor and Dobbs had left me more shaken than I'd realized. When those shotgun loads were ripping through the branches over our heads, I felt like pissing my pants. Sergeant Stingley would have grabbed the Tommy gun away from Harry and charged the bastards flat out, yelling obscenities and firing from the hip. All I'd wanted to do was burrow my way to China. Could I possibly handle Korea, when it was commie burp-gun bullets zipping toward me instead of birdshot? T-34 tanks and MIG-17s hunting me rather than a civilian float plane and a swabbie with a deer rifle? I'd thought that Parris Island had toughened me, erased my imagination along with my civilian personality. That's what it was meant to do. Stingley and all the other instructors told us again and again about young Marines in the Pacific island campaigns who'd thrown themselves on grenades to save their buddies. Gotten their guts blown out for the Corps. Okay, maybe it was sheer reflex, or a boy's inability to visualize his own death, but would I even be able to face enemy fire without crying momma? I could never admit these doubts to Harry or anyone else, not even Lorraine—least of all Lorraine. But I had to admit them to myself.

They were rainbow trout, chunky little guys no more than nine inches long, but game as hell, jumping clear of the water on the hookup, their red sides flashing in the sunlight. I picked them off one after another as I worked my way up the bank, and when I'd killed six, I stopped. Three each for supper was enough. Pan-fried along with thin slices of Flo's potatoes and a slivered onion. It wouldn't be Evangeline's ribs, but it would be wonderful.

Back at the canoe I picked some ostrich ferns, wet them down with cold water from the creek, packed the trout in layers, and laid them in the shade. Then I woke Harry up and grabbed forty winks for myself.

By late afternoon we were well downriver. No sign of the Beaver and none of Doc and Curly. The Firesteel widened here into a stretch of broad, slow meanders, broken up with long sandy islands grown dark and tall with aspens. A good place to stop for supper, while it was still light and no one could see the gleam of a cookfire from the river. We pulled over to one of the bigger islands and hid the canoe in the brush, then explored inland. There was an old cellar hole on the high ground. It was filled with fire-blackened timbers and shards of old-fashioned windowglass, wavy and dark-ened by heat and time. We wondered who'd lived there and when, what was their story, did they all die in the fire, or did it happen after they'd pulled stakes? Most of the old timers who settled up here, after the loggers had finished with the country, quickly learned that this wasn't farmland. The soil was all sand and stones and glacial muck. You could grow spuds and that was about it. Maybe a milch cow or two could sustain themselves on a quarter section, but the grass was poor if you could grow it at all. No big dairy herds of fat, glossy Holsteins and Guernseys like the Dutchmen raised in the southern half of the state. The would-be farmers soon moved on to better lands in the Dakotas and points west, leaving "Up North" to the tourists and weekend fishermen.

We made camp near the river where we'd landed, behind a low dune and well away from the cellar hole. It was too damned depressing there. I think we were both feeling kind of blue by then. The trip wasn't working out the way we'd imagined it. Doc and Curly were downright frightening, and apart from the girls, the Stoat interlude was no fun either.

"He's going to make trouble when we get back to town," Harry said. "You can hop a train west and the Marine Corps will take care of you, but Stoat sure as hell's gonna bitch to my dad and I'll be in the shithouse. Or j-j-jail, more likely."

"Tell him I fired the Tommy gun," I said. "That's the only chargeable act we committed, Hairball, and they shot first. We've got the wounds to prove it. Stoat can't run us in for something as laughable as fishing without permission. We didn't catch anything anyway, and the girls won't fink us out. Just taking a boat ride with his daughter and her friend is hardly a federal offense."

He laughed. "Yeah. And when you stop and think about it, they seduced *us*, d-didn't they?"

"College girls," I said. "They learn it all at school."

I dug a firepit in the sand, lined it with dry rocks from the shore, and built a cookfire of pine sticks and hunks of charred wood from the burnt-out house. The aroma of frying trout, spuds, and onions cheered us some. Our coffeepot burbled on the grate. When the fish and potatoes were crisp and brown, we dug in.

Night came on quick. For a while, all you could hear over the whisper of the Firesteel was chomping teeth and the clink of aluminum forks and plates. After we ate, Harry played quietly on the horn—quick, light little phrases, with subtle changes in inflection to counterpoint the sound of the tinkling rapids. The Firesteel Bop . . .

Then I heard something rustle in the bushes nearby. Harry froze in midnote. I eased my hand over to where the BAR stood leaning against a craggy aspen trunk. A black, wet muzzle loomed out of the dusk, nostrils twitching in the firelight. A pair of hungry eyes gleamed above them.

"Fuck!" Harry said. "Another bear!"

But as I grabbed the BAR, I heard a tinny rattle, and a big, ungainly mutt emerged from the underbrush, grinning merrily, wagging its stubby tail. It had a studded collar around its neck, from which license tags jingled. The dog—it looked like a cross between an Airedale and a Labrador—slunk into the circle of firelight. Its paws were huge.

"He's just a puppy," Harry said. "And hungry, too. Look at his ribs." He reached his plate out toward the dog and put it on the sand. Then he took the frying pan and slid the last remaining trout onto it—*my* trout, I might add. I'd been saving it for dessert.

With one swipe of his long wide tongue the dog slurped it down, all gone in an instant, then looked up for more. Eyes gleaming with joy. Harry reached into Flo's food box and pulled out a handful of jerky sticks. The dog settled down on his elbows and haunches and started chewing, growling with contentment and flailing his stubby tail like a runaway metronome.

"I wonder what his name is?" Harry leaned over and looked at the brass plate on the dog's collar. "Gayelord Schnauzer? What kind of m-monicker is that for any self-respecting m-m-mutt?"

"A play on Gayelord Hauser?" He was the author of a best-selling diet book called *Look Better, Live Longer*, all the rage among health food faddists at the time. Harry's mother, who was good-looking enough in my book without any outside help, worshipped his every word. "Who does he belong to?"

Harry read another tag. "Someone named Duluoz. But it's not a Wisconsin license. New York, it says here."

"He's a long way from home."

"Poor little puppydog," Harry cooed, rumpling Gayelord's ears. "Is 'oo lost? Is 'oo lonely? Is 'oo . . . housebwoken?"

"Don't talk baby talk to him," I snapped. "I can't stand it."

He looked up at me, wide eyed and batting his lashes. "Oh, Gayelord, is the big bad Mawine angwy wif us now?"

"Fuck you."

Then a new voice sounded from the darkness. "I gotta agree with the 'Mawine.'"

A short, stocky figure stepped into the light, and at first I thought it was Curly. But this guy was much younger, with short, dark, tousled hair, high cheekbones, dark, wide-set eyes, and built like a football player. He even walked like a running back, toes turned inward. He wore faded Levis threadbare at the knees and a blue chambray workshirt. Scuffed black motorcycle boots on big feet. "I'm Peter Martin," he said. He swung a bottle from his hand and held it out to us. "Have a drink? We're camped out down the other end of the island. I was just taking a little sundown stroll with Gayelord here. Digging the sunset. Then we heard your music and ambled over in this direction. Gaye musta smelled your food cookin' and decided to see what he could mooch off you." He smiled. "Sorry for the interruption, but c'mon have a snort. I know *I'm* getting a bit dry."

Harry stood up and accepted the bottle. Jack Daniels. We each poured a slug into our tin cups, sweetening the coffee, and Harry filled a third one for Martin. He sat down crosslegged beside the fire and raised the cup to Harry. "Cheers, man." He smiled again and I could see he was half lit already.

I gave him our usual riff about the canoe trip, leaving out the Curly and Doc bit and making no mention at all of our troubles at Twodoggone Lake.

"Peter Martin," Harry mused. "The owner's tag on Gayelord's c-collar says something different."

"Yeah, Duluoz. He's, uh, a friend of mine. Over in Brooklyn. He gave me Gayelord. Said the pooch was unhappy in New York, too big for a one-room apartment. I was gonna be on the road this summer, so he turned him over to me."

"Having a look around the c-country, are you?"

Peter Martin grinned, his dark eyes sparking. "Hey, man, it's the only way to go. Don't you think? Fuck the cities. New York's a frosty fagtown, confusion and nonsense, Chicago not much better, all clangor and stink from the stockyards. Money money money, all they think of. L.A., Frisco, Denver—screw the lot of 'em. The one true and noble function of our time is to *move*." He pulled a packet of Zig-Zag papers from his shirt pocket, tipped in a line of shredded green tobacco, and rolled a lopsided smoke. Lit it with a kitchen match snapped alive with a thumbnail.

"Boo?" he said through his teeth, holding in the smoke. He held the cigarette out to us.

Harry drew back in mock fright. "Please don't say things like that. I-I've got a weak heart and I'm scared of the d-d-dark enough as it is."

"No, no, no," Martin said. "Boojie. Bambalacha. Muggles. Some call it mohasky."

"I'm in training," I said. "Tobacco shortens your wind and I may have to run for my life in Korea."

"It's not tobacco," Peter said, laughing. "It's grass, tea, Mary Warner. Good for you. Some call it Mary Jane or moocah, or just plain loco weed. I like to think of it as blue sage, Indian hay. A sacred herb." He shook his head, smiling. "Jeez you guys are square. Have a toke and I swear it'll make your night nicer." He looked up at the stars, shining through the trees. "It's all an illusion, anyways." The guy was always smiling.

To oblige him we each took a drag, then another. Following Peter's example we held them in as long as we could, then exhaled slowly through our teeth. Gayelord sat before us in the good-dog posture, grinning as he inhaled the smoke. We passed the joint around until it was down to a nubbin. Peter Martin fed the stub to the dog. "Mellow him out," he said.

Peter lay back on an elbow and poured another cup of coffee sweetened with bourbon. "So you're in the Marines," he said. "I joined the Navy during the war, V-12 program, wanted to be a fighter pilot in the Pacific. But I couldn't take the drill, all those asshole regs. Everything by the book, by the numbers. Finally I wigged out. Punched the company commander smack in the mouth and went off to the library. Later I showed up naked for a dress inspection. That did it, spent weeks in the loony bin while they gave me all kinds of tests to see what kind of psycho I was, but then they gave me an honorable discharge. Unfit for service. But I still wanted to see the war. I signed on in the merch. The merchant marine? So I'm a kind of a marine too, but different."

I'll say.

Brush wolves howled from across the river, an eerie high-pitched chorus.

"Aaaah," Peter Martin said. "Coyote nowhere. The place for me."

9

THE FRIENDS OF
GAYELORD SCHNAUZER

Later that night, when the coffee and bourbon were finished, our new friend led us up-island to where his buddies were camped out in an old, prewar Airstream trailer. We brought some of our gear with us. Gayelord led the way through the aspen jungle, using his nose to sniff out their earlier backtrail. Peter was impressed with our hardware. "God," he said, "if Ol' Bull Lee could see these guns, he'd cream his jeans." Bull Lee was a writer friend of Peter's who lived in Algiers, Louisiana, just across the river from New Orleans. Peter and his friends were heading down there from here, once they could figure out a way to get back across the Firesteel. A dirt track had led them in to the river a week ago and they'd crossed to the island with the Airstream towing behind a battered gray '49 Hudson. But since their arrival, the river had risen and there was no way they could get back without waterwings. The Firesteel was falling now, sure, but still too deep to venture it.

His pals were an odd lot. A slutty-looking babe in her twenties named Marylou; a short, blond, criminal type called Dean, skinny and wild eyed; and a heavyset fellow named Hal who worked for the Southern Pacific Railroad along with Dean. They were sitting crosslegged around a Coleman stove when we pulled in, stirring a pot of canned chili con carne. Empty cans littered the ground. "The crackers are kinda stale," Dean apologized after offering us a bowl of it. "We've been marooned on Crusoe's Island for damn near eternity."

"No thanks," I told him. "We just ate."

Peter went over to the Hudson, leaned in, and turned on the car radio. He fiddled with the dial, zooming up and down through ethereal static, until he picked up a faint but clear signal. Jazz, it sounded like. "From New Orleans," he said. "At night we sometimes pick it up. You can hear all of America in the dead of night if the atmospherics are right. St. Louis, Kansas City, Omaha, even Denver sometimes. It's different music everyplace. You can put your thumb on the pulse of the country this way. And man, what a different beat. In New York you gotta go to the clubs to hear real American boogie. Dig that tenorman, wailing away at the stars. Just like those coyotes out there."

"Jack gets a bit carried away," Marylou said in a gravelly whisky-alto.

"Jack?" I said. I looked around.

"I mean Peter," she said. "Or do I mean Duluoz?"

"What's in a name, man?" Peter said, looking at me. Then he grinned at Marylou. "You oughta know, honey. A 'Peter' by any other name would taste as sweet, hey?"

"Fuck you, whatever your name is." She pulled out a Benzedrine inhaler, unscrewed it, shook out the six thin white strips of paper inside, wadded them up in little balls and popped one in her mouth, chasing it down with a slug of hooch. Peter and Dean followed suit. Hal ate two.

Peter put the tin bowls and the chili pot down on the ground for Gayelord to finish off. "Saves doing the dishes later," he said. Gayelord's tongue made quick work of it, missing not a morsel. We smoked more boo and drank powdered lemonade in water from the Firesteel, spiked with shots from another of Peter's bottles, and listened to jazz until Dean said we had to turn off the radio for fear of draining the battery.

The northern lights came on suddenly, flashing down in green tendrils threaded pink and blue, then blazing white and dancing back and forth across the skies in a rhythm that matched my heartbeat. At first I thought it was just my eyes playing tricks on me, maybe some side effect from the Mary Jane, but then the others began commenting on them. "Hey, listen up," Peter said. "They crackle! They hum. Do you hear that bass note? Hey, man, they're playing our song. Oooom mane padme oooooom! Dig it?"

"I always said you were a freak-o nutcase, Jack," Dean said, cuddled under a blanket beside the faltering stove with Marylou. "That's not the oom song. It's the *Nutcracker Suite,* sure as shit."

"You'd better turn off that Coleman pretty quick or you're going to run out of fuel," I said. "Can't you guys build a fire?"

"We're city boys," Dean said. "We only burn down buildings. Whole city blocks if we can manage it. Anything smaller's beneath our dignity." Hal giggled. Peter went into the trailer and came back with a pea coat, which he draped over his shoulders, turning up the threadbare collar. "From my days in the merch," he said. "Ah, the sea stories this coat could tell."

"Yeah," Dean said, "like the time you got cornholed by the cook on the way to Liverpool."

"Fuck you," Peter said.

"Ooooh, I'd like that!" He leaned over and turned off the stove. At once the chill of the night air hit us. There was no warmth in the aurora.

Harry had brought the sax and now he ran changes up and down the valves, a hard sound, no vibrato, as if he were leaving that effect to the Wurlitzer buzz of the northern lights.

I got up from where I lay on top of my sleeping bag and gathered some firewood. Kicked out a shallow depression in the sand and got it going with a couple of dry pine cones for kindling. I reeled a bit on my feet as I stood there looking up. The lights *were* singing, urging me to join in the dance. I could hear Harry laying a dark blue line down beneath the tickle and tinkle of the Firesteel where it sluiced over the stony ford, a castrati choir of alien voices. I could almost see the lights swaying over the water where it glinted below the stars. Or maybe it was just the night fog rising. From far upstream came the splash of a rising trout. Harry heard it too: he blew it a gentle blat.

These people were what in those days we called Bohemians. Later they'd be called Beats, the Beat Generation,

Beatniks after the Russkies launched Sputnik, and even later, hippies. They belonged in the city, any city, the scruffier the neighborhood, the better. Greenwich Village or San Francisco's North Beach. "That's their natural habitat," Sergeant Stingley said. "They fit in perfect with the rats and roaches." Commonists, he called them. "The only way they know how to shoot is *up,*" and here he'd wink and depress an imaginary plunger into the crook of his elbow. Out here in the boonies they'd starve to death, I thought, or die of exposure if the weather suddenly took a turn for the worse. Well, that's their lookout. Or so I believed in my jarhead mode.

I lit the fire, waiting until it was going good, then walked back down to the river to get some more wood for the night. Harry got up and came along. Gayelord followed us.

"F-f-freaks is right," Harry said when we were out of earshot. "I don't like that Dean guy. He's creepy. Did you see the way he was eyeing the g-guns?"

"Guy like that's likely to cut our throats during the night," I said. "Maybe we ought to trade off watches again. Or just say fuck it and drive on."

Harry looked out at the river. "Too foggy," he said. "There may be r-rocks and whitewater downriver."

"Let's check it out." I led the way down the bank. Gayelord ran ahead, picked up a stick, and came back to drop it at my feet. "Thanks, pooch," I told him, "but let's pick up firewood on the way back, hey?"

"I think he w-wants you to throw it for him," Harry said. Gayelord was sitting and looking up at me, head cocked to one side. I sidearmed the stick out into the river. It landed with a heavy splash, invisible in the fog.

"Fetch!"

Gayelord hit the water in a flat racing dive and disappeared into the mist. "Oh fuck, I hope he can find his way back."

We heard him swimming around out there, chugging and puffing, but in a minute he was back, the stick crosswise in his mouth and his eyes gleaming with pride. He dropped it at my feet, then shook himself off. They always wait to do that when they're close enough to spray you. Doggy altruism. They love the water, so of course you must love it too.

"Hey," Harry said, "he knows his job. Must be the Labrador in him." He threw the stick, farther this time, and again Gayelord found it in short order.

"This could go on all night," I said, pushing on down the island. A short distance ahead we came to a deep, narrow, weedy inlet. Out in the fog I could hear ducks talking, low and slow as if they were sleepy. Gayelord heard them too, ears peaked and his head cocked quizzically. We eased down the shore and then we saw them, a big raft of migrant waterfowl, mallards or blacks by their size and shape. Probably a mixed flock of both varieties, with greenheads predominant. Maybe some blue-wing teal mixed in with them for good measure.

"Man, what a setup," I whispered. "We could sneak down here before first light, one of us on each point of the bay. Then get them flying between us. Limit out in five minutes. And with Gayelord to help us, we wouldn't lose a bird." The dog whined his assent. He was sitting on my feet and I could feel his stub tail whipping back and forth.

"Except we've only got one shotgun," Harry said. "M-mine."

I'd forgotten for a moment that Curly still had my Remington.

"Still, we ought to try it. You get well hidden with the gun in some brush near the point, and I'll sneak around the other side. Then when it's light enough, I'll jump up and spook 'em toward you. If you can reload fast enough you ought to be able to drop at least four of them, maybe six or eight if they're knotted up."

"It's a p-plan," Harry said. "M-maybe a game warden will hear me shooting and come over to check our licenses. He could help get these people off the island, and maybe put out an alert to the state troopers for D-Doc and C-C-Curly."

"Yeah, but maybe he's already had an alert for us. From Stoat & Co."

"Hmmm." Harry scratched his head. "Well, I s-still think we should do it. I'd rather be hauled in by the l-law than m-murdered by those b-bastards. Wouldn't you?"

When we got back to the Airstream freighted down with firewood, the gang was buzzed and incoherent on Benzedrine, booze, and boo, still gabbling up a gale. Words swirled around in a bluewhite dustdevil—satori, nirvana, Buddha, delusion and illusion, along with references to New York jazz joints like the Apollo, Kelly's Stable, Small's Paradise and the Savoy up in Harlem, all the cool clubs on 52nd Street. They nearly got to slugging it out over the merits of their champions. Basie, Lester "The Prez" Young, Dizzie Gillespie, Charlie Bird. Harry's ears perked up. And then into writers. William James, Dos Passos, Saroyan, and not surprisingly that long-winded jabbernowl Thomas Wolfe. I never could read him. Peter thought he was God. Well, the way they were going it was clear we wouldn't get any sleep around there.

I looked at Harry and shrugged. He nodded. We stoked up the fire again, picked up the horn, the Thompson, and the BAR, and eased on out of there, taking Gayelord with us back to where we'd left the canoe. The dog seemed to prefer our company. Or maybe it was just the smell of the guns. He didn't once look back.

We traded off watches during the night, not taking any chances. It was cold and dank, but we built no fire. If Doc and Curly happened past, let them see the other fire and put ashore with Peter and his pals. We'd hear them long before they found us. I woke Harry in the dark when the sky to the east was just starting to lighten toward gray. We loaded the canoe and shoved off, with Gayelord in the bow alongside Harry. The fog had thinned but still lay close to the water. When we slipped past the trailer, the coals of the campfire glowing eerie in the dark and reflecting blood red off the aluminum, Peter and his pals were all dead to the world. They'd probably sleep until noon.

We pulled ashore just short of the inlet. Harry set up at the point with the Winchester and a box of 4s, and I made my way through the woods to the other side, Gayelord at my heels. The ducks were still there, starting to stir as dawn neared. The sound of their muttering voices set Gayelord to shivering. He knew something was up, and deep in the Labradorian recesses of his brain he knew it was going to be good. He whined once, but I hushed him and he never uttered another sound. Instinct.

When I was halfway up the far side of the inlet, I pushed quietly through the brush, crouching low, and had a look-see. A pink streak low in the east was brightening quickly to red and the last stars winked out like dying fireflies overhead. Another cloudless day. The ducks, maybe fifty or sixty of them, were knotted up in the middle but closer to me than to Harry. I couldn't see him in the alders that grew down close to the water, but then I caught a glint from his gunbarrels.

Okay, we were ready. "Let's get 'em up, Gayelord," I said. We bulled noisily through the brush, down to the edge of the water, and as I started waving my arms and yelling, Gayelord joined in with a loud, deep bark I hadn't heard before. The ducks exploded off the water, jumping straight up, quacking in chorus and winging out low—straight toward Harry. His gun banged twice, hollow in the distance, and three ducks dropped with a splash at his feet. A pause while he reloaded and it banged twice more. More falling bodies. Then I saw him spin around, reloading again, and fire both barrels, bangbang—chasing shots, but they told. Two more birds fell, in the mainstem of the river this time. Yes indeed. Crisp extractors on old Ollie Winchester's masterpiece.

Gayelord and I were running full tilt back around the inlet. Harry called the dog and made a throwing gesture out into the Firesteel. He wanted those river-killed birds first, before they were swept downstream on the current. Gayelord must have spotted them, maybe even marked them down when they fell, because he hit the water running. I was breathing hard when I came up beside Harry, and the dog already had dropped the two birds at his feet.

He fetched five more while I caught my breath. Seven ducks in all, five mallards and two blacks. We'd eat well tonight.

"Good shooting," I said.

"I t-tripled up on that first shot," Harry said. He was beaming. "N-never done that before. Two of them flew smack into the same pattern, and I got the other one on the second barrel. Then it all happened so fast I can't remember. All I saw was flying brass, more birds, and the muzzles bucking." He ran his hand over the tubes. "The b-b-barrels are still hot. Feel 'em." They were.

"What do we do now with Gayelord?" I asked.

He looked at me, dubious. "Are you thinking what I'm thinking?"

"Traveling around America with a bunch of dope fiends is no life for a dog. Not as good a guy as this one."

"Well," Harry said, "we beat up a b-blind man, stole a couple of machine guns and fired them at people, sank a rich man's b-boat, c-committed statutory rape—or d-damn near that. Do you know how old the girls are? Oh, and I almost forgot. We v-violated a 'no fishing' regulation and smoked marijuana, not to mention that we're both too young to be drinking. I think d-dognapping would be one of our l-l-lesser offenses."

"Let's go," I said. I clapped my hands. "Come along, Gayelord."

"Wh-what the hell," Harry said, picking up two of the ducks and his gun. "It's all in the great American outdoor tradition."

❖ 10 ❖

MARLOW'S LEAP

The rest of that day reeled off without incident. At least not the sort we'd come to expect of the Firesteel. Rather it played out into a waterborne idyll, the kind of trip we'd hoped for all along. The weather could not have been better: clear sunny skies dotted here and there with bright, fat cumulus clouds that ambled across our track at a walking pace from west to east; the air cool and dry, scented with pine needles, old wood ash from ancient fires, and rotting apples from the occasional abandoned orchards along the river. The river ran fast but smooth, with a few easy stretches of riffle and whitewater inserted here and there by the Canoe God to keep us alert.

Wherever the going was easy, Harry reached for his horn and blew appropriate tone poems, tossing kisses at the passing scene. They were lyric riffs, gutsy and dissonant by turn. I could feel him reading the country. There was a rhythm to the water, but it wasn't a 4/4 beat, more like 5/4 shifting to 7/5 and back again, then uncountable changes as we hit whitewater, easing out smooth and sweet when we'd cleared the run.

Gayelord proved a natural in a boat, stretching himself out on top of the duffel bags with his head on his paws, watching the landscape pass by. He sat up now and then to raise his head and test the breeze, nostrils working like a wine connoisseur wrapping his tongue around an interesting new vintage. We had the flyrods rigged, and when a productive piece of cutbank presented itself, we'd move in close to it while either Harry or I cast to the pocket water with a muddler, a hopper imitation, or a woolly worm. Gayelord stood up and whined when the first trout hit. A rainbow, it vaulted high from the water and set the drag screaming. The dog growled and was about to dive in and retrieve it when Harry grabbed him by the collar. It was a small trout, maybe ten inches, and when I'd brought it alongside and unhooked, I let him have a sniff before I released it. He gave me a puzzled look, but then settled back down on the duffel.

"They taste better cooked," I told him. "We'll catch you a couple for lunch."

He was alert to every bird that flew past. Flocks of migrant redwings and grackles and cowbirds; crows and raucous ravens; a red-tailed hawk swinging high overhead on a thermal. Fast-moving strings of ducks traded up and down the river, and Gayelord whined at their passage. When a great blue heron transformed itself from a bedraggled, upright snag along the riverbank by unfolding its impossibly long wings and flapping away ahead of us, slow and clumsy with his long legs trailing behind, the pup's eyes popped and his glance flashed from Harry to the shotgun case and back again. He barked his frustration that no one was blasting such an easy target.

We caught a few more trout, killed them, and started looking for a good place to land. At about midday Harry pointed to the left bank. "Good spot for lunch," he said.

We put ashore at another of those old apple orchards. They dated back to the period just before and after World War I when farmers were still trying to hack a hardscrabble life out of this sour, sandy, glacier-scrubbed country. Many of the old trees still survived, thick trunked and gnarled, but in some cases bearing fruit. You never knew from one apple to the next if they would taste any good. The trees were of old varieties rarely grown anymore in this age of long-keeping but sawdust-flavored supermarket Delicious—varieties like Red Spy, Blue Pearmain, Macoun, and Wolf River. These antique varieties had cross-pollinated over the course of time. The apples they now produced were unique, a melange of flavors not to be found in any arbor but their own. Harry and I had discovered how good some of them could taste from hunting grouse in the old orchards around home. Nothing tastes more refreshing on a hot, sweaty October afternoon, after a day of pounding the briers for partridges, than one of these cool, white-fleshed, winy-flavored mutants, even if it has a few wormholes in it. We hoped to find some tasty ones here to stuff our ducks with for dinner that night.

"Let's bring the shotgun," Harry said. "Could be some grouse in the trees."

"I don't know. We've got ducks enough for the next couple days. And anyway, why advertise our presence?"

"Right." But both he and Gayelord looked crestfallen.

"Oh, fuck, bring it along," I said. "We can always smoke some of the birds. We might need 'em later the way this trip is going. You never know what lies ahead on the Firesteel."

"Yeah, maybe a blizzard will snow us in before we reach the lake. Then you wouldn't have to go to Korea."

But I wanted to go to Korea. Little did I know . . .

I emptied a canvas tote bag to carry the apples in. Hornets buzzed underfoot, feeding on the apples that nearly paved the ground and made walking under the trees a hazardous business. It was like trying to balance on loose, lopsided ball bearings. The air smelled like hard cider, sweet with apple rot. Gayelord ranged ahead, quartering among the trees but always checking back on us. When he got too far out, Harry whistled him in, then sent him out again with a hand signal. This dog was born to hunt.

I'd filled about half the bag with crisp apples—they looked and tasted almost like Winesaps—when Harry said, "Look!"

Gayelord had stopped on what looked like a flash point, then he tiptoed forward with his head low, as if treading on eggs.

"Get . . ."

"R-ready. Yeah, I know."

Gayelord crept forward, one step, another. . . . A grouse roared up and out from beneath the tree, in two wingbeats placing the thick, gnarled trunk between itself and the gun. Harry leaped to one side, raised the Winchester, and fired. The grouse tumbled in a gray puff of plumage. Gayelord was on it in a flash, picked it up still flapping, and trotted in to us, head high. He was grinning around the mouthful of hot meat and feathers, a few of which trailed away from the bird like falling autumn leaves. He dropped the grouse at Harry's feet. Harry picked it up and spread the tailfan. "Cock bird," he said. He pointed to the unbroken dark band near the end of the tailfeathers. Hens' tailbands are mottled in the middle of the fan.

"He'll eat good, fat with apple seeds."

Harry gave me the gun and returned to the canoe with the bag of apples, now much heavier with the added weight of the partridge. I hunted on with Gayelord. At the far end of the orchard, where it tailed off into a thick stand of young quaking aspens, the dog started acting birdy again. "Get 'em up, boy," I whispered. He nosed into the popple whips, and a pair of woodcock flushed on twittering wings, one beside the other like two ascending helicopters. I waited until they'd cleared the tops of the aspens and shifted to horizontal flight. At the pause they were lined up perfectly for a Scotch double—one shell, two birds. *Pow!* It worked.

Gayelord was reluctant to pick them up. Woodcock have a strong, musky smell that most dogs dislike at first. But I picked one up and pressed it to my face, inhaling deeply. "Mmm-mmm, good," I said. He wasn't about to be outdone and mouthed the other with wrinkled lips, though very carefully. "That's not so bad, is it, Gayelord?" He wagged his tail, then spat the bird down at my feet.

When we got back to Harry, the trout, dusted in flour, were frying in a dollop of clarified deer marrow from one of Florinda Wakerobin's mason jars. He'd sliced some of the apples to sizzle alongside. I cleaned and wrapped the birds while our shore lunch browned to perfection. Gayelord approved. He polished off his trout and apples in short order, devouring the paper plate for dessert. Harry and I were a little slower, if only because of fastidiousness over the fishbones. Then we were back on the river.

The rest of that day remains a blurred memory of utter satisfaction. Clear light on green, fast water; whispering currents and the pull of paddle blades and the warm, supple stretch of limber muscles; full bellies and the subconscious knowledge that we had enough food and strength in reserve for the future, the near one at least. We were young animals working together, two men in a boat not to mention the dog, immersed in action and movement, with the scenery changing at every bend of the Firesteel. The paddling itself was pleasantly hypnotic, the canoe leaping ahead with a faint hiss at each synchronized pull and follow-through. Behind us spun the whirlpools of our strokes. We were one with the flow of the current. For the moment at least, all was well with the world. We'd outwitted or outrun our foes, made love to a pair of nubile maidens, rescued a prisoner who'd since proved to be a valuable ally, and now we were headed home.

In late afternoon we came to a place where the Firesteel flowed between low limestone cliffs. The river narrowed and increased its speed. We thought these buttes must be the remains of a preglacial mountain range. Here the water was clear as the air. We could see fish swimming among the boulders thirty, maybe forty feet down in the deepest pools. It was hot between the cliffs, which masked the slight breeze that had cooled us during the hours of nonstop paddling since our lunch stop.

"We've made good time already today," I said. "How's about we stop for a swim?"

Harry was ready for a break. We tied the canoe to a juniper growing at the base of the western scarp, then put on our fins and face masks and slid in. The water was cool but not chilling. We dove again and again down the limestone walls of the chasm, working our way deeper with each dive, peering into pockets and crevices, feeling cold seeps spilling out of some of them, then dropping to the bouldered bottom, where we chased big trout around big white smooth-polished rocks and through the cracks between them. After we'd had enough, we dried on a rock ledge across from the canoe, where the sun was still hitting. The shelf was wide and deep, with a vaulted roof that glowed like marble. There was driftwood piled by the current, stacked against the corner where the ledge met the cliff face.

Harry looked up at the overhang that bulged above the ledge. "This might be a good place to spend the night," he said. "There's plenty of firewood, protection from wind and weather, and no one's likely to spot us here before we spot them. Unlikely that any b-b-bear's gonna disturb our beauty sleep."

He was right. I swam across to the canoe and retrieved the map. We spread it in the sun and looked at it. The cliffs were marked there, sure enough. "Marlow's Leap," the legend read.

"Who's Marlow?" Harry asked.

I turned the map over. On the reverse side was a list of place names.

"'Marlow's Leap,'" I read. "'Roger Marie de Merlons (1688-1771) was a French-Canadian voyageur and coureur du bois who explored the Firesteel in the wake of Sieur du Lhut (see entry above) and established a fur trading post at Heartbreak Rapids, near an Indian village called Chechemanguego ("Place of the Muskrat"). In the winter of 1724, pursued by a hostile raiding party of Santee Sioux, perennial enemies of the Chippewa with whom he was trading, de Merlons (or Marlow, as he was later known to the English who followed him into the region) ran a purported "sixty leagues" on snowshoes through the frigid forest, but was finally brought to bay, surrounded on the cliffs that mark the river here. Shedding his heavy pack, musket, snowshoes, and even his wolverine overcoat, retaining only his knife and a tomahawk, Marlow took a long running start and cleared the river in a single bound. Or so say the Indians. After "thumbing his nose" at his frustrated pursuers, Marlow threw the tomahawk and split the skull of the Sioux chieftain. Thus

runs the legend. A pleasant view of the river here, though diffi-
cult to reach nowadays.' "

Harry looked up at the gap overhead, the band of sky
above it going already from blue to lavender.

"Yeah," I said. "I'd make it about forty feet. A world's
record in the broad jump that'll never be beat."

"Some guy, that Marlow."

"I guess."

We pulled the canoe up onto the ledge for the night; there
was plenty of room. Harry rigged a reflector oven with tinfoil
and roasted three of our ducks for supper that night—two black
ducks, blood rare, for Harry and me, and a mallard (ditto) for
Gayelord, who we figured wouldn't notice the difference. Our
birds were stuffed with tart slivers of the apples I'd picked, and
a double scoop of the wild rice Florinda had included in her care
package. Then we rolled into our sleeping bags, leaving them
unzipped because the heat of the sun and our cookfire had sat-
urated the limestone ledge on which we slept and would have
kept us warm enough without covers. But the bags were soft,
the rock was hard. Before dossing down for the night, we
wrapped the grouse and woodcock, stuffed with apples, in
riverbottom clay and placed them in the hot ashes of the cookfire to bake overnight. Harry blew taps on his ax. From somewhere far to the north, coyotes chorused a mournful answer.

It was the first full night's sleep we'd had since we started. I
dreamed of Lady Day, her sad, hoarse, sweet voice echoing down
the lonely ashcan alleys of the night. Strange fruit, indeed. . . .
We relied on Gayelord's ears, nose, and menacing growls to
alert us to any prospective danger. The dark cloud that loomed
in the back of my mind was a small one, and it lay low on the
horizon: How long could all of this good fortune last? Through
that night it held, and well into the following day.

Not until then did the weather change.

AFTER THE STORM

I n the morning we shoved off at the first wink of daylight. We ate in the canoe. Not even time for coffee. Instead we ripped chunks from the baked gamebirds, alternating mouthfuls of tender meat with the still warm apple stuffing, which had absorbed the birds' juices while they cooked. We scooped river water between paddle strokes to wash it down. Gayelord ate the picked bones when we were finished. We'd left plenty of meat on them.

The reason for our haste was the tautening bind between time and distance. According to the map, Lake Superior was fifteen river miles to the north, an easy day's paddle flat out. But the map didn't show all the kinks in the river. And we might have to portage around a rapids. A two-lane state highway crossed the Firesteel just above its mouth. Our arrangement with Mr. Taggart's truck driver was for him to meet us at the trestle bridge near sundown of the 20th. That was today. He might wait around for us a few hours, but knowing the man, we had our doubts. So we'd have to paddle hard if we were going to make the rendezvous and still have time to fish for the big, bright steelhead that entered the Firesteel at this time of year to spawn. Steelhead are rainbow trout that grow up in deep water, either the ocean or a sea-sized lake like Superior. Their colors are oceanic as well—chromed mirrors, hence the name.

It's a hard, vigorous, fish-eat-fish life out there in the fathomless blue, and as a consequence steelhead have to get much larger and stronger than river trout. And they have to get that way quick; otherwise, they're chum for their fellow predators. Big fish, little fish, that's the menu in steelhead water. Neither of us had ever fished for them.

According to our source in the Tomahawk tackle shop, the steelhead didn't often spawn above Heartbreak Rapids, a rugged, Class IV run about five miles upstream of the outlet. The old Indian village and trading post were long gone. For a while a thriving sawmill town named Chemango (pop. 1,000) had stood on the spot, but it burned out in the big fires of 1923 and no one bothered to rebuild it. The Tomahawk guy said that even the two-pump gas station and general store had closed down after the state decided not to pave the county road that once terminated there. That was about eight months ago. There was talk in the state legislature every year of building a bridge across the rapids, but nothing ever came of it. If we could get to Heartbreak by noon, we'd have the afternoon to mess around with steelhead, so we put our backs into it.

By midmorning I noticed the sky overhead growing streaked with high, lacy fingers that sparkled in the sun. Stratocirrus—a sure sign that a front was approaching. To the west some ominous blueblack clouds were just showing their ice-plumed domes over the horizon. Thunderheads? What else? We were overdue for a storm. Harry noticed the weather signs too, and now we really dug in. Half an hour later the cumulonimbus covered a quarter of the sky to the west. We could see lightning bolts flashing between the anvils, and Gayelord's ears perked to the boom of distant thunder.

"We're gonna get wet," Harry called back to me. "Maybe parboiled too, j-just for good measure."

"There's time yet before it gets to us," I said. "Let's keep paddling as long and hard as we can, then pull over to whichever bank looks most protected. All we can do is pray until it blows through."

"Check." But he sounded dubious.

The air had gotten humid now, and the sun felt heavy on our heads and shoulders. Not a breath of breeze. Deer flies appeared from nowhere to halo our heads, swarming out from the shore, biting fast and hard, taking big chunks out of us, but we didn't dare break the rhythm of our paddling to swat at them. Much good it would have done anyway. Gayelord snapped at the flies, bit at his back and tail, but finally gave up the unequal struggle and nosed his way under the tarpaulin that covered our gear amidships. His growls under there were soon drowned out by the approaching storm.

A few minutes later I looked to the left and saw the cutting edge of the wind moving toward us. Closing fast. The spiky tops of the jackpines and spruce bent to its sudden lash. Ahead, not a furlong upriver, a tree toppled into the stream, and a flash of blinding white lightning whipped out of clear air to blast a nearby spruce into a column of steam, splinters, and sizzling needles. Thunder cracked loud and close and Gayelord whined as if doom were upon him. We were rounding a sharp bend. I saw whitewater ahead—Heartbreak Rapids already? Harry looked back at me. I pointed my paddle to the left bank and we dug for it.

Ahead the river opened out to a new view, and I thought I saw something flash red and black, metallic, against the far bank. Then—*pop, pop, pop*—what sounded like distant gunfire but could have been breaking branches. Right then I couldn't concern myself with that, and the sound was drowned out anyway by the shriek of wind, followed by a blinding sheet of rain and hail the size of hen's eggs that laced us hard as we swept in under the overhanging branches of the shoreline.

We were out of the wind and most of the hail, in the lee of a man-high riverbank. Now all we had to worry about were toppling trees and lightning.

The storm blew through fast. The hail died away, moving ahead with the storm front, and the rain steadied down to a rapid thrum that lashed the river into froth. Already the water was discolored, stained with tendrils of graybrown clay sluiced from the banks. Branches, leaf litter, rafts of pine cones and needles bobbed past us, with now and then a whole tree thrown in for good measure, trailing its rootball behind it like a sea anchor.

We were drenched to the skin, of course, and I could feel knots coming up on my head where the ice balls had bounced off of it. The air turned chilly. No. Downright cold.

As the line squall boomed away toward the east and the rain eased off to a drizzle, all we could hear was the patter of icy water from the trees overhead and the rush of the river. Then that popping came again. Gayelord, who'd emerged from under the tarp, turned to look downriver, his ears peaked again.

"You hear that?"

"G-gunfire you think? Maybe duck hunters?"

"Doesn't sound like a shotgun. Too sharp. That's a rifle. Maybe two different ones." I remembered that red and black flash I'd seen along the bank ahead of us--like lightning reflected off painted metal. My God, could it be Stoat's Beaver? We'd last seen it heading north. Maybe it had crash landed and Dobbs or Sailor was firing shots to attract attention.

I told Harry about it.

"Christ!" he said. "The girls! Th-they were all supposed to be heading back yesterday."

More shots in the distance. Four quick, throaty blasts that sounded like they came from a source close by, about where I'd seen what might be the Beaver, then two sharper cracks from a greater distance.

"L-let's get on down there," Harry said, picking up his paddle.

"Wait a minute. Someone signaling for help would fire three measured shots, then pause, then fire three more. That's definitely two different rifles. One's only about two hundred yards away and the other's farther out, maybe twice as far."

"How can you tell?"

"We spent a lot of time on the rifle range at Parris Island."

"So—what do we do?"

"Let's slip down there and have a look. Not in the canoe. Through the woods. And let's bring the Thompson and the BAR, just in case."

"In case what?"

"One of those rifles sounds like a Springfield. Curly's weapon of choice."

We tied the bow line to a spruce root and worked our way downstream through the dripping woods, keeping well in from the bank for cover. It was thick in there. Gayelord came with us. I thought of leaving him tied to a thwart in the canoe, but he might bark when we left him and give us away. He knew something serious was up, probably from the tones of our voices, and stayed close behind me. We heard more firing, not fast this time, but single, sporadic shots, as of snipers firing at movement. When we were about opposite the nearer rifle, we got down on our hands and knees and crawled toward the river.

It was the Beaver all right, moored in a shallow cove on the far bank. No sign of any people, but they'd all be under cover. Downstream about a quarter of a mile I saw what was left of the town of Chemango—a few blackened brick chimneys poking up from the second growth, and the abandoned general store cum gas station, hard by the riverbank. There were holes in the roof and the pumps were those old Mobilgas bubbledomes, faded red. A sign dangled cockeyed from a chain overhead: "The Sign of the Flying Red Horse."

"Keep your eyes skinned for a muzzle flash over there by the plane," I told Harry.

It wasn't long in coming. We both saw the lance of flame spurt from behind a big, downed pine on the south side of the cove. The other rifle fired at the muzzle flash and bark flew from the pine trunk.

"C-could you see where that second shot came from?"

"No, but by the sound of it he's maybe in the store, or behind one of those chimneys. Downstream from our gang, at any rate."

"*Our* gang? S-Stoat wants our scalps, remember?"

"Curly and Doc want 'em worse," I said. "Our balls as well. And the girls are over there near the plane, by the way. If Curly hasn't shot them yet."

"We've got to get over and help them. They need our fire-power." Harry meant business now. No stutter this time. "We'd be in Curly's sights if we tried to cross right here. Easy meat. But maybe we can haul the canoe upstream, above that last bend, then cross over and reach them through the woods."

"Good idea."

Wading chest-deep up the shoreline, we towed the canoe upstream under the cover of overhanging branches. It was hard going, slippery rocks underfoot and the current working against us, but when we were masked from Curly's view by the river-bend, we piled in and were quickly across. We pulled the canoe up on the bank and stopped to consider our next move.

"Sounds like our guys only have one rifle," I said. "The one Sailor was carrying the other day when we saw them fly over. But they probably have those shotguns, too. Saving their fire for close shots. I hope the hell they don't cut loose when we come up behind them."

"We'll work in close, keep under cover, then yell to them."

I hadn't thought of that. Harry fed more .45 slugs into the Tommy gun's drum and stuck the rest of the box in his shirt pocket. I draped the bandoleer of BAR magazines over my shoulder. Then we moved out, into battle.

When we were within a hundred yards of the pine log, Harry yelled, "Mr. Stoat, hey you guys, it's Harry and Ben. We've come to help you."

Silence. Then Stoat yelled back, "Do you still have that submachine gun you fired at me?"

"Yeah," I shouted. "And a BAR, too. With plenty of ammo for both weapons."

Another long pause. What was this? An audition? A job interview at Stoat's goddamned bank? Then we heard the women's voices arguing with him. I could make out Cora and Wanda, but Mrs. Stoat was the loudest, and she was chewing her husband out in no uncertain terms. He grumped back at them, something we couldn't make out, but it sounded from his tone of voice like he'd caved in.

"Come on in, boys," Mrs. Stoat yelled to us.

"And keep your heads down." That was Flo talking. It was good to hear her voice. "Curly can pick a gnat's nose at three hundred yards."

"Yes, *please* do be careful!" Wanda and Cora chiming in. Even better.

12

THE SIGN OF
THE FLYING RED HORSE

They were all huddled in the protective lee of the pine log, the girls and Mrs. Stoat grinning at us as we bellied in. Stoat glowered and looked away. He chewed savagely at another of his fragrant Upmann's. Flo had their rifle—a Model 99 Savage, the lever action with the five-shot rotary magazine. A lot of empty brass lay scattered around her. Sailor was down flat on his back with a bloody bandage wrapped turban style around his head. His eyes were glazed with shock, but he smiled up at us and raised a thumb. "Cavalry to the rescue," he said. Dobbs was at the far end of the log with one of the Brownings. Stoat had the other next to him. Neither of them looked at us.

What had happened, as we pieced it together, was about what I'd figured. Dobbs refused to use the tainted avgas at the lodge and was heading for Superior to tank up. That electronic repair we'd seen him making the other night was on the Beaver's fuel gauges but his fix hadn't worked and they didn't realize they had too little gas for the flight. They'd put down on the river with the engine sputtering. "Then these outlaws attacked us," Mrs. Stoat said. She shuddered. "That Dr. Haugenbusch is a discredit to his profession. I shall certainly report him to the American Medical Association."

"Mother," Cora broke in. "He's not a *real* doctor. That's only his nickname, as Florinda told us. He's a bank robber."

"How are you doing for ammo?" I asked Flo.

"Half a box left," she said.

"What caliber is the Savage?"

"Aught six."

I handed her one of the magazines from the bandoleer. "Here's twenty more." I'd have given her the BAR but it had iron sights. She'd be more accurate using the four-power scope on the rifle.

"Where are Doc and Curly holed up exactly?" Harry asked.

"In that building there by the river," Flo told him. "The old store with the gas pumps in front. Anyway Curly's in there. Doc isn't shooting, being blind like he is, but he's probably right in there with him. He's carrying that pump gun of yours."

I popped my head over the log for a quick look. Curly fired just as I dropped it again. The bullet smacked the bark and whined away into the woods.

"There's that old dirt road right ahead of him," I said. "He can't come across it without exposing himself. What do they have for a boat?"

"That canoe you shot up," Flo said. "Curly patched it like I knew he would. They were paddling upstream toward us just before the storm hit. Mr. Stoat spotted them first and said, 'Good, help's on the way.' When I looked over and recognized them, I told Sailor to right away cut loose at them. Thank God he did. Otherwise they'd have come right in here and slaughtered us." She shook her head. "Curly nailed poor Sailor as it was, a snap shot from two hundred yards away in a moving canoe."

"Did Sailor hit them, put a few holes in the canoe anyway?"

"I don't think so. Before I could pick up the rifle they'd ducked in behind the riverbank, by that dock there just next to to the store. Since then it's just been a sniper's fight."

I was trying to anticipate Curly's next moves. "He'll probably wait until dark, then move out of the store. Maybe circle back through the woods and try to outflank us." There went our afternoon of steelhead fishing. And probably our ride back to Heldendorf as well.

"Have you radioed for help?" Harry asked.

"Dobbs tried to climb back in the cockpit but Curly made it too hot for him," Flo said. "He couldn't even wade out to the float before bullets were splashing all around him. Anyway, with the storm screwing up the atmospherics, he probably couldn't have raised anyone anyway."

"Wonder why he hasn't shot up the plane?" I said. "He's mean enough to do it for sheer spite."

"Maybe they want the Beaver," Flo said. "They'll have to clear out of this country now, figuring you fellows blew the whistle on them. The cops could show up any minute. And Doc knows how to fly—he was in France with the Lafayette Escadrille during the First World War. He liked to talk about the time he used a Flying Jenny in a bank robbery out in Kansas. That was back in the twenties. Could be he figures on handling the controls while Curly acts as his eyes in the co-pilot's seat."

"Pretty risky," I said.

"They've got nothing to lose."

"Well," Harry said, "they can't fly it now without some gas."

Flo thought about that for a moment. Her eye was glued to the scope through all this, and now she squeezed off another shot. Then cursed. "Stick your head up again, you bastard," she said. She resumed our conversation. "No, unless there's some fuel left in the storage tanks at the gas station. Float planes used to land here back in the forties, guys flying in to fish the lakes in the Chequamagon country."

So we had the plane, they had the avgas. The trick would be to sneak in there and filch some of it. But how?

Now Stoat piped up. "When are you fellows going to begin shooting? You have those machine guns, why don't you use them?"

"They're our element of surprise," I told him. "Doc and Curly don't know we're here yet, and that we have automatic weapons. Flo thinks they also may be sitting on a supply of avgas, in one of those pumps at the store."

"Well, we must get some of it then. Time's a-wasting. I have to be back at the bank by nine a.m. tomorrow. You're a bold young Marine. Charge them singlehanded, or take Mr. Taggart with you. Root them out of there. Surprise them with firepower. With those guns it should be easy as pie." Dobbs looked over at me and smirked. His look seemed to say, Now you know what I have to put up with.

But maybe it would work. I could leave Flo back here with the BAR to provide heavy covering fire while Harry, Dobbs, and I worked our way up along the riverbank, under cover. Then one of us could shoot up the store with the Tommy gun while the other two dashed for the gas pumps and filled a couple of cans with high-octane avgas.

"Do you have any gas containers on the plane?" I asked Dobbs.

"Two ten-gallon jerricans. Empty. And they're in the back of the cabin. We'd never be able to fetch them, not the way that guy shoots."

"I think I can do it," I said.

The Beaver was moored by a single line to a tree on the bank, floating about twenty feet out from the shore. I told Flo what I wanted her to do, then stripped to my racing trunks and crawled down to the river. It was an easy underwater swim to the far float, the one on the upriver side from Curly's vantage point. I looked back to Flo and gave her a thumbs-up. Wanda crouched beside her, eyes big with worry. Flo racked the lever of the Savage and started pouring shots into the storefront. I pulled myself up on the float, then scrambled into the portside hatch. As Dobbs said, the empty gas cans were stowed in the rear, under a couple of tarps. I grabbed them and crawled back. In the water, I unscrewed the caps and let them fill halfway. That way they could travel with me to the shore, underwater. Curly wouldn't see them and would have no idea what we were planning. Anyway, I hoped he wouldn't.

Back behind the log I emptied the jerricans. Now came the hard part. I explained my plan to the rest of them. "Is twenty gallons of fuel enough to get you out of here?" I asked Dobbs.

"Yeah, as far as Ashland anyway. Maybe even Duluth."

"Well, let's go get it."

The pilot looked at me and frowned. "It's not in my MOS, but what the hell." He smiled. "The Japs couldn't kill me. I don't see why a renegade Marine like this guy Curly should be able to." Spoken like a true movie flyboy. John Wayne, maybe, in *Flying Tigers.*

Harry and I flipped a coin to see who would carry the gas cans. I won, for a change. He'd hang back at the riverbank and provide covering fire, alongside Dobbs with the Savage. Flo's BAR would give us a crossfire. I'd rush the pumps with the jerricans. They were the old-fashioned kind of pumps with a manual crank and didn't require electricity. I'd just have to pray that our guesswork about Doc's intentions were correct, and that there was indeed still some avgas left in the tank.

"Give us ten minutes to get in position," I told Flo. "Then open up with all you've got."

"Shouldn't you synchronize your watches?" Wanda asked. "They always do it in the movies." Cora nodded her solemn corroboration.

I didn't have a watch, but Dobbs did. Waterproof, too. Stoat unstrapped his Patek Philippe and handed it to Flo—"Be careful, that timepiece cost $5,000!"—and we synchronized them to Wanda's satisfaction. Then we slipped once again into the Firesteel's icy water.

As we worked our way down the bank, we could hear Flo popping a few desultory rounds at the store. She had the BAR on single fire. She'd flip the selector to full automatic when the time came. There was no difference Curly could detect in the sound of her fire. Both weapons shot the same round.

When we reached the dock, Harry went up the bank first with the Tommy gun. He looked over the top, then signaled us up. We had four minutes left on Dobbs's watch before H-hour.

"I think I can sneak around behind the store," Harry said. "There's a big pile of snags back there for cover. Captain Dobbs can shoot from here, and with Flo firing from the front they might panic. They ought to. Hell, they're surrounded."

"That drum on the Thompson's supposed to hold a hundred rounds," I told him. "It's probably less. Try to keep your bursts short and sweet, conserve ammo, light finger on the trigger. The cyclic rate of fire on that bastard is about six hundred rounds a minute, so you could empty the drum in a hurry if you don't watch out. Just . . ."

"Alright already," he said. "I get your drift. Nag, nag, nag."

"Three minutes to go," Dobbs said. "You better get a move on. When you hear my first shot, start blasting."

I said, "And remember . . ."

Harry gave me the finger and crawled over the top. He ran in a low crouch to the rear of the store.

"Which pump is the avgas?" I asked Dobbs. He looked at them and shrugged.

"The colors are too faded to tell for sure, but I think it's the near one. If there's a price schedule left on them, it'll be the one that's most expensive." He looked at his watch. "A minute."

It was a long one. I tightened the laces on my sneakers and tied them tight in a double knot. I loosened the caps on the gas cans. I started taking deep breaths. It was about twenty yards to the gas pumps.

Dobbs counted down. "Five, four, three, two, one . . . Go!"

As I topped the berm I heard Flo cut loose on full automatic. Splinters flew from the front of the store, long silvery gray ones, and what was left of the glass in the windows shattered to bits. I heard the Savage crack behind me, then a chugging, four-round burst from the rear of the store. Then I was at the pumps. The first one I came to had no price listed, but it had "Hi Test" painted in white letters on the faded red cylinder. I unscrewed the cans, lifted the hose from its rack, and started pumping the handle. At first there was nothing but air, the stale smell of old gasoline fumes. But then I heard a gurgle, and a trickle of pale gold petrol spilled from the nozzle.

Fuck! At this rate of flow I'd be jacking off an hour!

But then it started gushing. I flailed at the handle like a mad masturbator, bullets flying every which way around me, the roar of gunfire everywhere, even from the front of the store, where Curly was returning fire. He hadn't seen me yet, though, too focused on Flo's muzzle flash to look to his right. Then I heard a shotgun blast from the back of the store. Doc had gotten into the act, spraying buckshot blind in Harry's direction.

Suddenly Dobbs appeared beside me and grabbed the pump handle. He handed me the rifle and Flo's half empty box of bullets. One gas can was full, and we switched to the other. He pumped while I reloaded the Savage, holding the pump nozzle in the mouth of the jerrican with my knees. The whole area reeked of gas fumes now. The hose was leaking.

"Almost full," Dobbs said.

I saw the muzzle of Curly's Springfield poke out of the glass-fanged hole that had been the front window. Flo's fire had stopped. She must be switching magazines. The muzzle swung back and forth, like the head of a snake licking the air for a taste of its prey. I raised the Savage but then thought better of it. This close the rifle's report would tip Curly to our presence at the pumps. With all the high-octane gas soaking the ground, one whitehot bullet fired at us could touch off an inferno.

"We'd better call this good enough and run for it," I told Dobbs. He nodded and screwed on the last gas cap.

"It's damn near full already."

Curly's muzzle swung back fast to the front and steadied. He had a target. Looking down his line of fire, I saw something galloping toward us. Something lanky, longlegged, and rusty brown. Gayelord! He must have spotted me at the pump and broken away from the girls, who were supposed to be holding him. The ground between the store and the plane was littered with stumps and old slash, all interfering with Curly's aim. But in a moment Gayelord would reach an open patch only fifty yards away.

I raised the rifle, tried to calculate where Curly would be behind the muzzle of his Springfield, and fired. Instantly the rifle disappeared. Did I hit him? We ran for the bank, the jerricans swinging heavy from Dobbs's hands. I looked back and—shit!—saw Curly lean out of the shattered window. He glared straight at me. The Immortal Jarhead. He tossed the Springfield from his right hand to his left, or open side—a good Marine marksman can shoot off either shoulder—and drew a bead on me. But at that moment Harry burst from behind the store, ran around to the front, and firing from his hip cut loose with the Tommy gun.

"No!" I yelled.

Sure enough, a spark from the Thompson's muzzle blast hit the spilled gas. Ignition . . . Harry saw it happen, figured it with a flash, spun around and sprinted toward us. The flame flickered for an instant over the rainbow-hued puddle, blue and yellow and ghostlike, then the whole shebang went *WHUMP!*

The explosion blew me into the river. Harry landed on top of me, still clutching the Tommy gun. When his head popped clear of the water, his eyebrows were gone, along with the hair on the back of his head. Dobbs stood up to his waist in the water, holding the gas cans clear of it. The heat from the fire reached us even under the bank. We slogged back fast toward the plane.

Cora and Wanda were weeping when we slogged in from the river, while Mrs. Stoat hovered beside them, murmuring words of comfort. Gayelord had somehow gotten back and cowered now, shivering, at Flo's feet. His hair looked kinkier than ever.

"Well, well," Stoat said. "Our Johnnies come marching home. Rather bedraggled but none the worse for wear."

The girls ran to us, so did Gayelord. Quite a reunion.

While Dobbs waded out to the plane and began refueling, I looked back at what had once been Chemango. The store was a plume of fire. A greasy black cloud writhed above it. No way Doc and Curly could have survived that holocaust.

Harry had brought his horn up from the canoe. He played a few sweet bars—the opening notes to a favorite of ours: "My Old Flame." The Spike Jones rendition, with Peter Lorre on the lyrics. Spike Jones and His City Slickers . . .

Back in grade school we used to play those old 78s in Harry's rec room during our nonstop Ping-Pong matches, which the Hairball always won, 21 to 6. Or maybe 10 if my reflexes were sharp. He riffed around those basic notes for a minute or two, then skyed off into noodling arpeggios, high intervals overlaying low ones, blats and flats and fresh sweet lyrical phrases that spilled from his horn as if there were no limit to his invention, sounds that would have left the Bird himself flightless in their wake. He looked up and winked at me. Behind him the flames of the Flying Red Horse quavered all over the sky, red black and yellow.

13

CROSSING THE BAR

After Mrs. Stoat and the girls had treated our burns with salve from the Beaver's first aid kit, we helped carry Sailor aboard. He was much better now. Curly's bullet had grazed the side of his head, leaving him with a bloody but superficial wound, a concussion, and a hell of a headache. Dobbs had refueled the plane, filtering the old avgas through a chamois cloth to remove any crud or ground water that might have accumulated during its months of underground storage. We pulled the nose of the Beaver in close to the shore and cranked the prop a couple of times to prime the engine. Up in the cockpit, Dobbs hit the ignition switch. The big DeHavilland rotary sputtered, coughed, hiccupped once or twice, and then lit off in a loud cloud of dirty blue exhaust.

"Why don't you two come with us?" Cora asked over the roar of the engine. "Bring Gayelord, too. There's room enough on the plane for all of us, and you could always come back later for the canoe. We'd drop you off on the river at Heldendorf."

I could tell from the look in his eyes that Harry was tempted.

"Thanks," I said, "but we have an appointment to meet a guy downriver." It was only early afternoon, and I might have added: "A couple of steelhead, too."

"Y-yeah," Harry said. "M-my dad would skin me alive if we stood his t-t-truck driver up."

Oh hell, his stutter was back. He really wanted that plane ride.

"Hey," I said, "I could take the canoe the rest of the way. It's not all that far. Why don't you and Gayelord go along with them?"

I could see him debating the options. He must have decided that there wouldn't be much chance to make out with Cora on the plane, not under the eye of her parents.

"I'd b-better not," he said. "We started this together, let's finish it that way." He turned back to Cora. "I've got your address at Bryn Mawr. I'll write you when I get back home."

Stoat came up to us. "Well, boys, I don't know what to say. You sunk my float boat, but then you salvaged it. You abducted my daughter and her friend and poached my priceless muskies. But then you saved our bacon from those . . . those murderous canaille." He gestured toward Doc and Curly's funeral pyre, which by now had about burned out. "All I can offer you is my *half*hearted thanks and the *whole* hearted suggestion that you never darken my door again. He turned and helped his wife onto the float. The girls followed them into the cabin. Wanda looked back from the door and blew me a kiss.

"Here's the BAR and the bandoleer," Flo said, handing them to me. "There's only a couple of full magazines left." She picked up a sheaf of herbs and weeds she'd harvested after the firefight, ingredients for Mrs. Stoat's potions. "It's been nice working with you. And one last bit of advice, boys. It might look like Doc and Curly are burnt bacon in that little bonfire over there, but I've known them both long enough to realize that nothing's for sure with those jokers. So watch your backs."

She climbed aboard and slammed the door. We grabbed one wingtip of the Beaver and helped turn it around, facing outboard toward the Firesteel, then stood watching as Dobbs taxied out into the current, bucking it upstream to get enough room for his run. They turned again and took off downriver in a roar of flying spume. Dobbs didn't waggle his wings good-bye.

"D-do you think she's right?" Harry asked. "They c-couldn't have lived through that fire, c-could they?"

"We could go over there and rake through the ashes, I guess. Might turn up some bones. Or we could go fishing instead."

We went fishing.

Heartbreak Rapids was dicey, but the Firesteel was high after the rain and the canoe was light now. We ran the vees like slalom racers. This was a whole new river, deeper, colder, loaded with power, and paved with huge gray granite boulders. The water was still turbid and we couldn't see the bottom at first, but then a mile or so downstream it started to clear.

"Let's keep our eyes on the bottom when we can," I said. "These steelhead will hold down there, in the lee of the boulders. Look for a long silver flash."

We paddled on for another half hour. Then Harry saw one. And then another, and another. A whole damn pod of them, holding at the bottom of a deep, fast riffle. We pulled over to the west bank and debarked. Judging by the sun, it was about two o'clock. We had at least three hours in hand and the lake was only that many miles away.

We stripped the floating line from Harry's rod and bent on a fast-sinking cored flyline. Harry tied a heavy leader to it, with a 2X tippet.

"What fly should we use?"

"Why not the old r-r-reliable? The Firesteel C-Cannibal-Killer."

"We don't have it anymore. Remember? I broke it off on that muskie."

He unzipped a pocket in his fly vest, pulled out a streamer box, and produced the fly in question. "Once again, *Voilà!*"

"How . . ."

"I t-tied another one last night, when we stayed in that cave on the c-cliff. You woke me up, snoring, and I didn't have anything better to d-d-do. The l-light was bad, but it came out okay."

I took the fly and examined it. "The wraps aren't as tight as they were on the original, and the whip finish looks like a booger. You're losing your touch. Let's just hope it has the same magic."

It did. On his third cast, stripping in slow and deep past the boulders where we'd seen them lying, Harry's rod tip bent in a sudden arc and line ripped off the reel. "H-holy shit!"

The steelhead ran him up the riffle, Harry stumbling and skidding over the rocks along the bank, then down it again. I saw bright, quick streaks across the bottom as the other steelhead cleared out of the pool. I could swear they were breaking the sound barrier. The hooked trout kept Harry sweating for fifteen minutes before he brought it in to his feet. It was a long, sleek, bright fish that glowed in the water like a silver ingot. Harry worked the hook free and held the steelhead facing upstream until it revived. "Y-you oughta feel this g-guy. He's hard as a rock." I reached down and the trout was gone at the first touch of my fingertips—flat disappeared, upriver to join its buddies.

We moved down to another pool. It too held steelhead, but they looked hard to reach, so we continued toward the lake. Two pools lower, the bottom looked studded with them, like hobnails in the sole of a boot. My turn. I cast up and across toward the lie of what looked like the biggest one. He took on the first pass. I'd never felt such strength in a fish before, not even the muskie came close. Once again it was a footrace to keep the backing on the spool. I fell twice on the rocks but didn't even feel the bruises.

"K-k-keep your rod tip up!" Harry yelled, smirking.

"Up yours," I grunted.

"N-now you know what it f-feels like."

A dirty gray herring gull swooped down over my head as I knelt to release the fish. When I looked up, the sky was full of them, white gulls and brown ones along with the gray, all screaming their lonesome cries. The air was colder here, I noticed, with that icy bite of the big lake on it. I was about to comment on it when the water at my feet jumped. A sharp crack followed, from upstream.

"*C-C-Curly!*" Harry was pointing to the top of the riffle we'd just run. There the bastard stood, on the rocks above us, working the bolt of the Springfield. He was four hundred yards away. I could see the other canoe, nosed up on the bank. Doc sat in it, his face wrapped in bandages like the Curse of the Mummy.

I popped the fly out of the steelhead's mouth and ran for our canoe. Harry was there before me. Another bullet smacked off the center thwart, shattering it. Gayelord, who'd been nosing around in the shallows for crayfish, jumped in and dove under the tarp. I slung the rod into the Old Town and we shoved off, paddling up a froth.

"We've got to get around that next bend. Right now!"

"'W-watch your b-back!' she said. G-goddamit, we *d-didn't.*"

"Dig!" I yelled.

Two more bullets hit us before we swept around the next bend. The first one holed the canoe just forward of where I knelt. The second ripped across my back, throwing me forward onto the duffle bags. A hit like a blow from a sledgehammer. It knocked the wind out of me. No pain, not at first, but a sudden eruption of fear that started my water. How bad was I hit? The paddle started to slip from my hands, and I only just saved it from going over the side.

Then I came back to my senses, dug in again and kept paddling. They'd be after us in a minute. Our only hope was to get to the highway bridge and hope the truck driver was waiting for us. Maybe a cop would be parked behind him, writing him up for obstructing traffic. Fat chance. I could feel blood soaking into my waistband. Maybe we could get far enough ahead of them to pull over to the shore near the truck, break out the automatic weapons, take cover behind the bridge abutments, and turn Curly back before he drilled us both. Doc couldn't help them much, he looked way too weak from his burns from what I'd seen.

"H-how far are we from the highway?" Harry yelled back.

"A mile and a half, maybe less. Hey, listen. Curly nicked me. In the back. I'm bleeding but I can't see the wound."

He turned around, eyes wide.

"No, no, keep paddling. You can't do anything for me, and if it was bad enough I'd be unconscious." Or dead, I thought. "I just thought you ought to know, in case I pass out or something. If I do, pull over quick and grab the BAR and the bandoleer. Then head for cover, a boulder or whatever. Leave the Tommy gun with me. I might be able to play possum long enough to kill the fuckers when they get within range."

"Shit."

"Hey, there's no time-outs in this ballgame."

We swept into another bend. The river got faster here, and whitewater showed its teeth up ahead. Way off to the north I could see sand dunes, humped like camels in the hazy distance, and a creamy line of breakers beyond them. Blueblack water. Gitche Gumee. . . . We were damned near there. The bridge might be visible once we cleared the next corner. There were empty shacks along the river here, gray boards, rusty tin roofs, tumbledown places, but one of them might provide enough cover for us to make a stand. I looked over my shoulder. No sign yet of Curly's canoe.

Then the pain began. Dim at first, no worse than a bee sting, but it widened and deepened with each stroke of the paddle. It was the twisting motion that did it. I should never have looked back that first time. But then I turned again. And wished I hadn't. There was Curly, coming fast, less than half a mile behind us. Much less. Doc was slumped in the bow. His head was up and he was dipping his paddle in the water, but once for every five of Curly's strokes. They were token gestures. No strength in them.

When I turned to the front again, I felt woozy. Silent star-bursts behind my eyeballs, tiny ones but many of them. I was no better off than Doc. Worse, maybe. The bottom of the canoe was red now, a shallow pool of blood swirling with ice water, sloshing side to side with every paddle stroke. My khakis were soaked with the stuff. I was bleeding out . . .

"There's the bridge," Harry yelled. We came around the last bend into the straightaway. "And the truck is there too." His voice sounded faint and hollow to me. Over it I could hear or maybe feel a hollower, rhythmic pulse. My heart? No, it was the sound of the surf. Only a few hundred yards more to go.

The driver—I remembered that his name was Ted, or Ned, or maybe Red?—was leaning on the bridge rail, watching us approach. Harry waved to him. He didn't wave back, just looked at his wristwatch. 'Nuff said. He spit in the water.

I must have blacked out then, just for a second or two, but the next time I looked up, the bridge was looming ahead of us, over us. We were centered on it, not heading in to the bank. The current was too fast to turn. I heard a faint, far pop and a bullet spanged off the concrete abutment. Ted or Red didn't hear it. He had his back to us, showing his cool, looking out at the lake. We shot under the bridge, into momentary darkness, then emerged again—out into the turmoil of the lake.

"Oh shit," Harry yelled. "Look at that wave!"

It was mountainous, a skyhigh haystack to end all haystacks—the wind from the North Pole driving half of Gitche Gumee up over the sandbar at the Firesteel's mouth. I could hear Curly's rifle again over the roar of the surf, much louder now. He must be right behind us.

Our bow slewed to the right as we neared the Haystack. Harry couldn't control it alone. Somehow I dug in my paddle—a twenty-five-mile hike with full field pack, Sergeant Stingley waxing his mustache as he cursed out the cadence—and we hit the comber head on. The Haystack loomed above, waiting to devour us. Water crashed from its leering face, ice cold. The Old

Town wallowed, her gunwales nearly awash. But then she responded, good old water sow. Raised her bow to the cloud-streaked sky, hovered for a moment as if she was going to topple over backward, then toppled over the crest. We were clear, and still afloat.

I'd heard another shot as we peaked the top of the Haystack and a simultaneous thwap as it hit the tarp in front of me. I looked back. Doc and Curly's canoe disappeared behind the wave and I saw it broach to, sideways to the crush of falling water. It rolled.

I was feeling sick now and leaned over the side to throw up. There was no blood in it, thank God. Then I saw a sight that has never left me in the fifty years since that day. Doc Haugenbusch was sinking through the depths, his face turned upward, empty eyes staring, big blisters on his face, even on the old scar tissue. The bandage around his head unfurled and flapped in the lake's rips and back eddies. Something big and silver darted out of the bluegreen dimness and grabbed the end of the cloth. Doc spun on his axis as the steelhead made off with the bandage.

Harry's urgent voice brought me back.

"We're sinking!" he yelled. "Can you make it?"

I nodded yes. He looked doubtful.

"Gayelord, it's time to go!" Harry lifted the tarp. There was a bullet hole, smack in the center of it. Under the oiled canvas, Gayelord lay in a pool of blood. It spilled from the top of his head into the red-clouded water that filled the canoe.

Harry looked up at me, aghast. He stood in the bow, up to his shins in lakewater, with the blade of his paddle braced against a duffel bag. I thought he was going to weep.

Then, with the suddenness of a porpoise, Curly boiled up from the waves, right beside our foundering canoe. His Brillo pads bristling, he reached for the gunwales.

Harry raised the paddle like a maul and smashed his skull. "You fucker," he screamed, "you shot my dog!" The paddle blade split and Harry drove the splintered end of it deep into Curly's throat. He left it there as Curly sank.

Thus perished the Immortal Marine.

Gayelord, I saw, was still breathing.

I passed out then, but remember feeling Harry's arm around my shoulder and chest as he swam us ashore. He had Gayelord by the collar in his other hand. Somehow he dragged us through the slambang surf and up onto the cold, cold sands. I must have grabbed the saxophone case while we were sinking. It was still in my grip when we hit the beach.

Harry had me roll over onto my chest so he could examine the wound. "Not so bad," he said, tracing the length of it lightly with his forefinger. "I was afraid it might have hit your kidney. It's not even bleeding that bad anymore. We'll stop at the clinic in Ashland and have the doctor sock a few stitches into you and Gayelord, maybe a shot of penicillin for both of you just to be safe. Hell, you'll be good as new by the time you hit Korea."

Gayelord was sitting beside me, groggy but licking my neck.

The cold water must have stanched the blood flow for now, and it had numbed me enough so that the pain was nearly gone. But I still felt sick. Unable to control the nausea, I rewarded Harry's welcome news with a gallon of Gitche Gumee over his cold blue feet.

We trudged up the beach through ankle-deep sand to where the truck waited. I leaned on Harry's shoulder and carried the horn. That's all we saved from the journey.

"Well, boys," said Ted or Red as we came limping up, "I see ya got a puppydog along the way. Was it a pleasant trip?"

"Pretty good," Harry said, his stutter forgotten. "A bit chilly though. You wouldn't happen to have a cup of hot coffee, would you? Two would be even better. And maybe a dog biscuit?"

ENTR'ACTE:
IN THE FOREST
OF THE NIGHT

❖ L'enfer, c'est les Autres. ❖
—J-P. Sartre

The road north was lined with fruit trees. It was late October and they had shed their leaves. A few persimmons still hung from the boughs like puckered oranges. The days were sunny at first, Indian summer weather, but skim ice formed on the rice paddies overnight. Fires burned on the sawtooth mountains to the north where they were headed. Some of the more impressionable Marines imagined a great dragon brooding up there, watching and waiting, its breath kindling the grassfires, but it was only napalm.

By 8 November there was frost in the Funchilin Pass and the next night they had their first snowfall. A week later the wind from Manchuria was blowing hard, as it would all winter, and the temperature dropped to fifteen below. They called it the Siberian Express. The wind tasted of sleet and fine dust. Manchurian camel dung, the old China Marines said. It stung their eyes and gritted in their teeth when they stopped to choke down their C-rats—wienerwurst, lima beans, fruit salad.

Supply sergeants broke out cold-weather gear. The wool socks and shoepacs with felt insoles were welcome, but the long, alpaca-lined parkas tangled their legs as they marched.

At night men cut firewood with their K-Bars. The wind died and they heard strange music from the mountains. Whistles and bugles. Distant dissonance. There were red deer and bear on the slopes and some said tigers too. Once they reached the high plateau they could see a big lake half a day's march to the north. Steam rose from black ice. Marines bought Red Dot stogies, two for a nickel, and smoked them to ward off the cold. That's where Ben acquired the cigar habit.

Yes, the Crotch takes care of its own. Thanksgiving dinner was traditional—from roast turkey and mince pie to fruitcake, shrimp salad, mixed nuts, stuffed olives, cranberry sauce—the works. But Field Marshal Winter disapproved of such largesse. The gravy froze first, then the sweet potatoes . . .

They moved north.

On the following evening, the night of 25 November, the Chinese launched their assault. No one was prepared for their coming.

General Douglas MacArthur's staff in Japan had repeatedly assured Washington that there were no more than 16,000 to 30,000 Chinese troops operating in North Korea, all of them mere "volunteers." In fact the CCF (Chinese Communist Forces, as they were officially known) numbered 300,000 troops.

Across the Taebek Mountains a hundred miles to the west, General Lin Piao's Thirteenth Army Group, eighteen divisions strong, slammed into Lieutenant General Walton Walker's Eighth Army. Regimental commanders issued urgent orders to their battalion C.O.s who passed them on down to company level—How Able! "Haul Ass!" The doggies reeled back to the south, toward Pyongyang.

Two days later, east of the mountains, General Sung Shih-lun's Ninth Army Group with a dozen divisions, hit Major General Edward Almond's X Corps, which consisted of the First Marine Division and part of the U.S. Army's Seventh Infantry. The Marines held.

Up past the reservoir, near a village called Yudam-ni, the sky looked like Christmas come early. The moon was lopsided, four days past full. American tracers were red, the Chinese green, and those used by the North Koreans were blue. They crisscrossed in the air. Orange sparks gushed upward from mortar tubes firing illumination rounds. The flares popped overhead, lit the mountains all around in a hard white glare, and squeaked as they drifted down. Now and then a white phosphorus round from the mortars would send quick orange-tailed snakes slithering over the snow.

You could smell the Chinese coming, like a gust of cold stale garlic breath. Even their gunpowder smelled different, like burning hair.

Their basic infantry weapon was a 1918 Mauser-style rifle in 7.92mm, manufactured in China, but they also carried Mauser machine-pistols, American Tommy guns, and Russian PPSh 41 burp guns. Some of their light machine guns were Japanese Nambus captured during World War II. They threw long-handled potato-masher grenades. To arm them they had to unscrew a cap from the bottom of the wooden handle, then pull a strip of cloth to light the fuse. These caps often froze, and in advance of an attack the grenadiers could be heard tapping the handles on a rifle butt or even the frozen ground to loosen them for action. Most of the grenades were frags, but the Chinese used a lot of concussion grenades too, perhaps in order to take more American prisoners.

Over and through it all, a cacophony of bugles and whistles, drums and cymbals. This was how the Chinese officers maneuvered their troops.

Sergeant Stingley had joined the regiment at Wonsan. He spotted Ben right away. "Slater," he said, "I want you for my platoon. Most of these men are candyassed pogues—Reservists. The rest have been in country too long, from Pusan through Inchon to Seoul. They've gone Asiatic on me. You're fresh meat.

I know I can trust you. Hell, I trained you myself." Stingley arranged the transfer.

Ben was assigned as a BAR man. He already had plenty of experience with the weapon. A loaded Browning Automatic Rifle weighs twenty pounds; its ammo belt with twelve magazines—another 240 rounds—weighs nearly as much. Ben fired them all that first night and many more. Twice the Chinese broke through their perimeter, but Stingley rallied the men and drove them back. He moved the platoon higher on the ridge they were defending and formed a tighter perimeter, on the crest. Ben not only carried his BAR but dragged the body of a dead Marine with him as well. Marines didn't leave their dead or wounded behind.

Another platoon was already on the hilltop, or anyway what was left of one. All of its officers had been killed or wounded. Stingley was senior N.C.O. He took command. The position was anchored by four .30 caliber Browning machine guns, one at each end and two in the middle.

They piled the dead Marines in the center of the perimeter, near the 60mm mortar tubes, and covered them with a tarpaulin. Not a man in the outfit hadn't been hit. Many had frostbitten feet, hands, and faces. Corpsmen worked on the badly wounded, popping morphine Syrettes and dusting perforated bellies with sulfa powder. The men who'd only been nicked tended their own wounds.

At first light an L-19 spotter plane circled their position, and a few minutes later three gull-winged F4U Corsairs roared in low with 20mm cannonfire, five-inch rockets, and napalm. The Chinese faded into the surrounding hills. Pine trees blazed in their wake brighter than the rising sun. Mist rose from the frozen ground, writhing like ghosts. "They'll be back come dark," Stingley promised.

They counted eighty-five Chinese bodies on the slope below. Snow was falling. Soon the bodies looked like nothing more than hummocks on the landscape. Stingley's Marines had lost six, including Mr. Wittold, the platoon leader, who took a bullet in the groin and bled out before a corpsman could reach him. Ben helped the corpsman slide the lieutenant's body under the tarp. Hoarfrost bloomed like mildew on the faces of the dead. Even on their eyeballs.

All day they sweated it out under a bombardment from Chinese 82mm mortars and 76mm howitzers, firing from the reverse slope opposite them. ChiCom machine guns laced their position. The Chinese pulled their heavy Maxim MGs in two-wheeled dogcarts. The Marines dug their foxholes as deep as they could, not an easy job in that frozen, rocky soil. During a lull in the firing, Stingley sent out a work party to drag Chinese bodies upslope to their position. They drew sniper fire from the far ridge but no one was hit. Stingley had the corpses piled like sandbags around the foxholes. "Red revetments," he called them.

The ChiCom dead wore canvas tennis shoes with crepe soles and uniforms of quilted cotton. The uniforms were reversible, white on one side, mustard yellow or a murky pea-soup green on the other. Most of the Chinese had fur-lined caps with earmuffs. In their knapsacks they carried a four-day supply of garlic, rice, beans, and corn, along with eighty to one hundred rounds of ammo. Some of them also had plugs of opium and tins of Benzedrine tablets.

Know your enemy, Stingley said. This was true intimacy. The cold weather kept the dead from bloating but the smell was overpowering. The bodies exuded essense of garlic. "Eat enough of it regularly and it comes out through your pores," said Doc Magnuson, the Navy corpsman. "Eventually you'll get used to the smell."

On Stingley's orders they rifled the enemy packs for maps and scraps of paper. These were passed along to the ROK second lieutenant who traveled with them. He could read Chinese. From these papers the South Korean interpreter learned that the troops opposing them belonged to the Chinese Seventy-Ninth Division, part of Lin Piao's Fourth Field Army. A map showed that the Chinese objective was the southern end of the Chosin Reservoir, just north of Hagaru-ri and fourteen miles east of the Marine positions around Yudam-ni. The units detached from the ChiCom main force had orders to destroy the Marines, or at least pin them down so they couldn't blunt the assault on the reservoir. Stingley tried to radio this information to the intelligence staff at regimental HQ, but the surrounding mountains blocked his transmission.

A small shrine stood on a knob just to the left and a bit forward of the perimeter. Toward dusk Stingley crawled over to Ben's foxhole. "See that Buddhahead over there—no, not the dead gook, that stone thing on the hilltop. I want you to go up there with the BAR. From that position we'll have a crossfire on any goonies that come up the slope. Take your buddy Darwin with you. He can cover your ass with his M1 in case they try to come up behind you. Take plenty of ammo—four belts anyways. Slip over the back of the ridge and make your way up to the shrine from behind. Maybe they won't see you."

"When can I come back?"

"When we've killed them all."

Luke Darwin was a tall, lanky, jet-black PFC from Harlem. He was a bebop fancier. "Too cool for school," as he put it. Ben and Luke had hit it off from the get-go. Luke had brought a few platters with him, cushioned with cotton in his seabag, and in Wonsan before they moved out to the north they'd commandeered a phonograph in the Navy enlisted men's club. He had Dizzy Gillespie's *Manteca,* among others, along with Bud Powell's *Get Happy* and a number called "Epistrophy" with Shadow Wilson on the drums, Milt Jackson on vibes, and a new pianist named Thelonius Monk who'd composed the thing. Monk was a bluesy marvel, Ellington times ten. "The Loneliest Monk," Luke Darwin called him. They drank Old Overholt with beer chasers. It was a pleasant evening.

When Ben crawled over to Luke Darwin's foxhole, he found his friend in mourning. "Them goddamn Chinamen," he said, "they busted my platters. Lookit this!" He shook shards of black shellac out of his sleeping bag. "A fuckin' mortar frag. I've got to get me some revenge."

"You'll have your chance come nightfall," Ben told him. They slithered over the crest of the ridge and ran in a low crouch to the Buddhist shrine. Luke was draped in bandoleers and dragged a burlap sack of grenades along with his M1 rifle. They drew no fire from the opposite slope. They crouched beneath the Buddha, breathing hard. Ben pulled a few stones from the retaining wall and set up his BAR behind it. He spread the bipod and looked down the sights. With a short traverse he could rake the entire slope. Luke covered their rear.

The Buddhahead smiled down upon them. His broad calm face had been chipped by stray rounds, brow and chin. Two of the fingers on his upturned right palm were gone. He didn't seem to miss them.

Red and green flares began to pop on the far side of the pass. Then came the bugles and what sounded like a shepherd's horn. Dim shapes emerged from the rocks six hundred yards away. Too far yet for accurate fire. The Chinese mustered in the ditch on the south side of the road. Ben estimated their numbers to be more than five hundred, perhaps as much as battalion strength. The Chinese waited until full dark before moving out. A single bugle blared and was joined an instant later by the sound of a entire lunatic orchestra—drums, flutes, fifes, cymbals, pennywhistles—gone spastic on reefer.

"Dig it," Luke said. "We gotta bring some of these cats to Birdland."

"Whatever you say," Ben whispered. "Let's hold our fire until they're almost on top of us. 'Don't disclose your position.' That's the word from Sergeant Stingley."

Behind them, on the crest, mortar tubes chugged and illumination rounds popped high over the hillside, swaying as they descended, sending out long blue shadows that danced in the wake of their glare. The dissonant music stopped for a minute.

The Chinese slogged uphill with tiny mincing steps, in perfect
formation. The flares lent a jerky quality to their movement,
like something from an old silent movie. *Birth of a Nation,*
maybe. Some of the Chinese wore long olive-drab parkas that
trailed behind them in the snow. Those coats, Ben realized, had
been stripped from Marine Corps dead.

Up top the .30s opened fire, quick bursts, four or five
rounds at a squirt. Gaps opened in the Chinese ranks. M1s
joined the machine guns, measured shots, well aimed. A
Chinese officer yelled something through a megaphone and his
troops began to run, screaming as they came. More and more of
them fell. Bodies piled up on the hillside. The first wave fell
back. More Chinese emerged from the darkness beyond the
road and came pouring uphill at a dead run. Now mortar
rounds burst among them. They were only a hundred yards
away. Ben leaned into the butt of the BAR and flicked off the
safety. Fifty yards. Forty. He touched the trigger. . . . Chinese fell
in windrows. He emptied the magazine and slapped in another.

Ben saw a Chinese officer glance his way and yell to his
men. Then he blew his police whistle. Ben cut them down. This
time his muzzle flash caught other enemy eyes. An entire wing
of the assault formation peeled off and headed their way. Too
many, too fast . . .

"Luke, you better start pitching grenades!"

He heard the spang of the spoon popping free and Luke's
long arm lashed past the corner of his eye. The grenade blew the
first wave flat. More grenades followed. Steam rose from the
barrel of the BAR. Ben spat on it while he was reloading. The
spit exploded before it hit the steel.

Chinese potato mashers whirled their way, trailing tails of
blazing cloth from their wooden handles. Luke caught one in
midair and flung it back. Another fell between them. They
rolled away from it and the blast hammered Ben's eardrums. A
concussion grenade. He felt woozy, like he'd been coldcocked
by Jersey Joe Walcott.

Two Chinamen vaulted the retaining wall. Then three more. One of them stuck a bayonet into Luke's shoulder. He lay there unconscious from the grenade blast and didn't even wince when the steel slid in. A Chinese officer with a burp gun stood on the wall, staring down at Ben. Ben stared back. A police whistle dangled from a leather thong around the officer's neck. A gust of wind made the pea in the whistle rattle tinnily. The Chinaman smiled at Ben and said, "Nobody lives forever." He spoke perfect English. He shot Ben twice, *bup-bup,* in the chest.

When he woke up, Ben wondered if he was dead and this the beginning of an afterlife he didn't believe in anymore. He felt of his chest where the Chinese bullets had hit him. It was sore as hell but he couldn't feel any blood. There were holes in the parka but not a trace of red on his palm. He unzipped his parka and field jacket, pulled the OD wool sweater up to his clavicle, unbuttoned his heavy wool shirt, and found the two burp gun bullets lodged against his longjohns. No wonder their gunpowder smelled like burnt hair. It had no oomph.

Or had the Buddha saved him? Ben looked up at the statue. Its smug, peaceful smile seemed to affirm salvation.

Luke was gone. So was the BAR, Luke's M1, and the bag of grenades. Luke wouldn't have taken off on his own, leaving Ben behind. The Chinese must have him. Ben looked over the parapet. Dead silence. Bodies littered the slope, hundreds of them it looked like. It was quiet out there except for the moans of the wounded and the whisper of night wind. Quiet on top, too. No Marine voices barking orders or whoops of exultation at having repelled the Red Menace once again.

Ben stood up. His legs were wobbly but he could hear again. He had a hell of a headache and every time he took a deep breath his ribs grated high in his chest. He walked through the lopsided moonlight to the top of the ridge. Marine bodies lay in their foxholes and at first he thought the men were sleeping.

They were dead. Arbogast, Fleming, little Rojas from West Texas huddled over his machine gun as if in prayer, Cotwinkle's guts ripped open and his left arm lying ten feet away to the west, blown there by a mortar blast. The fingers were locked in the crusted snow as if the arm were trying to drag itself back to its rightful shoulder. Ben was looking for Doc Magnuson, or at least Doc's B-1 bag. The medical kit might have some aspirin in it. Maybe those big yellow pills laced with codeine. But he couldn't find the corpsman or his kit. Nor could he find Sergeant Stingley's body. They must have pulled out, back down the reverse slope, when the Chinese overran the position. Along with the rest of the survivors. There weren't enough jar-head bodies up here to spell Little Big Horn.

Ben searched among the dead Marines for a weapon. The enemy would be out there in the night. All over the mountain-top. He could hear Chinese voices on the road that led to Hagaru. They were headed down through Toktong Pass toward the reservoir.

The Chinese had taken most of the weapons, but in a fox-hole over at the far western end of the perimeter he found an M1 pinned under the body of a marine from How Company. The jarhead was already stiff and Ben's head whirled as he stooped over to pry the rifle loose from its owner's grip. The clip had only one round left in it but he found a full bandoleer behind the foxhole. He reloaded, draped the bandoleer over his shoulders, and walked away.

There was nothing more he could do here.

Ben stayed to the shadows wherever he could. There were Chinese everywhere. He could hear their voices, singsong and far-carrying in the moonlight. The breechblock of the M1 was frozen and he thawed it with his breath, worked it a few times and replaced the eight-round clip, then carried the rifle with his gloved palm wrapped around the receiver. He'd taken a .45 pistol from Rojas and tucked it into the waistband of his windproof trousers. The spare magazines for the Colt he carried in his pants pockets to warm them. Frozen springs don't feed bullets when you need them.

He was trying to make his way to Hagaru, navigating by the North Star. There was sporadic firing off to the southeast and he recognized the slow heavy chug of an air-cooled .50 caliber machine gun. Chinese burp guns chattered like firecrackers. The Fifth Marines were down there, guarding Toktong Pass, probably surrounded by now like his outfit had been. Topping a ridge, he found himself looking down at the western shore of the reservoir. Where the wind had blown the snow clear, the ice shone black in the moonlight. He saw hootches along the shores of an inlet. No lights in the windows, no smoke rose from their roofs. Abandoned. If he could get down to them, he could hide out until morning. With sunrise the Corsairs would be prowling the skies and the Chinese would be hidden in the hills. Maybe he could make his way across the ice to Hagaru and 1st MarDiv headquarters.

He started down the slope toward the hootches but then thought better of it. The ground between here and the huts was open, treeless. In this moonlight, he thought, some Chink would certainly see him. Off to his right a ravine choked with shrubs and stubby pines snaked its way down to the reservoir. He hit for it, running hard in a low painful crouch. His headache was fading but his ribs still hurt where the bullets smacked them. From the grating sounds they made, they were probably cracked. He slipped into the shadows of the pines and sat down in the snow, catching his breath.

A small stream had cut the ravine but it was frozen solid. He was thirsty now, his mouth tasted of stale gunpowder, and he walked down the ravine hoping to find an open riffle where the fast water refused to freeze. It was eerie in there in the pine-scrub. The moon cast shifting shadows on the snow and he stopped often, looking for human movement. Ahead of him, where the ground fell away even more steeply, he heard water lapping. Must be a small waterfall. He moved toward it, but the closer he got, the odder it sounded. An even, rhythmic, steady sound, like a thirsty dog lapping water from a bowl. He stopped again and searched the shadows.

Something twitched down there. Something long and sinuous. And furry. It was a tail. It was striped. Then the lapping sound stopped and a huge white boulder, striated in moonshadows, raised up from the edge of the streambed and turned his way. The yellow eyes locked on his. The eyes were a handspan apart. His blood froze. For a long long moment they stared at each other. Then the tiger turned away and like smoke he was gone. Ben's blood started flowing again.

He walked down to the riffle and knelt in the tiger's paw prints. His kneecaps didn't quite fill them. He drank the racing water, ice cold. Then he backtracked the cat up the side of the ravine. Near the top he found what he'd hoped for, a fresh-killed red deer. He'd eaten nothing since morning. The tiger had consumed the deer's guts and most of one haunch but there was plenty of meat left.

With his K-Bar he skinned out the backstraps. He looked around. He was well concealed. He could risk a fire. He broke off a handful of dead twigs, gathered some pine cones for kindling, and kicked a clear spot in the snow. One flick of the Zippo and the fire was going. He skewered a slab of deer meat on the point of the knife and sat back, the rifle across his lap, while the meat seared. Fat dripped and sizzled in the flames. When the meat was half done, he wolfed it down, burning the roof of his mouth. The pain was worth it. He hadn't realized how hungry he was.

The meal warmed him inside and out but he knew he'd soon be cold again. He had no sleeping bag. He debated his moves. It was cozy in the ravine, away from the wind. He was getting drowsy. Should he wait out the night here and freeze his ass off or push on down to the hootches . . .

The edge of a knife pressed against his throat.

A voice hissed in his ear—"*You die, Maline!*"

Oh, Fuck! A Chink! Ben rolled away and grabbed for the M1.

Then the voice continued in a lower register. "Cool it, pogue. I taught you better than this in boot camp."

It was Stingley. He sheathed his K-Bar.

"Goddamit, Slater. I could smell that meat cooking halfway down the mountain." He stomped out the flames and kicked snow over the coals.

They headed downhill through the pines. Snow squeaked underfoot. A dozen Marines waited in a side gully. They were huddled together to share the warmth of their bodies. Sergeant Stingley slung the deer haunch to them. "Chow down, you pogues, before the meat's froze solid," he said.

"But Sergeant, it's *raw!*"

"Oh, is it? Good. Maybe it'll put some hair on your chest."

When the men had eaten, Stingley divided the remains of the meat among them. "Okay, saddle up," he said. "I reckon it's about ten or twelve miles to the Hagaru perimeter. But it's all downhill so the going should be easy." He turned to Ben. "Slater, you take the point."

Twice on the way down the ravine Ben heard Chinese patrols moving through the snow, big groups of men. Grenades rattled on their belts. They were close enough for him to smell them. The Marines lay flat and waited until the patrols had passed, then continued their way down the mountain.

They came to the end of the pines. Ahead the ground was open, bright in the moonlight. They could hear bugles and sporadic bursts of gunfire coming from Hagaru, the chugging blasts of Chinese grenades and the louder slam of 4.2-inch mortars replying. Illumination flares drifted down and columns of smoke rose from the scruffy little hamlet. The Chinese were hammering the place with all they had, wave after wave of them. They had plenty of troops to waste.

"How the hell do we get in there without being killed," somebody asked, "either by the Chinks or our own guys?"

"Who's got binoculars?" Stingley asked. A corporal from a How Company mortar crew produced a pair. Stingley scoped the scene. He fiddled with the focus. By the light reflected from the snow Ben saw that Stingley's chin was bearded in dried blood. His left eye looked swollen shut. "Goddamit, I can't see worth shit anymore," he said. "Here, Slater, you take a peek."

"What am I looking for, Sergeant?"

"The place where the gook lines are thinnest. They won't be looking behind them. If we can sneak up close and open fire, we'll have a chance of busting through."

Ben took the binoculars and scanned the Chinese lines. There seemed to be what looked like a command post behind them, a knot of officers in knee-high fur-lined boots carrying maps. He watched them for a moment as they dispatched runners to the front. Then his eye was caught by a group of men in Marine green field-jackets, about twenty of them, maybe two dozen. They were squatting or lying in the snow, most of them, guarded by half a dozen Chinese with burp guns. *Prisoners!* He focused on their faces and saw Luke Darwin among them, lying among the wounded.

"They've got a bunch of Marines down there, Sergeant. Right next to what looks like the Chink C.P."

"Are you sure?"

"Fuckin' A—I mean, yes sir. Luke Darwin's one of them."

"Let me see." Ben handed him the binoculars and pointed out the spot as best he could. Stingley looked for a long time.

"You're right." He handed the binoculars back to the mortarman. "That changes our priorities. Okay, here's the plan. . . ."

The Chinese command post was behind a low hill that rose like a crusted scab on the southwest flank of Hagaru. On their map it was designated East Hill. Gullies trailed off the knob, draining toward the Changjin River, which flowed into the reservoir just north of town. Stingley's men—about squad strength and armed only with rifles, grenades, and two BARs—bellycrawled across the snow to the nearest gully, taking advantage of the rolling terrain to keep out of sight. It took what was left of the night, and the sky to the east was brightening to dull gray by the time they were in position. It was 0500 by Stingley's watch. East Hill lay three hundred yards to their south, the command post perhaps a hundred yards closer. Easy killing range for Marine marksmen armed with M1s and .30 caliber automatic rifles. And all of them were marksmen. You didn't get out of boot camp until you'd qualified.

"Make sure your actions aren't froze," Stingley told them. "We're going to pick off as many Chink officers as we can. Rapid fire but accurate. Slater—you, Talia, and Holt are going to move up the gully till you're almost on top of those guards with the burp guns. Kill 'em all. Kill 'em quick. Kill 'em dead. Then spring the prisoners. Bring 'em back down the gully, fast. We won't open fire till we hear your shots. Don't worry about a thing. When all the Chink brass is dead we'll be covering your ass. Grab any weapons you can lay your hands on, grab ammo too. With those extra Marines we'll be about platoon strength and if they're all well armed, we should be able to fight our way to the top of that fuckin' hill. We'll hold out up there until help comes from town."

"Our guys must have that hilltop registered by now, Sergeant," the mortarman said. "What if they take us for Chinks?"

"Let's worry about that when we get there," Stingley told him. "Anyways, it's better to be killed by Marines than by these rat-fuckin' commie bastards."

Ben and the others bellycrawled up the gully. Talia was a big-shouldered, hawk-eyed Croat from northern California, a retread who'd served with the Old Breed—the Fifth Marines— on Peleliu and Okinawa during World War II. He was a CPA in the real world, but he hadn't lost his military skills. During the fight at the pass, Ben had seen him kill a Chinese sniper at nearly half a mile, and with iron sights at that. Holt was a tall, cool, lanky PFC from Chicago, a goof-off in most respects but a serious Bears fan. On the cruise from Inchon to Wonsan he and Ben had nearly duked it out one afternoon during an Armed Forces Radio broadcast of a Bears-Packers game. Green Bay had just scored on a forty-yard TD pass and Ben was inspired enough to exult out loud. But when Holt, his face gone red then white with outrage, clenched a fist and threatened to come across the messdeck table, Luke Darwin had told him to cool-breeze it. "Save that shit for the gooks, man." Ben hoped he'd saved some.

Near the top of the gully Ben signaled the others to wait and crawled to the lip of the berm. He took off his helmet before peering over. Then he slid back down. "Okay," he told Talia and Holt, "the guards are in pairs, two men to the right, two to the left, and the others on the far side of the prisoners. Holt, you take the left-hand pair, Talia the ones on the right. I'll pop the far pair, then run in there and roust those jarheads. The healthy ones can carry the wounded and whatever weapons and ammo we can find. You two cover us. With all this gunfire going on, maybe the other Chinks won't pick up on us right away." He looked from one to the other. "Questions?" They shook their heads.

"Okay, lock and load."

Bellydown behind the berm, they laid their sights. "On three," Ben whispered. "One, two, three. . . ." The M1s banged in unison, two quick shots each. The guards were down in their tracks. Ben slipped over the top and ran toward the Marines. They gaped at him, wide-eyed.

"Drop your cocks and grab your socks, jarheads, we're getting out of here. Grab those burp guns and ammo belts, whatever grenades you can find too. Everyone not carrying a weapon, help some of these wounded guys. We'll rally at the bottom of the draw. Down there." He pointed the way.

Then he ran over to Luke, who stared at him with a wide grin. "Fancy meeting you here, dude."

"Can you walk?"

"Yeah, but slow."

No counterfire yet. Ben could hear Stingley's men shooting and saw that most of the Chinese officers were down. A few Chinese in white quilts were running lumpily from the front line, their feet wrapped in burlap, babbling and firing occasional bursts in their direction.

"Here, hook your arm around my neck."

They made it to the gully just as a machine gun opened up. Bullets spanged the frozen ground, throwing shards of permafrost that stung like shrapnel. Ben felt blood running down into his eyebrows. He brushed it away. Can't let it get in my eyes. Not now when every round counts.

He felt Luke flinch and stagger beside him, the arm around Ben's neck clenched tight. He looked over. Luke's eyes were glazing.

"You hit?"

"Just a stitch in the side," Luke said.

His knees buckled. Ben saw blood darkening Luke's field jacket just above the kidney.

Ben stooped and swept him up in a one-armed fireman's carry. The bastard was heavy. Carrying the M1 in one hand, Luke with the other, he staggered back to where Stingley was waiting.

"You got 'em all?"

"We're the last ones," Ben said. "But Darwin's hit too hard to go up any hill. He caught a round from that m.g. right when we dropped in the gully."

"That's okay," Stingley said. "Change of plans. No way we can get through those gooks now that we stirred 'em up. We're going back down the gulch, then up into the pines again and wait. Maybe the Chinks will pull back to cover when the airdales get here. Then we can march into Hagaru unopposed."

Stingley looked around at the freed Marines. "Any of you guys a corpsman?"

A grizzled old guy stepped forward. "I'm Morgan, Pharmacist's Mate One," he said. "The Chinks took my B-1 kit, but I hid some sulfa and a few morphine ampules."

"Check this Marine, Doc."

A squad of Chinese charged the gully, most of them carrying nothing but grenades. But the rifles and BARs stopped them out of throwing range.

"They're testing our firepower," Stingley said. "Next time they'll send a whole lot more Chinamen. We've got to mount up, boys, and run for it. Right quick now."

Morgan stood up from beside Luke and stepped over to Stingley. "It's through and through," he said. "It may have nicked a kidney. No way I can stop the bleeding for long without at least a yard of gauze."

Stingley reached in his pocket. "Here's my snotrag," he said, handing Morgan a neatly folded Marine green handkerchief. "Don't worry, I haven't used it. Slater, give him yours, and you damn well better have one."

Ben did. Morgan dusted the handkerchiefs with sulfa and pushed them into the holes in Luke's sides. With his K-Bar he cut a long strip from Ben's parka liner and knotted it around Luke's waist. Luke was shivering hard. Ben took the parka off and stuffed Luke's arms into the sleeves, then zipped it up around him.

A white-phosphorus round from a Chinese 82 exploded on the lip of the gully. Marines fell back from the edge, batting at their uniforms, slapping handfuls of snow on their burns. But there's no escape from Willy Peter's bite.

"What about the rest of the WIA?" Stingley asked. "How many can make it on their own steam? We've got about a mile to go and we have to clear out fast."

"There's three leg wounds—fractures or torn ligaments. They'll have to be carried. One blind guy but someone can lead him. Major Thomason. . . . He's not gonna make it, gut shot, internal bleeding. With plasma and penicillin I could maybe save him." He shook his head. "Not got. The rest are mostly bullet and frag wounds, arms, legs, butts, faces, nothing life threatening."

Stingley called five men down from the firing line and told them to start humping the wounded toward the pine ravine. "You can help your buddy Darwin," he told Ben. "Move out, now."

When they reached the pines again, the sun was just clear of the horizon. Blood red, blink, bone white. The air sparked with frost motes. By 0900 the ground mist burned off. Long white snakes of Chinese troops were moving back toward the mountains but they'd left it too late. The first Corsairs of the day appeared. Two flights of three birds apiece. They roared in low with the sun behind them, hedgehopping the naked hills and the town itself, just clearing the two-story building that housed the mayor's office.

On the first pass they were firing their 20mm cannons, every third round high explosive, and tore long swaths in the Chinese columns. Distant bugles blared. The Chinese marched on, double-time but they didn't break.

The second pass was napalm. Fire flowers bloomed on the snow, red black and yellow. Little black and tan hulls littered the snow when the smoke blew clear. They were Chinese corpses, crisped up hard like the "spinsters" you find at the bottom of a popcorn bowl.

The Corsairs saved their rockets for the finale. They hit the heads and tails of the columns, hoping to take out officers and their Korean guides. The bombs flung dirty snow and body parts into a clear blue sky.

The Chinese marched on.

Ben watched it all from the edge of the pines where he sat beside Luke in the sunshine. The sun had little heat to it but at least it gave an illusion of warmth. He took off his shoepacs to check his sore feet. The frostbite was severe. His toes had the color and stench of incipient gangrene. Well, there was nothing much he could do right now but air them out and let his wool socks dry in the sunlight.

From the height of land he could see Marine engineers bulldozing the new airstrip on the south side of Hagaru. It was slow going. The ground was solid ice. The engineers had welded steel teeth to the dozer blades. Every few passes they stopped and knocked the frozen dirt clear. Even at this distance you could hear the clank of sledgehammers on the still, cold air.

He looked down the road to the south, toward Koto-ri and the Funchilin Pass. The First Marines must be fighting their way up it right now, he thought. Once Chesty Puller's boys get here the Chinese will realize they bit off more than they can chew. He saw the road that wound its way up to Yudam-ni. The Fifth and Seventh Marines were still up there. He could hear gunfire and the boom of 105mm howitzers. They'll have to be pulling out soon, rejoining the Marines at Hagaru. After that . . . well, it's seventy-eight miles back to Hungnam, fighting all the way.

The wind picked up and the sky turned gray. It started to snow. Ben put his still damp socks and boots back on. He pulled up the collar of his field jacket and shrugged down into it. Morgan used one of his last morphine Syrettes on Luke, and he was feeling no pain.

Pretty much out of it now, Ben thought.

In a way you're lucky.

Luke was scatting bebop riffs.

"Groovin' High."

"Cool Breeze."

Ben knew those numbers. Gillespie compositions. He picked up the beat, rolled frozen fingers on the rifle stock.

The bugles faded . . .

He heard a far, frantic, whinnying sound, oddly in tune with Luke's music. Some of the higher-ranking Chinese officers rode ponies—shaggy little animals with long manes and fore-locks, short coupled and sturdy legged. Now one of them ran across the snow, uphill toward where the Marines were lying. It was badly burned by the napalm strike. Twice it stopped to roll in the snow, then bounced to its feet again and galloped—trying to outrun the unrelenting hornets that were searing their way through its hide.

Ben raised his rifle and clicked off the safety.

"Good thinking, Slater." Stingley had moved up beside him, attracted by the screaming. "We can use the meat. It's already half cooked."

"I just want to put the poor bastard out of his misery."

Stingley laughed. Then he nodded. "That too."

They broke their fast on horsemeat tartare. Stingley said no fires. The pony meat was tough but hot, plenty of blood to put hair on their chests. They washed it down with canteens of ice water from the rivulet.

Nobody complained.

Stingley sent a work party with orders to bring back any weapons, ammo, and clothing they could find—even burned uniforms would do. Padded cotton was better than nothing. "If it don't fall apart when you touch it, you damn well better bring it in. It's gonna be a ballfreezin' hike into town and we gotta keep the WIAs warm."

When the last of the Chinese units had disappeared into the hills, Stingley mustered the men. Every man who could walk had a weapon now. The detail that went down to loot the Chinese dead had brought two sleds back with them, piled high with burp guns, grenades, ammo belts, and uniforms. Morgan lashed the worst of the wounded to these toboggans. Major Thomason was dead. The corpsman planned to bury him in the snow and mark the spot for later retrieval by Graves Registration. Stingley brought the Major's body along.

It took six men to drag the toboggans.

They were a strange-looking platoon when they set out for Hagaru, many of the smaller men wearing scorched Chinese uniforms, others with quilted jackets and trousers draped across their shoulders or tied around their waists. At Stingley's orders all the Chinese clothing was turned inside out, with the field green color showing, for fear that trigger-happy defenders in Hagaru would mistake them for another Chinese suicide squad and grant their wishes. It was a wise precaution. Twice on the march Corsairs peeled off and dove on them but checked their fire on closer inspection. Finally a Corsair pilot must have radioed Hagaru because as they neared town, a patrol slogged out to meet them. They were doggies—raggedy-ass troops of the U.S. Army's 31st Infantry Regiment. The patrol was led by a Jeep mounted with an air-cooled .50 caliber machine gun. Stingley called his men to attention. They snapped to.

"Hand salute," Stingley bellowed.

An army captain climbed down from the Jeep and touched the brim of his helmet with a limp, loosely cupped hand.

"What outfit are you men with?" he asked.

"The United States Marine Corps, sir."

Ben limped back down the line to the toboggans. Luke was on the second one. He was dead. The cold had killed him. Everyone on the toboggans was dead. Graves Registration was already there. They removed a dead man's dog tags from the chain around his neck and attached one to his ankle, the other around his wrist. Then they scribbled his name, rank, and serial number in a little Marine green notebook.

Gone but not forgotten.

Ben looked down at his friend's cold face. Hoarfrost bloomed on Luke Darwin's eyeballs.

Ben said, "Cool-breeze it, man."

PART II

THE SAME
RIVER TWICE

(Autumn: 2000)

Old men ought to be explorers . . .
—Eliot, "East Coker"

I

TIMOR MORTIS

L ike many doctors, I am reluctant—no, downright averse—to subjecting myself to an annual physical. In the first place, or so goes our reasoning, I am myself an ordained physician, fully capable of diagnosing whatever might ail me, prescribing the proper protocol to correct the problem, administering said treatment in the most efficacious manner, and thus in the fullness of time . . . of healing myself. This despite my seemingly limited medical specialty, which is the human eye in all its aqueous good humor.

In the second, I know that if I submit my frail flesh to the scrutiny of a colleague, the bastard will certainly find something wrong with me. This in turn will only lead to a lot of what my Jewish colleagues call *tsuris*. Once you're in our clutches, we never let you go. Not until the last shovel of dirt falls on your coffin lid. You can't really blame us, though. It's what we're trained to do. And, too, many of us are just in it for the money.

And I'm proud to admit that I made a bundle of it over my forty-year career as an ophthalmologist. By the time I retired from practice last year—the last year of the ultraviolent twentieth century (lots of ocular trauma!)—I'd salted away nearly a quarter of a gigabuck, most of it paper money admittedly, from market investments, and lived disgustingly well in the process.

After graduating from Marquette University med school in 1957 I served out my internship and residency in the U.S. Navy, first at the naval hospital in San Diego and then on an attack transport, the USS *Talladega* (APA 208) attached to Phibron Seven, home ported in Long Beach, California. On the Douche Boat, as we called her, we cruised the western Pacific, stopping at such exotic ports of call as Sasebo and Yokosuka in Japan; Inchon, Pusan, and Wonsan in South Korea; Taipei on the ChiNat island of Taiwan; Iwo Jima; Okinawa; and Guam, not to mention my favorite liberty ports, Dingalan Bay and Zamboanga and Olangapo-Where-the-Sewer-Meets-the-Sea in the sunny Philippine archipelago.

Most of the medical emergencies I dealt with in the Navy were of the gonorrheal persuasion, though now and then a whitehat would knock a shipmate's jaw adrift from its moorings, or fall down a ship's ladder in heavy seas, sustaining minor fractures and contusions. Once, in the midst of a typhoon en route from Pearl Harbor to Midway, a first-class bosun's mate named Boynton reported to sickbay with a bad bellyache.

The poor guy was running a temp of 103 and already starting to hallucinate. Classic signs of acute appendicitis. I palpated his hairy lower abdomen and discovered that the peccant appendage was about to rupture, flooding the poor salt's innards with poison. I sent a corpsman with word to the officer of the deck that I wanted to perform an emergency appendectomy before it was too late. Emergency surgery at sea, in the grip of a typhoon no less—this was the stuff that articles in the *New England Journal of Medicine* are made on, and thus reputations . . .

The skipper paged me on the 1-MC—"Now hear this. Doc Taggart, report to the bridge on the double. Doc Taggart to the bridge, ASAP."

The ship was wallowing like the pig she was, taking green water over the bow and tossing great swimming-pool loads of it eighty feet high onto the flying bridge. Each scoop of seawater hit with a crash that made the old tub shudder clear down to her keel. I scrambled up the slick wet ladders topside, squinting against waves of windblown drift that cut like a horsewhip, drenched to the skin by the time I reached the Old Man.

His name was Harold W. Becker, USN, a tall, square-shouldered four-striper, and the best skipper—the best man—I ever served with, military or medical. He stood there ramrod straight in his black foul-weather gear, swaying with the ship's pitch and roll like a white pine in a windstorm, the braid and scrambled eggs on his hat gone puke green with salt corrosion. He had the chinstrap pulled down tight under his lantern jaw, to keep the hat from going adrift in the breeze, and I was surprised to see by the light of the radar console that he needed a shave—but then, we'd been eighteen hours in the grip of this typhoon and he hadn't left the bridge in all that time, except once, the OOD told me, to take a whiz in his cabin.

"You want to cut this kid wide open, Doc?" he said. "In seas like this?"

"I have to, Captain, otherwise his appendix will pop and all the penicillin in the Pacific won't likely save him."

"Can you do it with the ship tossing like this?"

At that moment the Douche Boat pitched up her bow nearly to the vertical, then rolled almost perpendicular to the hollow of the seas. We both skidded ten feet sideways. I looked up. The slashing, moaning, white-maned crests of the waves were taller than the kingposts.

"I can secure him on the operating table with sandbags and strap him down tight, sir. Sedate him into cloud-cuckoo-land. Then if you can put her bow into the wind and hold her steady, I'll whip that nasty thing out, quick as a cat, pack him with antibiotics, and zip him back up again. Whole thing won't take fifteen minutes."

He gave me a dubious look.

"Level with me, Doc. You're not just doing this to get in the medical journals, are you?" He watched my eyes. His were like bright blue drill bits.

"N-no, sir," I said.

"Yeah," he said. "What would be your best considered alternative, if it came to that?"

"Well, sir, I could pack his lower abdomen in ice to reduce the internal swelling and lower his body temp, shoot him up with penicillin, and dose him with febrifuges. Then we could hope this weather blows through and head for Midway or Wake, whichever is nearest when we come clear. An appendectomy would be a cinch on dry land. But how long will it take us to get out of this weather, sir? How long to reach Wake or Midway?"

"Quartermaster of the watch?"

That worthy, who'd been listening in on our conversation as had all the watchhands, bent over his chart with parallel rules and protractor and quickly paced off the distance on a rhumb line.

"At least twelve hours to Midway, sir. Sixteen or more to Wake. That's figuring flank speed, maybe eighteen knots—all she'll turn without blowing a boiler, sir."

Captain Becker stroked his chin. It rasped, and he got a sour look on his face. "Can he last that long without popping his guts?" he asked me.

"I doubt it, sir."

He pondered a moment more. Then, "Okay, Doc. I can rig a sea anchor to hold her head into the wind and steady her down a bit more, once we've turned her bow into the seas. Lay below and have at it. Pass the word when you're ready to slice."

It never came to pass. Boatswain's Mate First Class William J. Boynton, USN, proved allergic to anesthesia. At the first whiff of ether he erupted from his bed of sandbags, ripped the mask from his face, burst the straps that bound him to the table, staggered to his feet on the heaving deck, and with a Gaelic roar came at the attending anesthetist, Dr. Heracles Zagoras, the ship's dentist, with clear intent to inflict grave bodily harm. My corpsmen had a hell of a time subduing him.

Once the boatswain was quiescent again, we had to fall back to Plan B. The icebags, antibiotics, febrifuges, and a mild diet of pablum and fruit juices kept Boynton's appendix intact until we reached Subic Bay in the Philippines. There he underwent an appendectomy in the naval hospital and was soon on his feet again. Indeed, the night before we left that port for Cap San Jacques in troubled French Indochina, I saw him outside the

Papagayo Bar & Grill in downtown Olangapo, the scuzzy brothel town that served Subic in those days when we still had a naval presence in the Philippines. The bosun was reeling with drink as he duked it out with a whitehat off another APA, our sister ship and squadron rival, the *Okanogan*. As I recall, Boynton was so well recovered that he knocked his opponent—splat on his keister—into the Shit River (yes, that was indeed its name), which slouched sludgily through town at that point.

I rather liked Boynton, not simply for his swift recovery from an infection that would have laid low a lesser man, but also because he reminded me of my old high school pal Ben Slater. I'd had only two letters from Ben since our memorable canoe trip on the Firesteel River in the fall of 1950. One was post-marked from Inchon, where he joined his USMC outfit that fall. Korea was a rathole, he said. Little kids everywhere selling chewing gum, Korean booze, shoelaces, and their sisters. Artillery fire w/ accompanying muzzle flash evident just beyond the hooches of town. The big surprise was when his nemesis from boot camp had joined his platoon—Sergeant Fuckin' Stingley, his old drill instructor. Their unit was deploying shortly for the east coast, he said. A place called Wonsan. That letter was dated October 24.

The second one reached me just after Christmas. He'd mailed it from Yokosuka, where he was cooped up in the big naval hospital, recovering from frostbite and a few "minor nicks and perforations," as he put it. "Nothing worse than after a foot-ball game." He'd been in the big fight up near the Chosin Reservoir, where the First Marine Division had fought its way out of a trap when the ChiComs invaded. "You think Wisconsin's cold in the winter," he said, "you oughta come to Frozen Chosin." When he was patched up, he said, he was heading back for the MLR—the Main Line of Resistance—up near the thirty-eighth parallel. "Trench warfare," he said, "just like France in '17 and '18. Ho-hum. . . ."

I got to Wonsan myself eight years later, on the *Talladega*. We were ferrying a regiment of ROK troops over there from Inchon. The fighting part of the war was long over, though sporadic ambushes flared now and then like endemic fever along the DMZ. The ROKs were tough, thieving little fuckers. They were desperate for anything they could swipe from us. One of them reached through the porthole in the navigator's stateroom while he was dozing in his fartsack one evening after chow. "I saw this arm come in and sniff around like a blind dog," he told us later in the wardroom. "The fingers touched the washbasin, just grazed my tube of toothpaste, felt and rejected a bar of soap, then glommed on to the blackout curtain over the port and lifted it. I jumped up and yelled. The steward's mates came swarming topside and nailed the guy redhanded. The OOD turned him over to the cognizant ROK authorities."

Next morning we landed the ROKs, and the crew of the first Papa boat that returned to the ship was whitefaced. "Jesus, Doc," the coxswain told me. "You know that poor ROK dogface who stole Mr. McGrath's curtain? They marched him behind a sand dune, jabbered a few words in gook, lined up a firing squad, and shot the fucker. *Bingo!* Like that." He snapped his fingers.

"Just saving face," I told him.

Later on that same visit I had to go ashore myself, to pick up some medical supplies. It was winter, black ice in the roadside puddles, corpses of homeless civilians who'd frozen or starved to death lying in the unpaved streets. I accidentally kicked one and he crunched like a popsicle. I had to carry a loaded Colt .45 on such trips, there were rip-off artists everywhere ashore, Koreans and round-eyes both. On my way back to the boat landing where the LCVP was standing by for me, a Korean in padded gray cotton pajamas jumped out from between two hooches and made a snatch for the satchel of drugs I was carrying—ampules of penicillin, mostly, but some morphine Syrettes as well. I fought him for it but he was stronger than he looked. I fumbled the .45 from its holster, let go of the bag, jacked the slide, and pointed the pistol at him.

"Hands up!"

"Fuck you, lound-eye." He flipped me the finger.

One of my Marine escorts shot him. His sternum collapsed as he fell, imploding inward. A concavity the size of a softball. He geysered blood from mouth and nostrils. His eyes stared up at me, glazing fast . . .

"Not to worry, sir," the SPs told me. "This guy's a Commonist, sure as shit. We've been lookin' for the fucker high and low. There's some wounded Chinks hid out somewhere in the boonies and they need medicine. "

Ah, the Navy. Those were the last of the biblical "seven lean years" for me. But it wasn't all Sturm und Drang. I loved the Navy, particularly being at sea, cruising independently from island to island, continent to continent, the timeless empty gray days of wind and weather, the Pacific spreading out unto eternity so that you felt you'd never see land again, and it was a good feeling; pilot whales broaching like enormous bubbles of black glass alongside and wheezing their misty spouts skyward; then the water going electric blue as we entered the Philippine Sea, porpoises flirting with the bow waves, flying fish skimming the trade wind and sometimes hitting the deck by miscalculation, flopping steely bluegray in the gunwales, and the Filipino mess boys scuttling to pick them up before they flipped themselves back overboard. . . . The Filipinos who prepared our wardroom meals of iridescent green beef and sodden gray potatoes always cooked up a mess of sticky rice, bamboo shoots, tropical greens, and fresh, stir-fried fish for themselves. My cabin was right up the ladder from the officers' galley, and sometimes in the late afternoons I'd be snoozing in my fetid rack when the aroma of their supper reached me. I would begin to dream of the Firesteel and the meals Ben and I prepared at night with the trout we'd caught—way back when, in our boyhood.

After the Navy I joined an eye practice in Santa Monica. It was owned by two old ophthalmologists who were looking for young blood. Old, I say. They were about forty-five. But already they'd earned enough, even in those days, before lasers, cataract surgery, and corneal transplants, to pull the pin. There's a lot of money in eyeglass frames. They wanted someone to buy out their practice and I was the golden boy. I'd met and married Kate during my last year in the Navy. Kate Winston, nee. She was a registered nurse at the naval station clinic in Long Beach, a leggy, bright, witty blonde from Des Moines, Iowa, with a taste for jazz. She caught me one night at the Blue Note West in Redondo Beach while I was riffing with some black cats from K.C. She dug my sax. She dug my sex. She scraped up the dough to help me buy out the old farts who ran the eye practice. She bore me three kids, two boys and a girl. Our daughter, Taffy, married well but moved to Wales with her husband, a professor of ethnology at Aberystwyth. We have made trips over there now and then, and it's not the same. One of the boys—Frank, the eldest and my favorite—was killed in the carbombing of the Marine HQ in Lebanon. October 23, 1983. I'll never forget that date. A Marine, yes, like my old friend Ben Slater. The younger son, Eddie, majored in economics at Berkeley, took an MBA at Wharton, and disappeared into the canyons of Wall Street. We hear from him three times a year, on our birthdays and at Xmas, tasteful Hallmark cards every time.

I piled up the shekels, year after year, bought IBM in the '50s, invested in offshore oil, caught Xerox early on, then Wal-Mart, cashed in on the Silicon Valley boom, made a killing in spousal abuse—every wife-beater left me a thousand bucks richer for each eye he blackened; I cheered them on. No, I didn't. I hate the bastards.

We built a house in Palos Verdes on a cliff overlooking the Pacific, a sprawling stucco hacienda with a red tile roof, all grown around with succulents and pampas grass, with a big slate deck and a kidney-shaped pool. Kate and I shot clays off that deck, hunted valley and mountain quail from El Centro to Bakersfield. Even up into Oregon sometimes. She was a natural wingshot, wiping my eye at trap and skeet with the nifty little 28-gauge Parker I gave her on our first wedding anniversary.

Later, we built another place, a redwood log cabin up near Bishop in the High Sierra. We fished trout there, but it wasn't the Firesteel by a long shot. I bought a forty-five-foot Norwegian ketch, a double-ender, clinker-built. Oak and pine, brass brightwork and teak deck, heavy and somewhat slow in stays but capacious and weatherly. We painted her hull bright scarlet and rechristened her *Red Orm*, for the hero of a Viking sea saga I loved, *The Long Ships*, by Frans Bengtsson. Kate and I cruised her whenever I could get away from the practice— long voyages, down the Baja to Cabo and beyond, clear up to Anchorage a few times. Once as far as the Cocos, off Ticoland.

I fished hard on those trips, always had a line or two out with a spinner trolling astern, stopped to cast a jigging rod whenever we saw albacore or bonita breaking; off the Revilla Gigedos, south of Cabo about two hundred miles, caught a yellowfin tuna over two hundred pounds, great sashimi, sliced still quivering from its flank, dark red fine-grained meat, cold as the sea herself, with plenty of wasabe and soy sauce; big wahoo as well, though not as good raw—and horse-eye jacks on the flyrod at night, under the searchlight on the transom, when we were anchored off Clarion that time, or was it San Benedicto? Up north, the big tyee and halibut that could break your arm if you gaffed them wrong, silvers and sockeyes on the Four Weight, strong tough swift steelhead in the Babine and Alaska's Situk River. But none of them matched the thrill of the Firesteel. Maybe it's the water.

I played my sax at dawn and sunset while we were at sea, did-dybopping with the gulls, summoning up cetaceans . . .

Kate died two months ago. July 10th of the first year of the new fucking millennium. A stroke, while playing tennis with her lady friends, five days after I'd sold the practice and retired. We were fitting out *Red Orm* for a long cruise this fall to the Marquesas, Tahiti, and the Tuamotus. I buried her, sold the ketch, and then started drinking in earnest. The kids made a one-day appearance for the funeral and then split. I don't blame them. No, I don't. Not a bit. I don't blame them at all. Really . . .

I found myself pissing six times a night. Thought it might be the booze. I quit. I still pissed, every hour on the hour. Good thing I'd sold the boat. I could never have single-handed her to the mid-Pacific unless I wore a diaper at the helm.

Diabetes? I tested my blood. Negative.

The Big PC?

There was no way I could palpate my prostate all by myself.

I went to Jack Trevanian, a urologist pal I'd played poker with for many years. Okay, against my better judgment. But what the hell. Tests. PSA through the roof. A mindboggling forty-five. The biopsy in Jack's office. It took only a minute, no pain on a local anesthetic. Rectally. With the "gun" that propels a needle very fast, like the tongue of a snake, into various areas of the prostate, nipping out samples with every lick.

These samples will not only detect a malignancy, but will show whether it's slow moving, "nonaggressive," or a metastatic meteor. Or somewhere in between. The scale runs from one to ten. With a ten, you might as well write yourself off.

I waited out the results of the biopsy. I went back to drinking and pissing. No, I'd never given up pissing. I was pissing my life away. Maybe I'd already done it. I was dying. Or maybe not. I didn't know. Or at least I didn't know when. All I knew was that I'd fallen into their hands. From here on out I faced a series of time-consuming, ever more depressing tests—sonograms, MRIs, bone scans, CAT scans, X-ray sessions, rectal prods and probes, clever, dancing fingers up the bunghole, and the sad, hopeful smiles of underpaid female assistants. Not to mention the bills I'd get from my compatriots, the ultimate reaming.

Timor mortis conturbat me.

Five days later Jack called. "Well, old buddy, I won't beat about the bush. It's positive. Six of the ten spots I tested. Looks like it's about a nine on the Gleason Scale . . . "

"Don't you mean the Richter Scale? Hyper-fucking-aggressive."

"Very."

"What's next?"

"Well, we'll have to see if it's metastasized, like into your bones or your colon. Hell, it could pop up almost anywhere, Harry. I'm afraid you're in for a lot of clinic time. Bring a book along—they're pretty busy right now. We'll start with an MRI . . . "

I hung up.

2

THE AFTERLIFE

I sat up late that night, sprawled on the veranda in a chaise longue, listening to the beat of the Pacific crashing the cliffs below. Now and then I blew some changes to the rumble of the surf, but the sax tasted dead in my mouth. The mouthpiece full of cold spit. Without Kate the music meant nothing anymore. I lay the horn aside and sipped Armagnac on the rocks. I was popping tranqs like M&Ms.

If it comes to it, I thought, like say a preexisting malignancy that's already metastasized from the prostate to maybe a bone cancer, colon, lung, liver, testicular, or whatever—should I check out before things get really rough, too depressing and grim? I could end up like my old fishing buddy Jim Jury, who never knew (or let on that he knew) what caused the cancers that devoured him.

Cancer: the ugliest, most frightening word in the English language. In any language.

What is it in other tongues?

Krebs in German, *le cancer* in French, *el cáncer* in Spanish, close to that in Italian.

But in the gentle koine of East Africa it's *jamii moja ya nyota.* Swahili. Almost musical. To die for. . . . Coming out of the tent at the crack of dawn, still cool before the sun cleared the acacias, and Wamatitu pussyfooting toward me from the mess tent with a tray of black, hot Kenya tea, smiling that broad, sweet Louis Armstrong grin of his, *Salaama, Bwana—habari gani? Chai, Bwana?* Beaded dew gleams like shards of diamond on the green canvas of the tent, and the air smells clean as cold canvas. Through the tops of the doum palms the snow-capped peaks of Kirinyaga float in the hard blue sky. A herd of Tommies is grazing out on the plain, their short white tails whirring like miniature helicopter rotors. The tails stop only when they die . . .

You'll never go there again, Doc. Have a Halcyon instead.

I picked up the saxophone and tried to play around it. It didn't help.

Checking out: Gunshot? Preferable: cheap, quick, painless, certain if you have a steady hand at the critical moment, and best of all no one else has to be involved. But it's messy. I wouldn't want the maid to see it later and feel obliged to clean up. Josefína would faint dead away before she even went for the mop and bucket. And what about the kids? Those images that yet fresh images beget . . .

Have another schnapps.

Drugs and poisons? Barbiturates, tranquilizers, rat poison, Drano, etc. An overdose, then? Of what? I've got whole drawers full of drugs in my office, freebies in a selection of delicious flavors from Roche, Pfizer, Schering, GlaxoWellcome, and all the usual suspects. But which flavor works best, and what's the optimum dosage to off oneself for sure? I could look it up. But there's always an element of uncertainty.

The Rope? Who cuts you down? Hanged men shit their pants. The dead always tend to void their bowels, leaving a terrible stink behind. Apt enough, but messy.

A car crash at high speed, à la *Death of a Salesman*? Too melo-dramatic, and there's always a chance of hurting someone else . . . in another vehicle, or maybe a pedestrian.

Disappear? Leave a farewell note? To whom? Jack Trevanian? It would be excessive, fucking romantic.

And after all, where would I disappear to? And what would I do when I got there?

I could drown myself. Swim out to sea like Norman Maine and never come back. Clichéd, and anyway I'm too good a swimmer. It would take me forever to sink. But then again, perhaps I might reach the Happy Isles, or anyway Hawaii . . .

Defenestration? I'm acrophobic. It would scare me to death.

Carbon monoxide in the garage with the Range Rover's motor idling? Not foolproof enough, I could end up half dead with brain damage. Picture it: an old fart in diapers, grinning mind-lessly, drooling, gurgling nonsense. Forget it.

I could update the Romans, open my veins in the hot tub. It's said to be painless, the heat of the water assuaging the sting. Do it at night, under a full moon, you'll have something to dis-tract the eye from the carmine cloud you're drowning in. They'd find me in the morning, a pale, leached-out hunk of flotsam adrift in a stale Red Sea . . .

But to hang on knowing that it's pointless, nothing afterward, going through the indignities of a long, slow, mindless, drug-dulled and terribly expensive death . . . it doesn't make much sense, except that it's "proper."

Think about it.

If it comes to suicide, I'd want some comfort along the way.

From whom? Kate's gone . . .

So when was the last time you thought about heaven, Doc? You haven't believed in it since you were ten. Now you're pushing seventy. Sixty-eight anyway. It's a nice idea all right if you can get in the right frame of mind.

I'm sure as hell getting there.

Have another schnapps.

Prosit Neujahr!

Who would you want to be there?

What would it be like?

Have another Xanax.

I'd certainly want my dogs, a dalmatian like Popsy, that coach dog my mother loved so much—yes, a coach dog, the kind that used to run along behind the fire engines when I was a kid, every firehouse had one; they were bred to run behind the coaches of the aristocracy, my mother's notion of high tone. Then Gayelord, who hunted well for me all through med school and finally died of leukemia when I was away in the Navy. Then Spunky, the fox terrier Kate and I adopted that time when the Douche Boat was in Mare Island Naval Shipyard near Vallejo and the pooch hung around for handouts, someone must have abandoned him there, and we kept him for a while even after the Navy, even though Kate was allergic to dog dan-der, and then gave him to a shipmate who said he had an uncle with a big chicken farm in Utah; then our black Lab, Peter, who

got chomped by that white-tip off Clarion on the Big Tuna
Cruise; and then freaky Max (the German shorthair, a great
gundog); and the big yellow Lab Simba, who took it as his droit
du seigneur to scarf the first quail of the season but fetched perfectly on every bird that followed; and finally his successor,
black Luke, the best gundog of them all, the best dog I ever had,
another cancer victim, and why the fuck am I crying now?

Then Kate died.

Have another schnapps. *Prosit Neujahr!*

Have a Nembutal . . . no, take two!

I'd want Kate there in heaven of course, lean feisty smart hawk-
ish—my blonde kestrel, no, my merlin—but not in her occasional combative mode.

Prosit Neujahr!

Another Percodan? Don't mind if I do . . .

And the kids?

Sure, why not?

But only if they're little still.

Pros't . . .

Maybe my parents if they could be nice to each other for a
change, and my grandparents, at least Frank Taggart and Rosa
Pueringer Seidel. But you don't have to have everyone in your
own particular heaven, that's the guilt-free beauty of it, those
you leave out will have heavens of their own, and maybe some

people can drop in from time to time, like my smartass cousin Maureen, and Captain Harold W. Becker USN, if he'd ever deign to spend time in the heaven of a mere doctor.

Ben would be there for sure. Even if he isn't dead yet, by God I'll have him in my heaven.

Here's to you, Ben. *Glück auf!*

Bird would be there, and Diz, and Coltrane, Max Roach, Lionel Hampton on the vibes, Lady Day diddybopping along with them, all in fluffy white robes and haloes.

And what would heaven look like? What would be the geography of it?

Well, it's *my* heaven, so I can make it anything I want . . . the best places I've ever known. Kenya in the early '70s; Baja ditto; Wisconsin in the '40s and '50s; Alaska now and forever; maybe even California in the '50s when we were first married, smog still a Bob Hope joke, and the earthquakes only spiced things up, but it would have to be a very big house to hold all those people, or a very big neighborhood, and the seasons would always have to be spring and early summer and September and October, and maybe a touch of winter. A kiss of snow . . .

There'd have to be a boat, of course, a ketch like *Orm* but lighter and quicker in stays, and Kate not prone to seasickness, and I'd have a wire snips with me when she got that fishhook through her thigh that I had to cut out, and I wouldn't offend the boys by drinking too much and pushing them too hard to hold a true course and shoot straight and cast with a flyrod, and I wouldn't argue against abortion when Eddie's girlfriend was within earshot not knowing that she'd had one, because Kate had kept that information from me, and I'd never be sullen or "out of touch."

Nor would my skin flake, nor would I ever erupt in blisters when I stayed out in the sun too long, nor would I ever piss more than twice or thrice a day, and never at all at night, and I'd still be six-one by 180, and my eyes would still be 20/10, and I could still clean-and-jerk two hundred pounds from a standstill, and I'd be able to hit every clay off the trap within ten yards, and every grouse that ever flew, and cast a streamer—a 4/0 Lefty's Deceiver—the length of a football field, with pinpoint accuracy.

With only one backcast!

And the wahoo would take it every time . . .

But none of the fish I caught would ever go belly up after the release.

Hell, I could fish and hunt and eat anything and everything any time I wanted in my heaven, drink and never get drunk, and win the Nobel Prize for medicine every Thursday.

This is pure shit: the pitiful idea of heaven. It's way too soppy-wish-fulfilling-sentimental. Pitiable is the word. My life was better than this implies.

Prosit Neujahr!

At sunup the next day I woke on the deck at Palos Verdes. It wasn't heaven. It was cold as an Inuit's igloo. The Pacific boomed good morning. Spray leaped halfway up the cliff, waves receded, regrouped, charged again. The whole house shuddered. The rhythms of the sea. I was reeling, still half in the bag. Salt water corrodes. The alto sax lay there on a chaise longue, beaded with dew. I fetched a towel from the locker and wiped it down, pulled the reed, licked it clean. Then I stood there naked with the dawn at my back, salt wind in my face, shivering, and wailed "Koko" the way the Bird blew it back in the '40s, that gutsy guttural line erupting into dazzle, hearing Diz on the trumpet in my mind's ear bopping behind me all around the chords. I needed someone to lay down the beat—Max Roach, maybe, Art Blakey? No, too showy, I wanted Ben there, tapping a smooth round riverbank rock like he did on the Firesteel, ticking out insect riffs on an empty tin can, rattling a hollow log beside the campfire . . .

Where was he when I needed him?

I laid down the sax. The empty fifth of brandy and a half full bottle of Xanax stood on the table beside the chaise. I tossed them over the cliff. And went in for some clothes and my Rolodex.

Ben called me now and then, every four or five years was his schedule, usually late at night Wisconsin time, sundown in California, slurred and mawkish—he'd taken up booze. Big time. When was the last time he phoned? I flipped through the Rolo. I usually scribble in the dates. There it was—two years ago. Before the shit hit the fan for me, but he'd already had a face full.

Ben's retired now too, from what sounds like a rollercoaster ride of a career as a building contractor. More downs than ups. Then his wife left him. That was what he called about last time we spoke. Lorraine was gone, after forty-six years of marriage. They'd been sweet on each other since high school. Lorraine, he often said, had an overdeveloped civic conscience. She was the kind of woman who, if she happened to run a red light and wasn't ticketed on the spot, would turn herself in to the nearest police station an hour later, checkbook and driver's license in hand, demanding instant justice.

"Lorraine's a *goodnik,*" he'd say. "Unlike me, the ultimate no-goodnik."

Why did she leave him? Men of our generation don't ask questions like that. If a friend doesn't volunteer how he got a broken arm or leg, you don't ask him how it happened. Nor do you ask a friend about his sex life, or what he paid for a new car, or gun, or pair of socks, or even what he's dying of. If he wants to tell you, he will. It's a simple question of honor between men.

Lorraine's living near their kids on the East Coast now Ben told me, somewhere below Philadelphia, and none of them will speak with Ben when he calls. He's all alone in a big, empty house of his own construction in a priggish, sleepy little hick town, Bonduel, with only his dog Jake, an aging yellow Lab, for company.

The Korean war scarred him for life, I think: that wicked winter fight during the Chosin Reservoir campaign, and later along the thirty-eighth parallel the "Diesels" and "Mercuries"— assault raids on the Chinese lines and ambushes in No Man's Land—it all must have left him with suppurating wounds, a lifetime of bitter flashbacks. The fact that we didn't win that war was worse. It turned him sour, surly, hair-triggered. He'd never admit it though. Ben's no whiner. But his life has been wasted. Now with his wife gone he drinks too much and eye-balls the gun cabinet—*mon semblable, mon frère!* All that keeps his finger from the trigger, he tells me, is the continuing love and presence of his dog. He figures that after Jake dies is time enough. All that keeps my trigger finger still--so to speak--is the memory of the Firesteel.

I picked up the cell phone, punched in his number, and flicked it to speaker mode.

Brrrring . . . Brrrring . . . Brrr . . .

I set the sax to my mouth.

"Yeah?" His voice was thick, blurred, drowning in phlegm, though it's already midmorning in Bonduel.

I wailed a line from "Salt Peanuts" . . .

A long pause, then:

"Well, you old son of a bitch! Long time, no hear. How the hell are you, Hairball?" He was suddenly awake.

"I have only one word for you, pal. Firesteel."

Another silence, then:

"You know, I think about it too, more and more these days."

"How is the old river?"

"I haven't been up there in—Christ, must be ten or twelve years. And then only to fish the estuary. You know, that lower run by the Haystack? But it was still good, Harry. Damned good. Since they put those Pacific salmon in the Great Lakes, there's plenty of action year round. Kings, silvers, steelhead, you name it."

"What about the upper river where we took those big brookies?"

"I don't know firsthand, but it shouldn't be too fucked up yet. Most of the city folks want lake property, and the state's kept the rivers up north pretty clean since the loggers cleared out."

"How about the bird hunting?"

"Still good. Woodcock are falling off, thin on the ground these past few years, but that's true everywhere. Habitat loss, I figure. Everything growing up to climax again. But this should be a peak year for ruffs, top of the cycle. And there's Huns now up on the Firesteel. Not to mention ducks and geese."

We were quiet for a moment. Then I said, "Kate's dead."

A long beat . . .

"Oh, shit, Harry. I . . . What can I say?"

"Look, let's do that trip again. What do you think? I could fly into Green Bay tomorrow, we'll buy ourselves a new canoe, Kevlar, light and strong, my treat. We'll outfit the bastard, and hit the Firesteel all over again."

"What did she die of?"

"Death," I said. "A stroke. It was quick, thank God for that."

"If it had to happen . . ."

"It happens."

I heard him cough, clear his throat.

"The Firesteel," he said. "One more time . . . What did that Greek guy say? 'You can't step into the same river twice'?"

"Fuck him, Ben. He's long dead. Don't mean nothin'. Drive on."

Ben laughed. "Why not?" he said. "It was a great trip, 'the worst trip I've ever been on,' I guess. We'll name the canoe *Sloop John B*. We were young then, guy—Great Lakes Beach Boys, strong and ignorant, not a clue to what was lying just down the pike. And maybe we'll finally catch that muskie."

"Fuckin' A."

The rest of the conversation was details. I'd bring my sixteen-bore Purdey and a trout rod or two. Ben had a tent, sleeping bags, and plenty of camp gear. We'd worry about food later, after I got there.

"You bringing that saxophone of yours?" he asked. "Your ax, as you always called it?"

"Couldn't die without it," I said.

He laughed. Then he started coughing, another gobbet of gunk . . .

"Frog in my throat," he said at last. "Too many cigars, I guess." Then, "Hey, Hairball! I'll carve me up some drumsticks, special for this jaunt! Shagbark hickory, there's a tree in the backyard I've had my eye on. Jake's been pissing on it for eleven years now so the wood'll be cured to a fare-thee-well."

Jake would come along, of course. A great last hunt for a great gundog, and perhaps a great trip for both of us as well. Maybe it could be a new beginning. Or a fitting finale.

3

PREPARATIONS FOR
GETTING UNDER WAY

Y ou move when the mood is upon you. That night I
caught a red-eye out of LAX for O'Hare, then galloped
the length of the airport to connect with a puddle-
jumper that got me into Green Bay at midmorning. The flight
north was high and smooth. Lake Michigan sprawled slate blue,
flecked with whitecaps beneath us. Off the port wing the
Wisconsin countryside was going gold and red to the touch of
approaching autumn. Milwaukee came and went, the story of its
life. Lakes winked in the morning sun, and slow brown rivers
seamed the flats. Then, ahead to the northwest, I saw Lambeau
Field. I could swear I smelled bratwurst and sauerkraut as we
banked, swept the fields, and landed. Austin Straubel
International Airport—its name is longer than its runways.

Ben was waiting at the arrivals gate, tall and gaunt, paler
than I'd ever seen him in his youth. The last time I'd laid eyes
on him was in the early '70s, before gas prices skyrocketed from
35 cents a gallon to their present stratospheric altitudes. He and
Lorraine had driven out to California and we'd spent a week in
my ketch, cruising the Santa Barbara Channel, fishing albacore
and tuna, and diving for abalone in the kelp beds off Catalina
Island. He was tanned, fit, and happy then. Now he looked like
he'd spent the past quarter century hiding under a cesspool lid.
But he grinned his old, wry grin when he saw me, and his grip
was still strong. He wore the old timer's uniform of the day
that's become de rigueur in contemporary society—Air Jordans,
sag-rumped black sweats, and a Packers ball cap. His white hair
spilled over his ears—no, make that his ear. The left one was
gone, sheared off by a mortar frag up near a town called Koto-
ri. That was during the Chosin campaign. The scar tissue
gleamed like a snail track.

"Baggage claim will take half an hour at least," he told me. "It may be a small airport, but its motto is 'Slow Is Beautiful.' Let's grab a Milwaukee orange juice while we're waiting," and he steered me to the cocktail lounge. The barkeep knew him, plunked down a boilermaker and his helper before we'd even got seated. Dickel and draft—Leinenkugel's. The barkeep, whose nametag proclaimed him "Red," raised an eyebrow at me. He wasn't a man to waste words, unlike the rest of the Badger State's population. "I'll have the same," I told him. Ben took a sip of his beer and poured the bourbon into the glass. I tossed my shot back neat, gagged, then drank half the beer in two swallows. "At this rate," I said when my gorge had settled, "we'll be lucky to find Lake Superior, much less the river."

"Don't tell me you've become one of those Californicated pussies," Ben said. "All mesclun and balsamic vinegar, designer fizzy water? You haven't wussed out on me, have you, Hairball?"

He took off his cap and I saw that he was bald as the proverbial billiard ball, apart from the shoulder-length white fringe that masked his missing ear.

"Jesus, Ben, I just flashed on our old pal Curly. He wore the same kind of hairdo you've got. You've got to give me your stylist's name."

Ben downed his beer and tapped the empty glass on the bar top—ordering up another. "Just the Dickel this time, Red," he said.

How many had he downed before I got here?

I'd packed light this time, the shotgun and rod cases, the horn, and my old Navy seabag full of outer- and innerwear. Thinking ahead, I'd brought along a cache of drug samples to treat any-thing that might ail me during the course of the trip, with heavy emphasis on some new pills called Micturatrol to calm my ner-vous bladder. Prolonged use of them might fuck up my plumb-ing, but I was damned if I'd embarrass myself in front of my boyhood chum. Picture us halfway down a run of whitewater with me yelping, "Hey Ben, pull over to the bank—I gotta shake hands with the mayor!"

Anyway, long-term effects were not a concern of mine.

Ben slung the seabag over his shoulder and I carried the rest of my gear. We walked out to his truck, a rust-scabbed black Ford F-250, vintage '92, I'd guess. The short-bed model. We stowed the gear under a tarp and headed northwest.

Ben's place, a split-level ranch built of Lannon stone, stood on the crest of a low hill just north of Bonduel (pop. 1,210). To the north lay the Menominee Indian reservation. The driveway was lined with Norwegian pines, the lawn needed mowing. Old Jake ambled out from the backyard to greet us, a big yellow Lab who'd gone bonewhite around the muzzle. He sniffed me up and down, then caught a whiff of the gun case. Now he looked up at me and grinned, a sparkle in his rheumy brown eyes. His thick otterine tail thumped hello. Hunters always sniff one another out.

"Woof," he said. You'll do.

Ben opened the garage door. Inside sat a boat trailer with a canoe on it, already loaded. "A Mad River, from Vermont," he said. "Kevlar, just like the doctor ordered. Sixteen foot of it. I thought of getting a Mackenzie boat, but they didn't have any in cedar."

"I told you I wanted to buy the canoe."

"What, you're going to paddle it back to California? I'm not dead broke yet, Hairball."

I ankled over to the canoe and eyeballed the supplies. Much of the space was taken up by a nylon sack full of water-fowl decoys, but the rest was as I remembered it: sleeping bags; cook pots and fry pans; a box of sulphur-tipped kitchen matches; a blue-and-white-speckled stoneware coffee pot full of aluminum knives, forks, and spoons; two pairs of swim fins and face masks; a spear gun; a roll of mosquito netting; and a leather-sheathed cruising ax. I hoped it wouldn't need sharpening this time. Somewhere he'd even scrounged up a few orange crates and filled them with the foods of yester-year—Hormel chili, Chef Boyardee spaghetti and meatballs, Quaker Oats, Dinty Moore beef stew, and a mason jar full of brown sugar. Elsewhere in the load I spotted tins of Carnation milk, Aunt Jemima's pancake mix, a tub of crunchy Skippy's, and three loaves of Wonder Bread. Up in the bow, where I usually paddled, sat a big gift-wrapped box, tied with a broad pink silk ribbon.

"Open it," Ben said, deadpan.

"What the fuck?"

Brisling sardines, bread-and-butter pickles, Ritz crackers, strawberry jam, mayonnaise, anchovies . . . and a new addition, a magnum jar of pickled herring in sour cream.

"Oh, darling," I said. "You remembered!"

We went inside for a look-see. The living room was hung with the heads of deer Ben had shot over the years, the best of them a twelve-pointer with brow tines as long as an elk's. Above the limestone fireplace hung a steelhead the length of my forearm. "From the Firesteel," Ben said. "That trip I told you about, back in '85. I took her on a duplicate of our Cannibal-Killer, best I could remember it. Maybe a bit more orange in the tie."

This is getting creepy, I thought. The poor old bastard lives in the past. What a memory, though. I couldn't have retied that fly on a bet. But what the hell, how many times have I redreamed the Firesteel? Every night of my life, or so it seems of late.

"Hey, Benjamin, I almost forgot. I brought you something from the Quaking Smog." In my carry-on I had a cedar box of Rey del Mundo Coronas, and now I presented it to him. "You said you were into cigars these days, didn't you?"

"Christ, Harry, these are Cubanos." He plucked a fatboy from the carton, sniffed it, and grinned. "Where the hell do you get them?"

"Same place I get my Cuervo Especial." Of which I presented him a bottle. "My 'Mexican connection.' The barkeep at Hussong's Cantina, down Ensenada way. No big deal in the Land of the Big Enchilada. They trade with the Beard all the time. Getting these smokes back into the States is the problem. But until recently I had a boat."

And a wife, I thought.

He must have read her in my face. He clipped the corona and lit up. The smoke wafted blue and fragrant across the room. Then he cracked the Cuervo. He looked over at me, no pity in his eyes, just the naked truth.

"This is my life since Lorraine left me. Booze and brown weeds." He raised the bottle.

He smiled all the sadness in the world.

"Skoal, partner."

By high noon, with Jake wagging between us, we were pouring north—toward the Firesteel and our fate.

Despite my globe-trotting and seeming sophistication, I retained a fondness for Wisconsin. There's always something left for the place you grew up in. To be sure it was Hicksville, a tiny, stale little swatch of flyover country, smelling of cheeseheads and crackers. The big timber, its only redeeming feature, had been cut off long ago. Oh sure, the good burghers still make the best beer in America and they have an interesting football team, the Green Bay Packers, but their minds are as stumpy as their long-gone trees. Love and religion, family chicken dinners, bowling alleys, bratwurst and pretzels. Beer and brandy and well-coached bowels. Most of the folks Ben and I were raised among were of German origin, still others from the eastern reaches of the old Austro-Hungarian empire.

When I was growing up there were still some very old people—smelly geezers who'd lost at least partial control of both sphincter and bladder (my future in six or eight months, if I should live so long), gimpy hausfraus with only two or three gold teeth remaining in their dry, pinkgummed mouths—who crossed themselves or indeed shed salty tears at the mention of Franz Ferdinand's assassination in Sarajevo back in 1914. The old women would say, "How schweet she vass, his vife *die Erzherzogin*, riding dere in da carritch mit him. Vy did that madman haff to shoot her?"

After stopping in town to pick up my nonresident licenses, we headed north, following the same route that I'd driven in college and med school—ah, that sleek old Studebaker ragtop of mine, a '48 she was, battleship gray, with a spaceship's nosecone worthy of reentry, but slow as redemption when it came to pickup—avoiding the new interstates that would have saved us hours of driving time. Ben's V-8 Ford ate up the road.

From Bonduel we angled northwest on State Route 45 through dairy country to Shawano, then northwest through the Menominee Indian reservation. In the old days it was all tarpaper shacks, the big, bleak, yellow brick orphanage, and that comfortless church at Keshena; roadside stands that sold flimsy toy birchbark canoes and headdresses of dyed turkey feathers and moccasins that fell apart in the first rain; a few fat young Indians in dirty Levis and gray shirts sitting and staring into the gloomy pine woods—the Romance of the Red Man. Now the Rez was prospering. Tidy new housing units sprouted in the clearings, clustered around a neat new tribal headquarters and clinic. The Menominees owned 240,000 acres of climax white pine and hardwood forest, and it all looked healthy as ever. Tribal logging trucks hogged the winding, two-lane road.

"The red man's *Dauerwald*," Ben said.

"Doh?"

"Yeah, I read a piece about it in the *Journal* awhile back. In Germany they're trying to maintain 'Perpetual Forests' with the same mix of trees— conifers and oaks for the most part—that grew in the days of Arminius. You remember old Herman the German, don't you? He's the guy who wiped out those Roman legions in the Teutoburg Forest. Well, the Menominees had the idea first. They've kept their woods intact since 1854, the way it was when the white man first showed up in these parts. Selective cutting's the key. The Indians take only twenty million board feet a year. With the price of lumber these days, it's enough to keep the tribe in clover."

We crossed the Wolf River, fast and cold as it slashed through the dark woods. Ben and I had fished it now and then in our old canoe, the one that ended up on the bottom of Gitche Gumee.

"How's the Wolf fishing these days?"

"Still plenty of big fat brookies, up near the headwaters mainly. You've got to hire an Indian guide, and I figure they keep the best water for themselves."

Out of the reservation we entered the cutover country around Langlade and Lily and Pickerel—country that only a century earlier had stood skyhigh in white pine, the birthplace of the Paul Bunyan myth, now laid flat and stumpy, regrown in weak popple and birch, jackpine and alder, like a woman with lovely hair who has lain with the enemy and then had her head shaved. A sandy country, the glacier had taken it down to bedrock during its slow grinding retreat ten thousand years ago. And then we emerged—abrupt, marvelous, rolling down the windows—into what I really considered up north: the road shooting straight and dusty through dense stands of spruce and tamarack, with muskegs sprawling right and left, stippled with crooked, wind-silvered snags on some of which perched eagles and ospreys, erect and wild-eyed, and always more frequently the crooked lakes and flowages glinting hard blue and brown in the sunlight that—Up North—still seemed to me cleaner and harsher than anywhere else on the planet, a sharp wind out of the northwest kicking up whitecaps on the open reaches, and old wooden rowboats painted dark green tied up to cockeyed piers, with cabins of peeled spruce logs squatting, smoking, back in the woods, and always a lone man in a red-and-black-checked lumberjack shirt fishing from the shore—casting and reeling, casting and reeling, again and again and again . . .

We blew through dumpy, grungy little burgs where the boys and girls, largely of Baltic blood, all looked pale and misshapen, with bulging foreheads and washed-out eyes, as if they'd sprouted from potato bins, and the sour stink of pulp mills invaded the car. In most of the towns Golden Arches tainted the atmosphere with the reek of hot, rancid fat, K-Marts and WalMarts sprawled in jampacked parking lots, and car dealerships on the outskirts now waved their red, white, and blue plastic flags over acres of asphalt where once, in our youth, Ben and I had shot ducks—mallards and pintails, bluebills and redheads. Now Neons and Prizms floated there, on heaving seas of blacktop.

At Rhinelander we turned west . . .

"Too many fucking people," Ben said.

"No, too many people fucking. Do you realize that when we were born there weren't even two billion human beings on earth? Now it's up to six billion, and that's not the end of it."

He grunted and lit up another stogey.

"It all needs a good stiff culling," I said. "When any animal population gets too big for its habitat, Nature arranges a die-off to bring it back in balance. She's trying to do it right now. Look at AIDS. Look at Ebola, and Hanta virus, and Legionnaires' disease. Look at the antibiotic-resistant strains of TB that we're seeing these days."

"I take it you're not a people person, Doc."

"Don't get me going."

"The world's gone to hell in a handcart, you figger?"

He glanced across at me and grinned. That gleam in his eye . . . I knew it of yore. The devil's advocate was emerging— Ben loved the role, he always had.

"But look how many things are better these days," he said. "In the old days, you bought a cuppa coffee, you could read the date of dime on the bottom of it, if you were dumb enough to drop one in. Now there's Starbucks everywhere. Even the supermarkets carry Costa Rican and Kenyan beans. And wine? Used to be nothing but Gallo and Manischewitz on the shelves. Now you got chardonnays and pinot grigios, from California to upstate New York, merlots and medocs. Beaujolais nouveaux up the gigi. Beer ditto. Microbreweries everywhere, not just that thin piss we got from the big boys, Miller and Pabst, Schlitz and Budweiser. And what about telephones? Answering machines, call waiting, caller ID, cordless phones you can take into the john with you if you've got a sudden urge. Fax machines, fucking e-mail . . . "

I snorted. "All that means is people can hassle you easier. Waste your time with bullshit. Telephonic junk mail's not even the worst of it. The internet makes it sheer hell. This is a consumer society, pal. And it's consuming us big time, guts and balls and brains, every fucking minute of the livelong day."

"Hold it right there." Ben reached above the sun visor and pulled down a CD, popped it in the deck.

The Bird blazed forth in all his long-dead glory, a remastered phoenix rising from needletracked ashes.

Ben grinned at me in triumph. "Scrapple from the Apple" he said. "Can you dig it, daddy-o?"

We listened. Then I said, "Pull over, Benjamin. I need my horn. Not only can I dig it, man, I'll gig it—like you never heard before."

It was an hour before sundown when we hit the Firesteel. We'd stopped only once along the way, for burgers and beers at the Little Bohemia lodge on Route 51 just south of Manitowish. Little Bohemia was the place where Dillinger and his boys had a big shootout with the G-men back in '34—shit, Ben and I were babies then and now it was ancient history. One fed was killed in the fracas, but Dillinger got away clean. The bullet holes from the fight were still there. Big ones, from Tommy guns. They had gear that belonged to the outlaws on display behind glass cases. Homer Van Meter, Baby Face Nelson, Tommy Carroll—famous crooks like that, but nothing that belonged to our old pals Doc and Curly.

The elderly frycook who served us told us that back in 1937, when Dillinger was still a big name, 51,687 tourists had stopped at the lodge to see the place. "Nobody knows from the Dillinger Gang nowadays," the old man mourned. Just old farts like us, was the implication.

"They don't know what they're missing," I reassured him.

Ben had arranged for a carpenter friend of his from Ashland to shuttle the truck to the mouth of the river. He left the keys under the left front fender and we lugged our gear down to the riverbank. There wasn't as much this time. Maybe we do get smarter with age. Or is it just weaker but wiser. No—the slimmed-down load was probably because I hadn't done the shoping for this trip. We dragged down the canoe, much lighter than our late lamented Old Town hog.

The country hadn't changed much that I could see. The old black trestle spanning the headwaters of the Firesteel was still standing, though it wore a new coat of lumpy, aluminum-silver paint. The woods had grown up, of course, then been cut again, and regrew a few times more in the half century since we'd last stood on this spot. The swamp was still there though. Amazing in this age of instant malls. "They paved paradise," as Joni Mitchell sang, "and put up a parking lot."

I listened for rising trout but heard nothing. Too many years of gunfire had dulled my ears. They must have been feeding, though. I could see clouds of mayfly spinners in the air—blue-winged olives most likely.

Jake charged down to the river, plunged in for a drink and a swim, came out, shook himself dry between us, then put his nose in the air and lit up. "He's birdy," Ben said, watching. "Go get 'em, boy."

Jake pussyfooted into the bankside alders. His tail snapped skyward, his head thrust forward, and he flushed two woodcock just yards from our put-in point. Then he sat and watched them go. A good omen for our trip.

"We've got about an hour of light left," Ben said. "What say we push on down through the swamp, pick up a trout or three for supper, then pitch camp in our old place."

"The Place of the Bear?"

"He's long gone," Ben said.

"If you can guarantee it, I'm game."

We strung up the rods and pushed off.

Maybe we took it too fast, maybe we didn't match the hatch, but we raised not a single fish in the whole spring swamp section. We didn't even see a rise or hear the splash of a feeding trout. But the spring pools were as thick as before with elodea, the mayflies and caddis just as abundant. Maybe the fish were sated on nymphs and emergers. Or perhaps an otter had passed through, putting them down for the moment. It was odd, though, to say the least. And ominous. The marl itself seemed to have washed out of the riverbed, leaving crevices of limestone visible through the water, crenellated ghost castles sprouting from the bony bottom.

As we paddled out of the swamp, we saw the lights in the distance. It looked like a housing development. Could the seepage from its septic tanks have altered the water? But the bugs were thriving and we did see a few dace and shiners.

Well, time enough to worry about it tomorrow. Right now we had to make camp.

4

NIGHT OF THE BULL NEWT

B ut of course we couldn't leave well enough alone. "Maybe they're feeding at night," Ben said, puffing another corona. "Like the cannibal brown on our first trip." Jake snoozed at his feet, sedated by a bellyful of Iams "Active Maturity," a crunchy, yummy, low-fat kibble for older dogs.

Euphemism is our middle name these days, even when it comes to dogfood.

We were lounging around the campfire sipping Cuervo after a hasty supper of chili con carne and Minute Rice. The tent was pitched—one of those nylon pop-tops with an external frame that opens like an umbrella: camping was sure easier nowaways, I'll give Ben that. The gear was all stowed, and the night was growing cozier by the minute. Our old campsite hadn't changed much, still plenty of deadfall firewood lying all over the place. But it wasn't scorched pine slashings this time, just spruce and windtoppled birch.

"She might have left plenty of offspring at that," I said. "Great-great-great-grandchildren, all with that cannibal gene. Big fish little fish. Maybe one of them ate up all the others and there's only one monster brown in the swamp. That would account for the dearth of activity."

"I brought along a couple of wet suits and an underwater spotlight," he said. "What say we swim up there and have a look-see."

I thought about it. Two old codgers diving alone at night in a dismal swamp, one of them dying and the other a lush who chain-smokes cigars. "Sounds scary," I said. "But we've got to get to the bottom of this mystery, and the only place to start is on the bottom. Let's do it."

We left Jake to guard the camp against intruders—Ben said he was hard on prowlers, tough enough to scare off even a bear— and snorkeled upstream toward the swamp, snug in our wet suits. Ben led the way with the spotlight to illuminate our route. Everything that lives in the water comes out at night. Crayfish scuttled across the bottom, blackshelled mussels lipped the current, big pink and golden carp with scales the size of silver dollars shouldered their way through the midwater. We even saw a few trout, browns mostly, about eight or ten inches long allowing for the face mask's magnification, and a couple of dark, fair-sized brook trout. They seemed stunned by the spotlight, swimming up to our masks and goggling at us. One of them hung there in the water, watching me, mesmerized. I reached out slowly and ran my fingertips down its flank. It woke up and flashed away in an ivoryblack blur.

When we got to the rapids just below the swamp, we had to crawl up them on our bellies. The water was too shallow to swim. It deepened as we entered the lower pool. Ben dropped back beside me and panned the spotlight beam across the bottom. It revealed nothing but limestone, eerie misshapen domes and minarets, fallen slabs of soft white rock like the ruins of some alien mausoleum.

Ben popped his head above water and pulled the snorkel's mouthpiece free. "I want to dive down there and look under those slabs. Why don't you stay up here and hold the spotlight, follow me along wherever I go. If anything flushes out from under the rocks, it'll probably kick up too much marl for me to see it. Watch where it goes."

"You got it."

He sucked a few deep breaths, charging his lungs with oxygen, then folded at the waist and dove, the big fins pushing him down fast. He was still damned good in the water. When he reached the bottom, he began pulling himself along, hand over hand, along the bed of slabs. He stopped every now and then to look under one, shoving a gloved hand in there, groping around. He stayed down nearly two minutes. So his lungs weren't shot yet.

I swam over when he popped to the surface.

"Nothing," he said. "It's damned weird. You'd think I'd have spooked out at least a few bottom feeders, carp or suckers or something."

"This whole place seems dead."

"Yeah, I saw a lot of fish skeletons down there in the marl. It's a boneyard."

"Let's go up to the next channel. That's where we hooked the cannibal."

We finned across the big pool and entered the channel. This time I went ahead, diving every ten feet or so in the light-beam and cruising along the rootbeds of the alders. The channel was about ten feet deep in here. I flushed a few small fish— minnows of some sort, or maybe they were fingerling trout— but nothing of predatory size.

We came to the end of the gut. The next pool opened out ahead of us. More slabs and falling castles. I swam over to the alders and broke off a branch to use as a probe.

"Good thinking," Ben said. "Reach in under there as far as you can. Poke the bastard out where we can see him. We can always come back tomorrow and nail him fair and square."

"Are there any alligators this far north?" I said. "Any freshwater sharks?"

"If there are, they'll be new to science. Think of it—you'll get in the history books. And I'll be sure to gather up your bones for a proper Christian burial." He grinned at me, the old Ben's grin again. "Go in peace, my son, and God bless you."

It was twenty feet at least down to the bottom and I had plenty of time to think along the way. I'd been kidding about gators and sharks, but there was something scary about this whole affair. The Firesteel below the swamp seemed to be in good shape, we'd spotted enough fish in our short swim upstream to confirm that. But here was this huge font of artesian water, rich in nutrients, grown junglelike with plant life, buzzing with insects, and yet no fish in it to speak of. The water was healthy, no doubt about that. So it had to be predation of some sort that had depleted the fish life. We'd seen an osprey nest on our way down through the swamp in the canoe, but no osprey—or even a squadron of them—could have emptied this fish bowl so thoroughly.

What could have wrought this piscine desolation?

Was it the . . .

I almost giggled . . .

The Creature from the Black Lagoon?

It was.

Here's how it happened:

As I probed the third crevice, the rotten alder stick broke off short in my hand. I still had air enough in my lungs to reach in for what remained of it. But when I extended my arm I felt something grab my hand. Something soft but strong and quick. Alive . . .

It clamped down hard on my wrist. I yanked my hand back, shredding the neoprene diving glove in the process, but the nightmare held on.

I flashed: *Moray!* I'd encountered them diving in the Caribbean, big ugly mottled graygreen eels with sharp-fanged blocky jaws like bulldogs. They lurked in caves in the coral, snapping up fish that swam by. If a diver reached into one of these crevices, feeling around for rock lobsters, maybe, the moray would grab him, its tail wrapped tight around a projection deep in the cave, and hold him down there till he drowned. But there couldn't be morays this far north. They were tropical creatures, sea-dwelling animals that would die in fresh water.

This thing—whatever it was—had me now. Its mouth felt slippery and cold, even through the ripped glove, with craggy nubbed teeth . . . like a mouthful of warts. It wouldn't let go. My air was going fast. I place my finned feet against the limestone slab and heaved.

As the creature emerged into the beam of the distant spotlight, I saw it clear . . . a wide lipless mouth, downturned at the corners like Edward G. Robinson's in the movies.

Mother of Mercy! Little Caesar! *Rico lives!*

I screamed through my snorkel.

Screamed like a girl.

Then the creature let loose and disappeared into the murk. I boiled my way to the surface.

"Holy shit!" Ben said. "What the fuck was *that?*" His face was whiter than bone.

"Don't know," I said, gasping, "but it wanted to eat me. It had no eyes, just a broad flat head covered all over with lumps. Let's get out of here—pronto!"

We swam, faster than we ever had on the Heldendorf swim team, looking back over our shoulders at every other stroke. We skidded down the rapids on our bellies, caroming off boulders, displacing sheets of gravel, and then we were clear. We regrouped in the deeper water at the bottom of the rapids, both of us puffing hard.

"I couldn't see it very well," Ben said, treading water and raising his mask to his forehead. "There were swirls of marl all around you, but that thing—it looked like it had legs."

"Yeah, short, stubby ones," I said. "With toes on them but no claws. He was covered with warts. When I hauled him out, he was all kind of brown and wrinkled and slimy, like an unhealthy turd—but a turd as long as a man."

"Are you hurt?" he asked. "Let's see your wrist."

"I thought you'd never ask."

I peeled off what was left of the glove and held out my hand. Ben played the spotlight across it, up and down.

"Bruises but no blood," he said. "No toothmarks even, but it's sure as hell swollen."

"The glove must have protected me," I said. "The bastard sure *gummed* me hard, like an old man working a chicken bone. And he had a helluva pair of jaws on him, a grip like a bear trap."

Ben shuddered. "Let's haul ass back to camp and stoke up that fire. I could use a slug or two of Cuervo, and you could too I reckon."

Jake had stood a taut watch. No ursine raiders this time. He growled once, low in his throat, as we emerged from the river but quickly recognized us. He came over to check me out with his lie-detector nose, just to be sure, but when he whiffed the slime on my wet suit, he wrinkled a lip and the ruff rose down his back.

"Easy, boy. I swear it's really me."

He kept a wary eye on me for the next few minutes anyway.

Ben threw more wood on the coals. We stripped out of our wet diving gear, got into our sweats, then poured ourselves a slug of Cuervo. I was still shaking. Delayed shock, I guess. Even the flames felt cold. You never know how sweet life is until the moment it starts slipping away from you. I know it's a cliché to say that, but the truism never felt truer.

"It couldn't have been a gator or a croc," Ben said. "Not in water as cold as this. But it had legs so it wasn't a fish of some sort." He clipped a King of the World, moistened it, annealed the wrapper for a moment over the flames, and lit up with a flaming stick. "Some kind of outsized otter or muskrat, maybe?"

"No fur," I said. "Its skin was covered with tubercles and slime. And it had a laterally compressed tail—narrow side to side but broad up and down, like an eel. Until I saw its legs I was thinking moray or conger eel."

"Did it have nostrils?"

"Not that I could see with all those warts. And it didn't seem to have any eyes either."

"Sounds like the Gollum in Tolkien. I used to read him to my kids when they were little." He frowned and took a pop of Cuervo.

"I'll tell you this, pal, I could have used a Hobbit to help me when that thing glommed on to my hand."

He laughed. "Well, if it wasn't a fish, a reptile, or an aquatic mammal," he said, "then it had to be an amphibian."

"What? The biggest bullfrog in the world? Some kind of giant newt or eft? Wait—I've got it! A mutant, man-eating toad created by radioactivity—A-bomb tests, illegally dumped nuclear waste? We're venturing into Godzilla Country here, my friend."

"Not really," he said. "Did you ever hear of a hellbender?"

"Can't say as I have. Unless you mean the kind I've been known to tie on every now and then."

"I'm serious, Hairball. Guys I knew in the Marine Corps, southerners mostly, used to talk about them. They're giant aquatic salamanders that live under river rocks in the Ozarks. They'll scarf down anything in the water—bugs, bass, crawdads, ducklings, low-flying bats, water snakes, even muskrats and nutria. They never come out in the daylight, but if you're fishing at night—for catfish, say—and you happen to hook one of these bastards, you're up the creek in more ways than one. They grow big, up to a yard long, and fight like hell. The hillbillies were scared shitless of 'em, used to shudder when they'd talk about the dread hellbender. Poisonous, they said. All covered with warts and deadly slime. They'd cut the line, or even throw away the rod when they saw they'd hooked one."

"Sounds like a tall tale to me. Those good old boys were funnin' ya, podner."

"Sergeant Stingley—you remember him, don't you, my DI at Parris Island?—he showed us a snapshot of one once. Carried it in his wallet right along with a picture of his girlfriend. Looked like a Gila monster, only uglier."

"The hellbender or the girlfriend?"

He didn't deign to answer.

"Old Stingley," he said, staring off into the dark for a moment, his expression almost dreamy. "Did I tell you? He showed up in Korea shortly after I got there. We fought through the Chosin thing together. One tough Marine . . ."

"Well, a snapshot doesn't prove a thing," I said. "Pictures can be faked. Remember those old stereopticon slides of Mississippi mudcats as long as a freight car?"

He finished his drink, got up and stretched. "I'm dead beat," he said. "Time to hit the rack."

"I'll stay up awhile," I told him. "Don't know if it's jet lag or too much adrenaline. You mind if I play the horn for a bit? Nothing loud, just some sleepybye music."

"Be my guest," he said, yawning. "Come on, Jake. It's bed-time." They went into the tent and I heard them shifting around awhile. Soon they were both sawing wood.

I took the horn and walked downstream aways. The moon was up now, filling to full, and the light on the water danced silver. Some trout were rising to spent spinners in the quiet water. I thought of getting my flyrod. But I blew some old riffs instead, on blues themes half remembered, quiet as the Firesteel in the moonlight, playing in the upper registers, letting the river set the beat.

"Death come a-creepin' in my room . . ."

5

THE CRYPTOBRANCHS

T he sun was well up when I woke the next morning. Ben was busy over the fire, fried trout and eggs from the smell of it, and the aroma of fresh coffee wafted into the tent. My right hand still felt stiff from the hellbender's love nip, and slightly swollen. I could flex my fingers though, and that meant I could work the flyrod. I crawled out of the tent and went down to the river to perform my ablutions. The water was cold and sweet on my face. I'd slept through the night, no sudden wake-up calls from my bladder. The pills were doing their stuff.

The sound of an outboard motor interrupted our breakfast. It was coming upstream. A blue, high-bowed Boston Whaler appeared around the bend below camp, spotted our tent and fire, and pulled in to shore. A Wisconsin game warden was at the tiller, and a woman sat up in the bow. She smiled and waved.

The warden was a short, blond kid with a cookie duster mustache and a fat blue Magnum on his hip. He didn't smile. He didn't wave. Instead, he marched up to us like something military, frowning, and for a moment I thought he was going to salute. But he only tilted the stiff brim of his trooper hat down over his eyebrows. He had cold, close-set gray eyes.

"Could I see your licenses, gentlemen?"

Just like that. No "Good morning, fellas," no "Nice day, isn't it?"

"Driver's, hunting, or fishing?" Ben asked him.

"Sir?"

"What *kind* of licenses?"

The game cop had to think for a moment. "All three," he said.

"Sure 'nough."

We broke out the paperwork. The kid studied it. His left eye was amblyopic—lazy—and kept slewing in toward the bridge of his nose.

"We were going to offer you and your companion a cup of coffee," I said. "Maybe *she'd* like one."

"I would," the woman said, smiling. She seemed embarrassed by the baby game cop's rudeness. "Cream and one sugar, if you please."

I poured it for her and walked down to the boat. She looked to be in her early forties, with sandy hair cut short and threaded with the first touches of barely visible gray. The boat was full of gear. I saw scuba tanks, coils of insulated wire, electrodes, a generator, and what looked like one of those bangsticks they kill sharks with.

"You'll have to excuse Ned," she said in a quiet voice. "He's new to the job and takes himself a bit seriously. My name's Molly Bellefont, by the way. I'm a fisheries biologist with the Wisconsin Department of Natural Resources." She offered her hand, a strong one.

"Harold Taggart. Pleased to meet you."

"Did you know that this area is technically off limits? 'Posted,' as they say?"

"No," I said. "We didn't see any signs."

"Maybe they haven't put them up yet, but we're conducting a study on this stretch of the river. A biological survey of sorts. Er . . . habitat changes, that kind of thing."

"As in, no brook trout left in the spring holes?"

She looked up at me, surprised, but then spotted the rod cases and nodded. She was a handsome woman, with wide-set blue-green eyes and a trim figure, an outdoors type from her suntan. She wore a khaki work shirt and no-nonsense canvas brush pants, only a hint of makeup, and well-scuffed green rubber Wellingtons.

"Have you figured it out yet?" I asked her.

"No," she said. "The water tested the same as it did five years ago, the last time we checked it for pollution and acidity. The pH is perfect for trout. There's an abundance of lesser biota—ephemerids, trichoptera, and the like."

"You mean mayflies, caddis, and stoneflies," I said.

"Oh, you're a scientist?"

"No, just a doctor. A medical doctor, that is. But I'm also a fly fisherman, and those terms come with the territory."

She smiled.

"I think we may have found the answer to your problem last night," I told her. I showed her my swollen hand.

"What happened?"

I told her.

She didn't seem surprised.

"My partner thinks it's a 'hellbender'," I said, "some sort of giant fish-eating newt from the Ozarks who wandered up here by mistake."

"No," Molly Bellefont said, flipping through a fat reference book she pulled from her backpack. "It's worse than that, I'm afraid. The hellbender's only about two and a half feet long. You say the animal you encountered was twice that size?"

I nodded. "At least."

She sighed.

She showed me a photograph from the book.

It was Rico, all right. I'd know that mug anywhere.

"It's *Andrias*," she said . . .

At that moment Jake growled. I looked over to the tent. The baby game cop was rifling through our gear—"tossing it," as they say on the cop shows—like we were a couple of dopers from the Inner City. I could see Ben was steamed. Jake snarled again, low in his throat. Ned stood up straight and put his hand on the Magnum.

"Don't even think about it," Ben said. He had the cruising ax in his hands, murder in his eyes.

"Then call him off," Ned said. His voice had gone squeaky. "I'm only performing my official duties and if he interferes I have every right to shoot him."

"Mister," Ben said, "if you so much as unsnap that holster, you'll be parting your hair down the middle."

"Enough of this," Molly Bellefont said. She vaulted out of the Whaler and strode up to the campfire. "Warden Maronski, get away from that dog. Behave yourself or I'll make you sit in the boat. You're here only to ensure my safety and he's no threat to me." She had steel in her voice.

Now she turned to Ben, all sweetness and reason. "Could I have another cup of this delicious coffee, please?"

Over the next half hour we learned a lot. Molly was a good teacher, though a bit pedantic. First things first, for instance . . .

Salmanders, she began, belong to the oldest order of terrestrial vertebrates, Caudata, which dates back more than 350 million years. There are 320 different species worldwide, all of them living in the temperate zone of the Northern Hemisphere. Most get no bigger than six inches long, but three species are giants— a "relict" or primitive group called the Cryptobranchidae—to wit, the Chinese giant salamander (*Andrias davidianus*), the Japanese variant (*A. japonicus*), and Ben's old pal the Ozark hellbender (*Cryptobranchus alleganiensis*).

The first giant salamander skeleton known to science was dug up in 1725, somewhere in Germany, and was believed to be a fossilized victim of Noah's flood. But the bones weren't human. They belonged to an extinct cryptobranchid named *Andrias scheuchzeri*. Since then, fossils of other giant salamanders have been found in Europe, Asia, Africa, and North America—every continent but South America and Australia.

Giant salamanders can live a long time, Molly said, up to fifty-five years in the case of one Japanese specimen.

Hellbenders are the most abundant species, but the Chinese giants are more widely distributed. They prefer fast, cold mountain streams in the tributaries of the Yangtze, Yellow, and Pearl rivers, spanning more than a dozen provinces and regions of China. They'll grow up to five or six feet long, sometimes reaching a weight of sixty pounds. They spend their daylight hours hidden under boulders or in rocky crevices along the riverbanks, facing outward for self-defense or to grab off a snack when some unwitting victim paddles past. They come out only at night, to hunt aquatic insects, frogs, crabs, fish, snakes, water rats, and turtles—almost anything that swims. They've even been known to gobble small dogs.

"The zoo in Cincinnati has some cryptobranchs, the Japanese species," Molly said. "They're breeding them using techniques perfected at the Asayama Zoo in Hiroshima. I've watched them feed. It's quite impressive."

According to Molly, the water literally erupts when a salamander dines. Depending on the position of its prey, the animal can open and close one side of its mouth independently—fast as lightning—and bend its jaw by as much as forty degrees. "You've got to look out when you're feeding them—you could lose a couple of fingers," she added.

I massaged my hand. Maybe I'd been lucky . . .

But like everything else that walks, crawls, flies, or swims in Asia, Molly continued, the big cryptobranchs often end up on slabs in the meat markets. "Stir-fried cryptobranch is considered a delicacy," she said, "and their body parts are used in traditional medicines. Both the Chinese and Japanese species are endangered and supposedly protected under international law, like rhinos and elephants, but as we know that usually doesn't mean much."

Unlike most amphibians, giant salamanders lay their eggs in early autumn. A small breeding migration begins in late August when "herds" move toward their nesting sites. A dominant male prepares and occupies each spawning pit, a submerged, sandy chamber at the end of a three-foot-long tunnel dug in marl or mud. "You can imagine the fights that take place between males over access to this scarce resource. Some of them lose toes and even legs in the battles. Some are mangled so severely about their heads and necks that they expire down there in the muddy dark."

"And some die of heartbreak?" Ben said. "The ones that are driven away?"

"That too, I suppose," Molly said doubtfully. Then she brightened. "But their sex lives are spectacular, when they get around to it—an elaborate ritual that takes place when a gravid female visits that carefully built cavern to lay her eggs. She swims in and looks it over for neatness, paying no attention to the waiting male. When she's good and ready, the female starts to turn and spin—it's a kind of mating dance, I guess you could say. The male joins her, almost hypnotized. Then other males ooze back into the nest to join the twirling couple. After a while she arches her back and squirts out a string of eggs—yellow beadlike things suspended in transparent jelly—for the males to, well, fertilize. Just picture it!"

Her eyes were fervid, her cheeks almost flushed.

"A huge spinning ball of amphibians that speeds up until all the eggs are spawned, and then slows as the males cover them with milt. This goes on and on, until she's deposited all of her eggs—four or five hundred of them. Then she swims away and leaves the rest to daddy."

"Wow," Ned said. "She's got it all." His left eye was doing that dance again. I could fix it for him in ten minutes with a scalpel, some fine gut, and a decent magnifier for the close work. Hell, it would be fun.

Molly frowned. "The eggs of several females may be deposited in the same nest," she said, "which the dominant male has to guard until they hatch out and larvae leave the nest in February . . ."

"So that guy who glommed me last night was probably a bull newt," I said, "guarding his kids?"

"Yes, Doctor, more than likely. Though he's not a newt, he's a . . ."

"Could he have eaten all the trout in those spring holes?"

"Not unless he'd been there for many years. Giant salamanders are like snakes; they have a slow metabolism and only
have to eat once every couple of weeks. According to the most
recent DNR survey of the Firesteel, there were thousands of
trout in the swamp only five years ago."

"Then maybe there's more than one."

"That's what I'm here to find out," Molly said.

THEORY & PRACTICE OF RIVERS

How did this trout-scarfing resident of mainland China happen to fetch up on the headwaters of a river in northern Wisconsin? Molly, ever the scientist, wouldn't even risk a speculation. But I sure could imagine some scenarios.

Theory #1: Both the U.S. and Canada trade with China. Perhaps some cryptobranch larvae had been pumped into the ballast tanks of a freighter when it was moored in the upper Yangtze, or any of those other big rivers, then pumped out again when the ship reached the St. Lawrence Seaway. That's the way sea lampreys, zebra mussels, and God knows what else found their way to America's Heartland. Once the larvae had grown to full size, they could easily have migrated up the Seaway into the Great Lakes, the way alewives did back in the '50s and early '60s. (I could still recall the stench of rotting alewives on Milwaukee beaches during their big summer die-offs, a problem that wasn't cleared up until the 1960s, when Howard Tanner of the Michigan Department of Natural Resources began planting Pacific salmon in Lake Michigan: the so-called Coho Miracle.)

But wait a minute. If they came up the St. Lawrence, why haven't these giant fish-eating vacuum cleaners turned up in other, more easterly tributaries? If they had, we'd already be hearing anguished screams from anglers throughout the drainage, from the Allagash in Maine to the Manistee and Boardman in Michigan. Trout Unlimited would be up in arms. Scare banners on the covers of *Fly Rod & Reel* and *Fly Fisherman*. This story would rank with "whirling disease" as a goad to nationwide flyfishing paranoia.

Scratch #1.

Theory #2 (a weak one): Molly Bellefont said the Cincinnati Zoo was raising giant Asian salamanders in captivity. Maybe a few had escaped and . . . But no, Cincy is on the Ohio River. Following that drainage there's no way that bull newts could have reached Lake Superior and thus the Firesteel. They'd more likely have invaded the cold water streams of Appalachia, ancestral home of their smaller cousins the hellbenders. Scratch #2.

Theory #3: Somebody put that creature there. God knows there are enough wackos in today's America to do it. Look at the jokers who plant computer viruses on the internet. And you can go back in history to find them too. Take Eugene Schieffelin, the well-meaning nineteenth-century Shakespeare enthusiast who tried to populate New York's Central Park with all the birds mentioned by the Bard, and unwittingly released *Sturnus vulgaris*, the English starling, on a wide-eyed New World. He should have left well enough alone. Anglers are some of the worst meddlers in this respect (or lack of it). At the end of a day on the water, thoughtless bait fishermen empty their minnow buckets into otherwise ecologically balanced lakes, populating them forevermore with shiners and creek chubs that in the course of a few years overwhelm the resident dace and minnows. Worse still are the northern pike freaks who transport their favorite fish, often in aerated tanks, to pristine trout lakes, hoping thereby to add zip to waters where they're too lazy or inept to catch brook trout or browns on a fly. Result: murder. Northerns spawn in the spring, browns in the fall. Baby northerns grow fast, they have big appetites and sharp teeth, and they chow down on newly hatched alevins like they were so much popcorn. In a year or two or three, no more trout.

But if someone had dumped a herd of Asian bull newts in the upper Firesteel, what would be his or her motive?

It had to be profit. But how? There was no big Asian population in the vicinity to make newt meat a sure-fire winner in the fish markets. What about brook trout, though, big ones like those that used to thrive in the spring pools? It's illegal to sell wild fish in the United States, and farm-bred species—usually rainbows—taste like the Purina trout chow they were raised on. Someone could have wanted to net, electroshock, or rotenone all the wild brookies in the swamp, sell them for quick bucks to swank, high-toned restaurants in Chicago, Milwaukee, or the Twin Cities, and cover their greedy butts by laying the blame to an invasion of giant salamanders.

Too far fetched . . .

"What are you pondering, Hairball? Time's a-wastin and the river calls."

Ben had been striking camp and loading the canoe while I sat beside the river with a last cup of coffee cooling in my hand. Jake was lying beside the canoe, staring into the nearby popples—doggy dreams of vaulting partridge and woodcock, no doubt. Molly and the baby game cop were long gone, headed up to the swamp to hunt out the bull newt and his buddies. They had the tools to do it right—diving gear, a bang-stick, and electroshock equipment if it came to that. Ned had made it clear that we weren't welcome on the expedition. This was state business, no taxpayers allowed.

"You're right," I said. "We've wasted two thirds of the morning. There are fish to catch, and miles to go before we sleep." I was just as glad to be shed of that game cop. If he'd found my pill cache, he'd have run us in for sure, for dopers if nothing else. I had amphetamines in my ditty bag along with some wicked downers, not to mention a bottle of "Navy gin"—codeine and cherry-flavored terpin hydrate—in case either of us got a sore throat along the way, plus a few ampules of morphine for broken bones or gunshot wounds. I'd come prepared for anything.

We shoved off with me in the bow, Ben paddling stern. He'd already rigged the rods—a no. 8 muddler cinched fast to my tippet, a bushy black Woolly Bugger on his. It was a day of strong light and sharp shadow, with the swamp maples going scarlet and the popples butterfly yellow. We ran down the shoreward edge of the flowage, casting up tight to the skinny shade along the undercut banks whenever we had a chance. In the glide below the riffle I'd serenaded beneath last night's moonlight, Ben raised the first trout of the journey—a chunky little brown of about ten inches that leapt once, flashing gold-flanked in the sun, then screeched a few staccato feet of line from Ben's drag before he brought it alongside and released it.

"I can hardly bear to kill them anymore," he confessed.

"We're going to need some trout for lunch though, aren't we? Or supper anyway."

"Let's worry about that later. I made us some sandwiches for lunch."

There was a sharp, fast right-hander coming up, full of tall white boulders and bouncing haystacks. Most of my trout fishing over the past fifty years had been with float guides on western rivers—the Rogue, the Green, the Madison. The guides do all the work on those trips and you just sit up there in the bow of the raft, like a maharajah on a swimming elephant, scoping the banks for good lies.

Now as we entered the rapids I felt a twinge of panic—could I still handle it?—but then we were busy with the paddles. It all came back. I hadn't lost my balance in a canoe, nor an eye for the vees either.

When we emerged into the glide below the whitewater, I picked up my rod and cast again to the bank, mending the line upstream in midflight. On the third throw I hooked up—another brown, but bigger than Ben's by the feel of him. He didn't break water except on the take, and as I brought him in, I wondered about my friend's newfound reluctance to take piscine life. I released most of the fish I caught, except when the dinner bell was clanging just down the road, but I'd never felt squeamish about killing them. Maybe his change of heart could be traced back to Korea, but I wasn't about to ask him. He'd tell me when he was ready.

As I brought the fish alongside, I could feel Ben's eyes on my back. I popped the barbless hook from the brown trout's jaw and turned him free. What the hell, there were more where he'd come from.

The old abandoned logging camps we'd seen on our last trip had by now decayed back into the ground they'd sprung from, leaving no trace of their existence; the scruffy second-growth stands of tamarack, jackpine, and popple had been succeeded by spruce, fir, and even an occasional family group of white pines: Ma and Pa and their tall, strong sons and daughters. Nature heals itself in a hurry, given half a chance. Would that mankind could do the same.

We passed the spot where Doc and Curly's shack once stood. The forest had reclaimed it. A stand of aspens rose from its ruins. Yellow leaves wigwagged in a high, cool breeze. A lone raven perched on a lightning-killed snag, nodding to us as we passed. Yes, winter's on its way.

If you live for half a century, as Kate and I had, in a lotus land with no distinct seasons, you forget the taste of fall. Autumn is bittersweet, like ice-cold applejack. It carries the summer just past, never to come again in exactly the same combination, those days that blaze like tigers, those nights of cold fiery stars. Winter is right around the corner: you can feel it crouching there with its claws of frost and its teeth of sleet, its blinding, wind-driven snows. Chilblains, despair. In some ways, at least in the higher latitudes, the year is like a woman. Her summer is fast and easy; her winter makes demands. Autumn teeters between them. It's the best time of year for fishing, the game birds have grown to full size and speed, the deer are fat with summer's glut and the sweetening fruits of beech and corn and apple. When you gut them out, your hands come away as yellow with grease as they're red with blood. Autumn is the killing season. Even the trees tell us so with their colors.

We came to a long easy run of pocket water, shallow enough to wade. It was almost high noon. "Hey, Benjamin, let's pull over to the bank and have our lunch. I'm getting a bit peckish and I'd like to work this water with a dry fly, on foot so to speak."

"Okay," he said. "Why not? We've got plenty of time in hand and no particular destination in mind anyway."

We wheeled into the bank and hauled the canoe out of the water. Ben had made me two sardine sandwiches on Wonder Bread, with jam and plenty of peanut butter. Thoughtful of him but I'd lost my taste for the combination. I ate it anyway, with an apple for dessert, slipped the crusts to Jake when Ben wasn't looking, then tied a 6X tippet to my four-weight Sage and waded out wet.

"You don't have to do that, Hairball," Ben called after me. "I brought along some hip boots that should fit you."

"I've got waders of my own in the duffel," I said. I wanted to feel the river. You lose that with dry feet.

The bottom was gravel, shifting and growling beneath my sneakers, and the water bitter cold. There were baetis emerging over in the shadows of the western bank, tiny things, about a no. 16 or 18 I guessed. I could see the duns drifting with the current, waiting for their slate-colored wings to dry. Then they flew off to the bankside brush.

I tied on a blue quill emerger and looked for the bulges of feeding trout. They were everywhere. I threw to one that was feeding from the lee of a submerged yellow rock, just nipping his head out now and then to take a shedding nymph, his mouth flashing pale as he ate. I could see by the rosy flash of his gill plates that he was a rainbow, laid out the fly about ten feet upstream of him, and let it sink to his lie.

Bump—he took it.

Tauten the line . . . now set it.

He sprang from the water like a bee-stung pup, shaking his head and throwing a quick comma of spray, then turned downstream.

I raised the rod tip and let him take line from under my forefinger. Then he was into the drag—no sweeter sound in the world. He jumped twice more, three times, far downstream of me, turned, and bored straight back again.

I stripped in slack like a speedcrazed spaz but it wasn't quick enough. There was still enough slack in it for him to throw the fly on his next leap, just opposite me, not five feet away. He was a nice fish, eighteen inches at least. I watched him flicker away, disappear like a whisper into a deep shadowed hold, up tight to the western bank.

My heart was pounding. I took a deep breath and shuddered. Adrenaline: it can kill you. But who was more spooked, me or the rainbow?

His run had put down all the fish in the near vicinity, so I reeled in, eased over to the east bank, and waded a hundred yards upstream.

The trout ahead of me were feeding on top now, quick slashing little rises. The hatch was at its peak. I clipped off the emerger and tied on a dun. My legs had gone numb from the cold and it hurt when my toes bumped the rocks. I waded out into midcurrent and threw a low, flat, easy loop to a riser working along the far bank. The first drift was too short. I waited until the fly was well below him, picked it up, and threw a bit more line. This float was right in the slot. He took it with no hesitation, jumped once, twice, then ran upstream in a hell of a hurry. The tippet ripped the water. I let the rod wear him down, brought him in, and held him there, close to my leg in the waist-deep water (sixteen or eighteen inches, almost as big as the one that threw the hook). His gills were pumping and I could see his eyes roll up to meet mine. I reached down with the pliers, slow so as not to spook him, and twitched the hook free without touching him.

He held there in the lee of my legs for a moment or two—unbelieving—then flirted away so fast that I didn't see him go. Blink of an eye. Just a cold quick roseate blur . . .

I looked back toward the canoe. Ben and Jake stood on the bank, watching me. He smiled and nodded.

"Get your rod," I yelled over to him. "They're all on the take."

"No," he shouted. "It's more fun seeing you fuck up."

Trout get more selective as a hatch progresses. It's an age-old practice of theirs, one you can count on. Far up near the head of the run I saw a big fish feeding. A twenty incher, judging by the breadth of his dark green back and his big square tail. Maybe better. I slogged up toward him, fighting the current and sloping into a crouch as I came within casting range. He was rising in a slow, steady rhythm. Time it—*rise*, two, three, four, five, six—*rise*, two, three, four . . .

I laid out the blue quill to fall a foot ahead of his rise form. The current—stronger up here at the head of the run, gnarly and braided—snatched it away in an instant, and the line dragged. But I'd mistimed my throw and he didn't notice the gaucherie.

I moved a few steps to the left to gain a more forgiving angle. On the next cast, I wiggled the rod from side to side, throwing a fat "S" of slack into the leader. No drag this time. The fly drifted down over him and I saw him rise to it. But instead of my blue quill, he sipped a natural that bobbed right beside it.

Twice more this happened, and I still hadn't put the big boy down. This luck couldn't last much longer, though. Time for a change. I replaced the blue quill with a pale morning dun. He paid it no heed. I switched to a blue-winged olive in an even smaller size. It was no go. In desperation now, I went to the old reliable—a no. 16 Adams.

All it did was put him down for good.

I waded back down to the canoe, chilled and dead beat. My teeth were chattering.

"Had enough?" Ben asked.

"It's never enough. I just got too cold is all."

"Figured as much. There's a pot of coffee waiting for you—just perked and piping hot."

We sat on the bank and watched the trout sipping mayflies as we sipped our coffee. Jake frisked the nearby thickets for patridge. We heard one roar away. The dog came trotting back, looking expectantly toward the gun cases. "Tomorrow, boy," Ben said. "It's too nice a day for killing."

The air was thick with new-flown duns. Caddises squirreled among them, big and clumsy as bombers compared to the tiny mayflies. Birds were working the hatch now too, bank swallows darting in to snap bugs in midair, with redwing blackbirds, iridescent grackles, cedar waxwings, and garlands of goldfinches scouring the brush to pick off the new arrivals. The grackles, with their angry yellow eyes, were loud and rude. A scarlet tanager flashed past like a meteor.

"There's nothing to beat it," Ben said. "Everything comes to the river in September. I could watch it forever."

"Let's pitch camp right here," I said. "We can grab a few zees, as they used to say, and there's bound to be a spinner fall toward sundown."

"What the hell, Hairball, why not? We've got no pressing engagements."

But nap time proved a nightmare. I dreamed of the bull newt. He rose to inspect my offerings but rejected them all. Not till I tied on a severed human hand could I get him to take. Yet whose hand was it?

7

A WHITE-GLOVED HOWDY

I woke with a foul taste in my mouth—stale coffee—and that sluggish feeling a bad dream leaves in its wake. A Dexedrine cleared out the cobwebs. Ben saw me swallow it.

"I take a lot of pills too," he said. "Vasodilators and calcium blockers every day for high blood pressure, along with a piss pill. It runs in the family. My old man had it. What's your problem?"

"Prostate," I told him. "The old fart's malady. They say that every man who doesn't die of something else first will end up with it. Fortunately it's a slow-growing malignancy," I lied. "I'll probably croak from something else before it gets into my bones or lungs or colon, but it's inconvenient as hell."

"You've got . . . cancer?"

I nodded.

"Why the fuck didn't you tell me? Shouldn't you be in the hospital? I thought you looked a bit fragile but figured it for jet lag. You shouldn't be paddling . . ."

"Lay off me, Ben. I feel just fine. If it hadn't been for the PSA test and the biopsy, I wouldn't even know I had it. Look, you just saw me wading wet in a fast cold current, fishing upstream for half an hour . . ."

"It was more like an hour and half," he said. He shrugged and nodded. "Okay, I guess I overreacted. But that's a scary word."

"Tell me about it."

The spinners were already working over the water, dancing up and down, glinting like flecks of bronze in the softening afternoon light, weaving their webs of airborne sexual magic. They mate in midair, then the females dive down like tiny kamikazes to drop their eggs in the current. Afterward they die, drifting downstream like so many miniature Ophelias. I'd like to think that they sing sweet crazy pastorales as they float to their collective doom, insect lyrics inaudible to human ears, way above the range of the saxophone or else I'd try it. Maybe I'd try it anyway. How else to explain the sadness of an autumn afternoon?

But trout aren't sentimentalists. They feed on these moribund damsels like the opportunists they are—that Nature has bred them to be. Already a few were working the spinner fall. Small trout leaped high to snag low flyers, others slashed the surface in quick little takes, slurping down whole rafts of the spent, clear-winged, rust-bodied victims. It was still too bright for the big trout to feed. But the sun was about to disappear behind the spruce and cedar of the western skyline.

We walked down the bank to the far end of the run. This time I wore waders. The cold of the afternoon's expedition seemed to have chilled me to the marrow. Too much California, I told myself. Too many trips to the Baja. You live in a bland climate, your blood's getting thin . . .

Bullshit. Don't kid yourself. It's the cancer at work.

We reached the end of the pool. "You had all the fun this afternoon," I told Ben, "watching me warm and dry from the shore while I beat my brains out on that big rainbow. So it's only fair that you should get in the water first this time. I could use a few laughs."

"Get ready to chuckle."

He waded out to midstream, heavy-legged in his chest waders, and started searching for risers. Ben had a slow, easy stroke to his casts, the classic metronome, and I followed the loops of his pale green flyline hissing esses in the sunset. It was hypnotic. He dropped the fly—a rusty spinner—about sixty feet up and across from where he stood. So soft a touch that there was no splash. The fly drifted less than a foot before it was taken. He tightened and raised his rod tip. A quick leap, two more, then he took the trout on the reel and brought it in, easing the fish away from the feeding line so as not to alarm the others. He released it and started casting again, air-drying the fly as he eased back out toward the far bank.

He took half a dozen more trout on his next six casts, easy as pie, then reeled up and waded back to the bank where I was sitting in the last random beams of sunlight.

"Your turn, Hairball," he said.

"Any size to them?"

"Ten to fourteen inches, but peppy little devils, full of bounce."

"I could see that from here."

"The big trout should start working soon, sometime within the next half hour," he said. "Maybe you'll tag that guy who gave you conniptions earlier."

But I didn't. Oh, I caught and released maybe eight or ten fish, all rainbows, but none of any real size. It got darker and darker. Colder and colder. Then, on my last backcast, I picked up a bat. He must have been cruising for the last of the spinning mayflies, and he hit my fly so hard that he made the reel sing. He flew off with it until the weight of the line slapped him down on the water.

I hate it when they do that. Not that I'm fearful of bats, but rather that I have too deep a liking for them. Ugly little fellows when you study them up close, but miracles of evolution—*die Fledermaus*, a German word that also means a flighty woman.

I reeled the drowning bat in and flipped him up on the near bank with my free hand. He was panting, poor little guy. I knelt beside him for a moment.

Ben and Jake walked down to where I was kneeling. "Are you going to give him mouth to mouth, Doc?"

"No, smartass, I just want to see how deep he took the fly." It was hooked in the corner of the bat's mouth, painful I'm sure but far from mortal. I reached down and clipped it loose with the scissors attached to my vest, just above the knot, taking care that he didn't nip me. I didn't dare pick him up in a bare hand

and try to remove the barbless hook with the needlenose grips. Even with an easy touch I might have crushed his bones. He'd throw the fly soon enough when he got airborne, just a few quick loops and chandelles should do it.

We went back a few steps and watched in the dying light until the bat flew away.

"You're getting to be a gentle soul, aren't you?" Ben said in a quiet, serious voice. "I don't mean that sarcastically. I'm not ribbing you. But you are."

The question took me aback. Was I going soft? Or perhaps this trip was rekindling gentler emotions that I hadn't felt since high school.

"I don't know," I said. "I have a sympathy for life, I guess, if that's what 'gentle' means. Maybe it comes with age. But you're a softy too it would seem. No trout for supper?"

"Think again, pal." He reached down into the grass and pulled up a stringer full of trout, stocky little ten inchers. "I'm not averse to killing a few fish now and then for a special occasion. I just don't want to kill all of them. Found these guys down at the tail of the pool while you were battling Count Dracula and they were too good to pass up. Just tiddlers, yes, but they'll taste mighty sweet from the frying pan."

Yes, they did. And it *was* a special occasion, I now realized. This trip was changing both of us for the better, bringing me back into a world more real than arid, success-driven California, and weaning Ben from self-pity and the bottle.

I stayed up late again that night, trying the capture the music of the spinner dance on my horn. I wasn't fast enough to do it justice, but some nice sounds emerged anyway—quick up-and-down riffs punctuated with buggy orgasmic flights in the lower registers, followed by sad melodic passages as the spent females drifted away downstream. But this number needed a quartet at least to do it justice—a light, quick keyboard for the braided sound of the river, John Lewis in his prime would do; a guttural trumpet for the climaxes (Diz at his best); Max Roach to mix the tempo; with the Prez and his tenor sax for the Lady Ophelia songs. I imagined the soloes as I sketched them out—the mind's ear connects straight to the tear ducts, and my eyes began to blur.

After a while I put the horn aside and watched the river race past. Large mayflies were spinning in the moonlight just below the riffle, twice the size of the baetis we'd seen during daylight hours. One of them fluttered to the bank and lit on my hand. I recognized it at once—an old friend of my youth, the White-Gloved Howdy. This outsized ephemerid is technically a subspecies of *Isonychia—I. Bicolor*—but its happier name derives from its forelegs. They're extra long for a mayfly and bonewhite toward the front end—what would correspond to the gloved hands and wrists of a Victorian gentleman caller.

Then I heard a sound from the top of the pool. *Ker-chung*! A big fish on the take. It was my nemesis from the early afternoon—had to be. The trout was feeding in the exact same lie. The rise rings spread as if someone had dropped a depth charge. I grabbed my flybox and searched it for a howdy match. The only extralong fly I had was a Hex tie, a mahogany-bodied imago of *Hexagenia limbata*, the so-called Michigan caddis, with long hyaline wings tied flat. It was big enough, a long-shanked No. 8, so it'd be worth the effort.

We'd been fishing 5X tippets to the baetis, with a breaking point of no more than two pounds. I'd need a sturdier length of terminal line than that, both to throw this fly accurately and to handle a really big trout if I could get one to take. Now I rummaged around in Ben's tackle bag and found a spool of ten-pound-test monofilament. I clipped off the old tippet back to heavier line, barrel-knotted the new long tippet to it, taking special care to ensure that the turns were wrapped tight, and greased the whole length with floatant. In situations like this it's unforgiveable to allow the leader to sink the fly.

The big 'bow was feeding steadily now, in heavy, hollow, headlong splashes that echoed back to me from the far bank.

Lesser trout were on the take too, all up and down the pool. No time for waders. I thought of waking Ben—he'd never forgive me if he missed this feeding frenzy—but that would take too long. These late-season falls of big mayfly spinners were over almost before they began. I slid down the near bank and crouched low as I angled my way across the slippery gravel. He was working in the shadow line of moonlight, close to the head of the pool. I squatted down, chest-deep in the current, and stripped line from the reel, enough—I hoped—to reach him with only one backcast.

I threw.

The fly blipped on the water, three feet ahead of him. I watched it swirl once, then drift down over him. He took it with the impact of a .375 H&H Magnum, a solid, no-nonsense hit that hooked him with its very velocity. He jumped high, shaking his head, gill plates rattling like a tarpon's, then jumped again—three, four, five times. He bored off up through the rapids and line melted off my reel. I couldn't turn him.

I'd have to follow or he'd spool me in no time. As I scrambled up through the rushing water and slippery boulders of the whitewater, holding the rod high over my head, I heard a shout from the campsite. I glanced back. Ben was standing there in his skivvies, with Jake beside him, pumping his right arm up and down. "Go, go, go!" Maybe I shouted on the hookup and woke him, or maybe he'd been watching me all along. But I didn't have time to yell back. I was too busy keeping my footing and fighting the onrushing current.

You're too old for this, Doc . . .

Somehow I made it up through the rapids though and into the slower water. The trout by now had taken me well into the backing. My knuckles were white on the corks, my hand cramping, I'd fallen twice, banged elbows to a high screeching tingle, and scuffed my shins on boulders. I'd lost one of my sneakers along the way. But unless the hook pulled out, I had him now.

Jake came running up the shoreline with Ben behind him, carrying a long-handled landing net. Ten minutes later we scooped him into its meshes. His heaving sides gleamed silver in the moonlight. A tiny, well-shaped head, broad shoulders, and a tail that looked a handspan wide from top to bottom.

"He's two feet long if he's an inch," Ben said. "And look at the girth of him—he's got to go eight pounds anyway, maybe closer to ten."

"Too much trout for us to eat before the meat goes bad," I said. "Let's try a little streamside CPR."

It took both of us to hold him upright into the current, kneedeep in the Firesteel, moving him gently back and forth until he righted himself. Blood was flowing down my shins, trailing off in black tendrils downstream. The trout tasted some of it on a back eddy, then sprang back to life. He rolled his eyes at us and zoomed away like an Exocet missile, into the darkness he'd sprung from.

8

SHIKAREE LODGE

I slept like a log that night. Literally. Flat on my back. No tossing and turning for me. Even rolling over was a pain. My
legs were not only stiff from all that upstream running but
sore as hell from banging into rocks. I'd doused the abrasions
with hydrogen peroxide, laved my shins with Neosporin, covered the worst scrapes with monster Band-Aids, then popped a
couple of Percodans and a tetracycline. I still couldn't sleep.

"You're gimpy, pal," Ben said the next morning as I
limped out of the tent. "'Slowly he turned, step by step . . .'
Maybe we ought to call it quits. There's a takeout spot a few
miles downriver."

"I'll be all right," I said. "My shins look like chopped liver
and my muscles are a little stiff, but I took an antibiotic and a
muscle relaxant. Half a mile of paddling and the kinks will
work themselves out. They'll record it in the medical annals as
just another case of 'Physician, heal thyself.'"

"You're the doctor. Anyway, we've got an easy day ahead
of us. The fishing sucks for the next ten miles—mostly hatchery
trout—so we can blow right through, dodging rafts and drift
boats all the way. There's a swank new resort down there by the
takeout—Septuagesima Island, right across from Stony
Creek—and they hammer the water for five miles either way."

"As in Septuagesima Sunday?"

"Yeah, seventy days before Lent. I guess one of the early
French explorers discovered it on that day. Duluth or one of
those guys back in the sixteen hundreds. They must have had a
chilly time of it, that time of year." He poured me a cup of joe.
"Those old voyageurs wouldn't recognize the place now.
Teeming with fat cats and their ladies, $500-a-day river guides,

whole herds of exotic critters from the Himalayas and Siberia—
Marco Polo sheep, musk oxen, argali, snow leopards, even
Asiatic brown bears, if you'd care to take one home as a 'trophy.'
They call it Shikaree Lodge. 'Thugee' would have been a better
choice. They charge 20K for a Marco Polo. I did some carpen-
try work there in the mid-'80s when the lodge was just opening.
You'll never guess who built the place."

"I give up."

"Your old squeeze Cora Stoat. Her third husband was
Lancelot Shrubb, a rabid big game hunter, a big bucks oil man
from Texas in more ways than one. She built the lodge for him
as a surprise, stocked it with critters suited to the climate, and
presented it to him on their fifth wedding anniversary. He was
surprised, all right. On his first day afield a Siberian tiger had
him for lunch."

"Serves him right for messing with my Cora."

"Anyway, with the Big Bwana gone she turned it commercial. With a capital 'C.' You'll know what I mean when we
get there."

Indeed I did. A few miles downstream we saw the first evidence
of Shikaree Lodge—an electrified game fence, twelve feet high
and topped with razor wire, that was meant to keep the wildlife
on Cora's property. Signs warned hunters to keep out under
threat of the direst penalties. The signs were better spelled than
Curly's similar warning of fifty years earlier.

The fence crossed the Firesteel, barring our way, and disappeared deep into the woods of the west bank. There was a gate in
the fence to allow river traffic through, and a guard shack on the
east bank. A guard ambled out of it as we approached, a tall beefy
guy in a rent-a-cop outfit. He carried a shotgun—a ten-gauge
streetsweeper, by the look of it. He gestured us in to the shore.

"Sorry, fellas," he said as we pulled up, "but I gotta check
you guys through—names, destination, time of entry, that kind
of bullshit. There's another gate at the far end to check you out."

"Is it legal to bar access to a public waterway?" I asked him.

"Beats me," he said "I only work here. But it's the boss's orders and I guess she's cleared it with the DNR. We've got a lot of valuable wildlife on the premises, some of it endangered species, and she can't afford to take no chances with poachers."

"She?"

"Miz Cora," he said absently, as if everyone in the world must know her. He was looking down into the canoe and had spotted the gun cases. He shook his head. "I'm afraid I'll have to confiscate your firearms, gentlemen. And the dog, too. They'll be returned to you when you leave the property."

"I'm afraid *not*," I said. "The dog is perfectly well behaved, solid to wing and shot, and what's more there's a priceless weapon involved—a rare English double worth more than $100,000."

He looked at me with new respect. "Your gun won't get hurt or ripped off, sir. We're bonded. Insurance up the ass."

"Up yours, my good man," I told him. I was getting hot. "No offense intended. Let me speak to your supervisor—no, better yet, let me speak to Cora herself. She's an old friend of ours."

He popped a cell phone from his hip, flicked it open, and punched a number. "May I have your name, sir?"

"Doctor Taggart. . . . No, tell her it's *Harry* Taggart from the fall of 1950, along with Ben Slater. Tell her we're the guys who sunk her daddy's Gar Wood."

He turned his back and walked up toward the shack, talking so we couldn't hear him. I caught a few words nonetheless. ". . . couple of old farts down here . . . rich fuckers . . . wanna talk to the Queen Bee . . ."

He nodded, waited, then snapped to attention and talked some more. He nodded a few more times, deep bows of respect, disconnected, and walked back down to us.

"She'll be here in a few minutes," he said. "Why don't you guys come on up to the shack, have a cuppa coffee while you're waiting? Bring the pooch too. I've got a Lab myself."

I looked at Ben. He shrugged—why not? We went.

228 + ROBERT F. JONES

The coffee wasn't half bad. Nor were the wildlife photos on the wall: A brown bear slapping salmon out of the Firesteel; a herd of yaks standing belly deep in a Wisconsin blizzard, circled up for protection with their horntips pointing outwards; a shaggy Asian argali sheep with a full curve and a half of horn, battling a pack of Russian wolves.

"Tell me about sinking that speed boat," the guard said with a wicked, complicitous grin. His name was Tony Mezzoni according to the tag on his chest, chief of what was euphemistically called the Grounds Crew. Ben gave him the rundown, with comic book sound effects. Tony laughed and hitched at his crotch, tears ran down his face.

We were standing outside the shack now, waiting for Miz Stoat. A monarch butterfly flitted past, drifting upstream toward the south. Tony's eyes lit up. Then the shotgun was at his shoulder—*POW!* Orange and black confetti fluttered on the breeze.

"Don't get a chance to shoot much on this job," Tony apologized. Jake went out and sniffed around, picked up a tattered wing, and dropped it at Ben's feet. I noticed that there were ragged lanes slashed through the brush surrounding the shack, all at shoulder height. "I love wingshooting. A few ducks blow through now and then, spring and fall, and of course there's always the robin migration. They taste damn good with pine nuts in a red wine sauce over pasta."

We heard the truck coming fast, bouncing down the two-track inside the fence. It was a Range Rover just like mine back in Palos Verdes, the same British racing green but filmed with dust instead of sea salt. It slewed to a halt in the dirt. Two women dressed in crisp, tailored safari clothes got out, both slim and well coiffed, and glinting with jewelry to boot. Cora from the driver's side door, and from the other . . . the Wickedly Wonderful Wanda. They walked toward us, smiling.

"Imagine!" Cora said. "Our knights in shining armor have returned, just in time to save us again."

"It's more like grungy sweat suits," Ben said, grinning. "But what do you want us to save you from this time?"

"Boredom," Wanda said. "And an elephant in *musth*."

Wanda and Cora were both widowed now. They had stayed in close touch since Bryn Mawr, getting together a few times each year for girl talk and shopping, in places like Paris, Milan, Palm Beach, and New York. Wanda had been married for fifteen years to a Philadelphia legal eagle, then divorced him when she caught him sleeping with a client's wife. She soon signed up for another hitch—this time with a commodities broker from Chicago who'd died a year ago of heart disease (too many pork belly futures in his past?). Cora hadn't remarried after Number Three's encounter with the tiger.

We learned all this on the drive to the main lodge, Cora at the wheel. She insisted that we stay the night there at least. Tony and the crew would bring up our gear, and dogs were always welcome at Shikaree. Up close the women showed their age, despite the most artful effects of more than one face lift apiece. The road wound through alternate woods and meadows, on some of which grazed mixed herds of wildlife—huge Indian sambhur fed beside tiny, tan, woolly-coated chiru gazelles from the plateaus of Tibet; English red deer as big as elk rubbed shoulders with bottle-nosed saiga from Mongolia. Alone on a grassy hillock stood a strange, brown, goatlike creature with horns like upright oil drilling spuds and a long black beard that blew back in wisps against a creamy white vest—a markhor, Cora explained, from the steppes of Uzbekistan. Wildlife from the former Soviet Union was a glut on the exotics market these days, dirt cheap except for the shipping costs.

As we neared the lodge we passed outlying guest cottages, some built like dak bungalows from the Indian raj, others styled after Mongol yurts. They were scattered among scenic groves of pine and aspen. Small islands of cedar and juniper dotted the grounds as well, scenting the hot noonday air with spices. There was even a petting zoo for children—baby sheep, fallow deer, wolf pups, and a lion cub among the cuddly attractions. They seemed to be getting along well together. Indeed, the lion was lying down with the lamb.

The main lodge was a dazzler—a miniaturized version of London's Crystal Palace. All glass and spires and Victorian gingerbread. It was surrounded by a wide moat on which I saw floating Muscovy ducks, emperor geese from Alaska, and slim, graceful black swans with red paddles and bills. "All the way from Down Under," Cora said. "They're native to Australia."

"How do they survive the Wisconsin winters?" Ben asked.

"Oh, we move them to an aviary out back. It's heated. We have all the 'mod cons' here at Shikaree."

"How much property do you keep fenced?" I asked her.

"Just under 13,000 acres," she said. "Daddy foreclosed on twenty square miles that belonged to a bankrupt lumber company. It went bust in the Depression. The parcel included Twodoggone Lake, where he built the old lodge."

"What ever happened to it?" Ben asked.

"Oh, it's still in fine shape," Wanda said. "I live there part of the year now, since my husband passed on. Summers mostly."

"And the Gar Wood?"

"We put it out to pasture after Daddy died. That was in '64. An aneurysm, but he died happy—fighting his last muskie. The Gar Wood went to Dearborn, I think—one of Henry Ford's museums anyway."

She parked in front of the Crystal Palace and we crossed the drawbridge. The lounge area bristled. Its floors and walls were covered with heads, horns, and hides, from wisent to yak to barasingha, Père David's deer to a full-body mount of the massive Siberian tiger that had done for Cora's last husband. As we entered, a familiar figure strode toward us—Florinda Wakerobin, as scowling, stout, and sturdy as ever though her hair had gone snow white.

"I knew I'd see you rascals again before I died," she said. "Only the good die young."

Then she smiled.

If I'd had the horn with me I could have played "That Old Gang of Mine."

9

THE ELEPHANT REVEALED

Pheasants, peacocks, and Northern European capercailzie strutted the lawns that led down from the palace's screened veranda to a nearby pond. I'd heard of capercailzie, the world's largest grouse, but never seen them before. They grow up to ten pounds, with dark plumage—almost black—and wide, fanlike tails. *Capercailzie* is a Scots Gaelic word meaning "forest horse." During the mating season, and to demonstrate dominance throughout the year, the males expand their bright red cheek pouches and boom like a herd of galloping stallions.

We watched the big birds strut their stuff as we lunched. Almost as colorful were the young waitresses in saris and caste marks who served us. They slipped to and from the kitchen bringing *bhagari jhinga* for starters—jumbo shrimp in a creamy pink sauce spiced with cayenne, coriander and jalapeños—followed by poached Firesteel salmon filets, early cohoes I think, seasoned with *panchphoran*, a mixture of five spices: cumin, fenugreek, fennel, and popped brown mustard seeds, along with a black teardrop-shaped number called *kalonji*, which tasted powerfully of oregano. Papadoms, pita bread, and basmati rice in abundance accompanied this humble repast. All of this was explained by our proud hostess. We washed it down with ice-cold steins of Old Milwaukee beer.

The waitresses said not a word and kept their eyes cast demurely downward through their comings and goings. "Don't be taken in by their Hindustani ways," Florinda whispered to me. "They're Chippewa girls from the rez, and all good Catholics. The waitresses eat what we do. That's why we're having fish—it's Friday."

Tony Mezzoni showed up with our duffel. After lunch we went out for a "post-prandial stroll" with the shotguns. "Good for the digestion," Cora said. She and Wanda carried light English doubles, round-action Dicksons with side levers, in 28 bore. The grounds were thick with game birds. Within a hundred yards of the lodge Jake flushed half a dozen ringnecks, a brace of chukars, and a covey of Huns, along with a flock of pale, strong-winged, grouse-like birds unfamiliar to me that flew out low and fast as sheet lightning. I emptied both barrels after them and never touched a feather.

"That's the rare Himalayan snow partridge," Cora said. "They're almost extinct in their homeland but adapt to this climate with exceptional vigor. Pretty soon they'll start outbreeding even the pheasants. They're already outfeeding them. You'd better not miss the next time, Doctor."

"So you allow your birds to breed in the wild?" Ben asked. "I'd have figured it was all put and take in these commercial operations."

"No, my gamekeeper sometimes stocks birds from the aviaries out back, but only after a bad winter. And then mostly pheasants or chukars. The Hungarian partridge do well here, too."

As we skirted the pond, Jake nosed into a clump of reeds and flushed a brace of woodcock—but woodcock twice the size of what he was used to. Ben dropped them with a nice right and left, and Jake fetched them both to his hand. "They're the European species, *Scolopax rusticola*," Cora said. "Much bigger than our timberdoodles. The only trouble with them is that, like their American cousins, they migrate—clear down to the Gulf Coast, or so I'm told. The U.S. Fish and Wildlife Service is rather miffed at me about that. Afraid they'll crossbreed with our native birds or some such nonsense."

Tony Mezzoni, who'd been relieved from his watch at the upper river gate, followed us along with a gamebag. Soon it was bulging.

"None of these birds go to waste," Cora said. "What the shooting guests don't eat or take home with them we contribute to soup kitchens in Ashland, Duluth, and the Twin Cities. Same with the excess meat left behind by the big-game hunters."

"Those towns must have the best-fed indigents in America," I said. "You'd pay $100 a plate for snow partridge under glass in Chicago, more for saddle of sambhur. Aren't you tempted to sell your game birds and venison to the restaurants?"

"Not at all," Wanda said. "She'll leave that to the Elephant when he buys her out."

"Is that the pachyderm in musth? The one you want us to rescue you from?"

"Yes," Cora said. "My next-door neighbor, Fritz Cardigan. You've probably heard of him. Cardigan Enterprises, second only to Microsoft in cyberworld skulduggery. He made his first billion before he was twenty-five—in weapon-systems electronics during and after Vietnam. Now he's into computers and he wants to buy this property for a new 'think tank.' His dream, he says, is to own the whole Firesteel from the estuary to the headwaters. He 'musth' have it!"

"Fritzie had a brief but intense flirtation with the counterculture during the late '60s," Wanda said. "Vietnam horrified him despite the money he made from it, and he hates what he calls 'the blood sports.' He equates hunting and fishing with war. Can't bear to see duck hunters or trout fishermen cruising 'his' water. The sound of gunfire gives him nightmares, he says. Yet his guards routinely put shots across the bows of passing boats. And the game wardens look the other way."

"You'll meet him tonight," Cora said. "He's coming to dinner. I invite him now and then, on the theory that while one should keep one's friends close, its wise to keep one's enemies even closer—the better to anticipate his moves, of course. But that doesn't mean he'll enjoy himself. He's a perfervid vegetarian, so I'm serving roast haunch of steppe wisent, blood rare."

"Fritzie's on to your tricks, hon," Wanda said. "He'll bring along a cooler of mesclun and Japanese seaweed, just like last time."

"What the hell is a steppe wisent?" Ben asked.

"It's the European bison, *Bison bonasus*," Cora said, launching into her tour guide mode. "They're nearly extinct nowadays except for a small herd, maybe 250 animals, in the Bialowiecza Forest of Poland. The Shikaree herd may be bigger than that by now. They used to range across all of Europe, from France to the Caucasus, and possibly well into Asia, but the last totally wild herd was wiped out for meat during the First World War. During the interwar period, the Poles used animals retrieved from zoos to breed replacements. Steppe wisents, in spite of their name, do well in the woods. They thrive here. In Poland they're prized by poachers, and with all the turmoil that followed the collapse of the East Bloc who knows how many are left there?"

"Don't you get poachers here as well?" Ben asked.

"Tony and his crew take care of that," Cora said. Tony smiled and nodded.

Cora had assigned us to a dak bungalow near the palace. After the shoot Ben and I took showers, shaved, and got dressed. A housemaid had unpacked and tidied our clothes. We donned freshly pressed khakis and went out on the screened gallery, where an ice bucket, glasses, and a bottle of single-malt awaited us. There were bowls of fresh-fried cashews to accompany our libations—*tale caju*, Wanda had called them, seasoned with salt, pepper, cayenne, and ground cumin seeds. We poured drinks and kicked back.

"What do you make of all this?" Ben asked.

"Like I've died and gone to heaven. I guess you're right after all. The present has a whole lot to offer that's better than the past."

He shook his head and reached down to scratch behind Jake's ears. The dog lay at his feet and mumbled through his

doze. The sun was sloping down toward the river, and a pleasant chill crept into the air. Muddy Range Rovers groaned past in
the distance, coming back from the field after a day of hunting,
their roofracks heavily laden with the carcasses of game—gut-
ted antelope, red deer, big bluegray nilghai, sheep, an enormous
brown bear. The bear's tongue lolled from its mouth, crusted
black with dried blood.

"I don't like it one bit," Ben said. "These birds and animals
don't belong here, no matter how 'wild' they're supposed to be."

"But if they weren't here they'd be nowhere. Most of these
species are headed for extinction in their native habitats, if
they're not wiped out already. There's no room for them anymore. It's like you said, 'too many fucking people.'"

"It's still wrong. A hunter should work for his shots. These
guys get driven to the pasture or woodlot where what they've paid
for is waiting. They get out, crawl on their bellies for a few yards,
and squeeze the trigger. The guide guts it out, winches it up on
the roofrack, and they're home in time for the cocktail hour."

"It's not that easy," I said. "You heard what Cora told us.
Sometimes it takes all day, all week, for some of these hunters to
connect with horns they're looking for. And sometimes they
never do."

"And that's all to her advantage though," he said. "She
charges sixteen hundred a day for these cottages, and really big
bucks on top of that for the animal. It's all commerce, Harry.
And that's not what hunting's about. You've got to *bleed* a little
to be worthy of taking a life. I'm never happier than coming
back in from a day of busting the brush for grouse, pounding
the hills from dawn to dusk, legs turned to wood, the backs of
my hands ripped by briers, grouse hunter's hands, and maybe a
bird or two cooling in the game pocket."

He knocked back half of his single-malt and made a sour
face. "That's when you've earned a drink, a good stiff belt of
Dickel on the rocks—not this seepage from a peat bog. And
maybe a handful of Planter's peanuts." He picked a few cumin

seeds from the nut bowl, then threw them back. "What are these, rat turds?"

"You know what you are, Benjamin? A Catholic masochist—a latter-day Saint Francis of Assisi pursuing stigmata in the grouse woods."

And you're envious of the rich, I might have added but didn't.

"I wish we were back on the river," he said at last. "This place gives me the willies."

There were two blue blazers hanging in the closet next to our shirts. The breast pockets bore tastefully stitched emblems depicting a topee-topped sahib blasting a tiger from atop a rearing elephant, and the words "Shikaree Lodge."

"Are we supposed to wear these?"

"I guess they dress for dinner around here," I said. "Look, they've even laid out a selection of ties for us. Regimental colors, old bean. With a name like Slater you should opt for the Royal Welsh Fusiliers. They quarry a lot of slate in Wales. I'll go with the Household Cavalry."

"Yeah," he said, "you *can* be a bit of a horse's ass at times."

We walked over to the palace. The evening was mild, with a soft afterglow suffusing the sky to the west. Strange horses impeded our progress—hammerheaded cayuses with stiff black manes and long, wild tails. The odd, pale yellow cast to their coats echoed the sunset. They spotted us, snorted, and hit out for the woods. Wild horses.

"This place gets weirder and weirder," Ben said. He looked up at the sky. "If we were on the water now, there'd be a spinner fall. A good one with the temperature like this."

"There'll be another tomorrow night."

"But how many tomorrows do we have left?"

A woman stood on the drawbridge watching the horses run. As we got closer I recognized her. It was Molly Bellefont, all spiffed out in a cocktail dress.

"Hi, guys," she said as we approached. "Mom said you'd be here. Those are Przewalski's horses, by the way."

"Who's Przewalski?" Ben asked, probably imagining some sausage maker from the South Side of Milwaukee.

"Nikolai Przewalski was a famous Russian explorer of the late nineteenth century, a major player in what the Brits called the Great Game. He named these horses when he found them in Sinkiang and Tibet. They're the only truly wild horses left in the world."

"They aren't anymore, not these anyway," Ben said. "Hell, we got within ten feet of them before they spooked."

"A more important question," I said. "Who's 'Mom'?"

"Why, Cora of course," she said. "She told me you were here when I got in this afternoon from upriver. She wants me down here to meet Mr. Cardigan. It seems he has designs on the river—a hostile takeover, she calls it—and she hopes I can help her in balking him."

"Did you and Ned ever catch that bull newt?"

"It's not a newt . . ."

"I know, salamander. Did you nail him?"

We went into the lounge. "Yes, Ned stunned him with the electrodes, along with two hundred or more larvae, just little ones. So that means there's a female in the river as well, but we couldn't find her."

"Could she be ranging downriver?"

"It's possible. But we zapped every pool in the swamp and found no others, so that means she can't possibly reproduce."

"But what killed all those brook trout up there? Two giant salamanders couldn't have eaten all of them."

"That's a very good question . . ."

The room was a blur of white noise—a klezmer band blaring in one corner, guests circling and talking, the clink of cocktail glasses, and the high piercing shriek of overdressed women in faux reaction to men's lame jokes. Molly pointed out some of the notables to us, sportsmen all. From Chicago, then, came the Hector Schechters and Pete Cosmolino, big in bonds down Windy City way; and a tall state senator from Madison named Dorsey Diffendaffer whom I'd known at Marquette, where he'd been a basketball star under Al McGuire; and Chalmers Caracal, who nearly died in a gliding accident last summer down near Odessa, Texas. And the Spudnuts, man and portly wife, both of whom had eight South African safaris under their ample belts; and Schuyler Fahnestock, the holder of the International Game Fish Association's all-tackle record—6 pounds, 4¼ ounces—on oyster toadfish (*Opsanus tau*); along with an extended family named Glimmerglass, from somewhere in Tennessee, who gobbled at everyone who passed. The Glimmerglasses, Molly explained, were ardent turkey hunters. They'd come to fill out their life lists of large dead game birds on peacocks, rheas, and capercailzies.

In a far corner of the room stood Gus Kohlfresser plotting stratagems for the morrow with his hunting partner, Durian Spleen. They were nibbling liverwurst cheesecake and chasing it with bock beer. Both men were big in organ meats, Molly advised us, and were here to experiment with exotic flavors.

The mob-connected Congonis were on hand from Detroit, along with Django Quagga, the noted Namibian rap star, whose objective on this safari, Molly said, was to lasso a Przewalski's horse and ride it bareback to a standstill. Django had a number already written, and a video crew from *Entertainment Tonight* was standing by, locked and loaded, to tape the epic struggle.

From Milwaukee came the Schornsteinfegers; Carlo Sears and Karl Garst with their wives; the Glomar-Fitch brothers; and O.B.G. "Whitey" Evergreen, the jet-ski mogul, wealthy industrialists all. Molly directed our attention to a table at which were gathered a conclave of Cheatweeds and Buelcks, pharmaceutical tycoons from Kenosha intent on cornering the market in anti-aging drugs. They were at Shikaree to "collect" a shaggy wild goat called the serow. Molly gave us her usual schoolmarm lowdown: "Native to China, the Himalayan massif,

Assam, Burma, and northern Honshu, the serow's meat is at best mediocre, but some parts of the animal are believed to have medicinal value."

Cora came bustling up to us. "Why didn't you tell me you'd met my daughter?" she asked. "And that you'd almost been eaten by that dreadful fish-eating warthog?"

"It's a *salamander*, Mother," Molly said. "How many times do I have to tell you?"

I chose to ignore the interruption. "Frankly, my dear," I told Cora, "we couldn't get a word in edgewise once you and Wanda started talking this afternoon. And you never told me you had a daughter."

Ben had slipped away. I spotted him in a far corner, tête-à-tête with Wanda. He was hooked, no doubt about it. Ben was right. We should have stayed on the river.

"Whatever," Cora said. "Come on, I want you to meet the Elephant."

You couldn't miss him. He towered over everyone else in the room, his gray hair cut short but balding, with a long massive face as smooth as a teenager's despite his years. He was dressed in London's finest and sipped his mineral water—Pellegrino by the size of the bubbles—with an air of faint hauteur that bordered on distaste. His bodyguards stood nearby, eyes flicking right and left, reading faces. I noticed Ned, the baby game cop, standing behind them, staring at the heads on the walls.

Cardigan's hand was limp when we shook, and he fluttered his eyelashes. "Cora has told me so much about you, Doctor," he drawled in an affected uppercrust lisp. "I understand you thpent a pleasant few hours this afternoon murdering birds."

"Pardon me?" I cupped a hand to one ear, feigning deafness.

"Slaughtering our fine feathered friends?" he bellowed. "You know—*bang bang*?"

"No, sir," I said. "One bang is usually sufficient."

He looked down on me with walleyed contempt. I was a hunter. I was a fisherman . . .

Fritz Cardigan not only swallowed his "r"s but elided his hard consonants.

"Vewy cwever, I'm sure," he sneered. "*Bwavo!*"

I smiled and bowed. "You know, Fritzie, I had a speech impediment myself when I was younger," I told him. "It's nothing to be ashamed of. A few sessions of speech therapy can clear it up, just like that. You'd be surprised what they can do nowadays. Look at Tom Bwokaw! You *musth* do something about it, if only to bootht your thelf-estheem."

His eyebrows shot up to his hairline.

"Excuse *me!*" he said, and turned away.

We watched him go his wide-assed way.

"That was rude, Harry," my hostess said, her eyes sparkling. "Good for you!" She wrapped her arms around me and hugged me tight.

For the first time in months I felt a tingle.

Cora and I went out on the veranda. Down below a chef was tending the barbeque pit. A huge side of roast beast turned on the spit, sputtering fat into the coals.

"How much has Molly told you about that problem upriver?" I asked her.

"You mean at the headwaters? Not much, only that this creature, whatever it is, seems to have wiped out the brook trout up there."

"Which means that the state has no grounds left for protecting the area. And if the river gets cleaned out of trout and salmon clear down to the estuary . . . it'll be open to developers all the way. But how did those monster salamanders get there in the first place? Somebody must have planted them. Molly doubts that they could have reached the upper river in any other way."

"What are you suggesting?"

I outlined my possible scenarios for her.

"Who could be bastard enough to do such a thing?" she asked. "And why?"

"For solitude?" I said. "For control of the river? Or in the way these rabid anti-abortion protesters can commit murder and claim it was necessary to save the lives of the unborn, a rabid anti-bloodsports type might kill an entire population of trout just to prevent anyone else from fishing for them."

"Of course," she said. "The Elephant. And he's not the dweeb he seems to be. Fritz has been suspected of worse than killing trout. A few years ago, when a young, virtually penniless computer nerd challenged his patent on some new software development, claiming Fritz had pirated it from him, the Juggernaut began
rolling. Literally. A double-rigged semi conveniently squashed the kid's 1962 VW bug one night when he was returning from court in San Francisco."

"Who did the rig belong to?"

"One of Cardigan's companies."

"Didn't the police suspect something?"

"Fritz feels he's above the law," Cora said. "A few megabucks dropped in the right laps and the investigation was declared a dead end."

A chill ran down my spine. This man was a megalomaniac, as dangerous as they come. How could we possibly get Fritz Cardigan out of the Firesteel Country without actually killing the bastard-or worse, getting killed ourselves? That was the scope of the problem.

10

VIOLATORS

Dinner was a Caledonian delight. Smoked Firesteel salmon for the fish course. A consommé of caper-cailzie. Braised woodcock breasts, studded with slivers of fresh ginger, served on crisp slabs of home-baked garlic toast. Dollops of well-seasoned haggis spooned from the boiled gray stomach of a sheep and consisting of the minced lungs, heart, and liver of said creature mixed with oatmeal, onions, and suet. Few tried it but it was good.

And then the pièce de résistance—Barbecue of Beast, blood rare, of course.

A whole new crew of waiters circled the tables now, men this time, bearded, clad in Scottish kilts and tam-o'-shanters, pouring room temperature ales and rare continental wines whether one was ready or not. Bagpipes crooned softly in the background.

I kept my eye on Fritzie, who had brought along his own eats. He nibbled at his mix of mesclun, artichoke hearts, radicchio, shaved fennel, and marinated sun-dried tomatoes, dribbling on occasional splashes of an extra virgin olive oil and lemongrass vinaigrette. But his proudly proclaimed vegetarianism was as suspect as his hoity-toity speech defects. At the height of the feed, when he thought no one was looking, I saw him snatch a bite of salmon from Cora's plate. A little later while her head was turned he filched a nibble of her woast wisent. The crispy curly part of course. Yet when one of his aides tried to sneak a bite for himself, Cardigan jealously poked his hand with a sharp-tined fork.

Molly was seated to my left and while we ate I tried out my salamander scenarios on her. As usual she wouldn't commit herself one way or the other.

"Your first theory is remotely feasible," she allowed. "Freighters and supertankers do indeed sail nonstop to the Gulf of St. Lawrence from Asia without pumping their bilges. We have investigative reports to prove it. And despite the best efforts of both the U.S. and Canadian governments they still blow their ballast in the seaway. How else account for this plague of zebra mussels? It's also possible that cryptobranch larvae could survive such a long migration through the Great Lakes, though it's not likely that many would make it all the way to Lake Superior, much less to the headwaters of the Firesteel. Our salmon and steelhead populations would pick most of them off like canapés, and trout would eat the rest. But yes—randomness being an ineluctable factor in all scientific calculations—it's conceivable that a pair of them might have reached the Firesteel, thus accounting for our breeding couple. Your secondary suppositions, however, smack of conspiracy theory, I'm sad to say. Too typical of laymen in many fields." She drained her glass, a pricey French Bordeaux that was, in my estimation, slightly "corked." So was Molly.

"Could you pass the wine please?" she queried with a tipsy tilt to her eyes and forehead.

I poured her another glass. "What's the matter? Has the baby game cop been giving you trouble?"

"Oh, that little shit," she blurted. "I saw him talking to Cardigan's bully boys before you got here. Thick as thieves. I think they're all in cahoots. The state doesn't have enough money to restock the headwaters of the Firesteel even if we do eliminate the cryptobranchs. Cardigan will snap up that property as quick as your so-called bull newt the moment we lift its sanctuary status. And Ned was looking at some videotape earlier this evening, provided by Fritzie's crew. It was all very hush-hush, but I gathered from what I could overhear outside the door of the screening room that it dealt with illegal hunting. On my mother's land!"

We didn't have long to wait for the trump card. While the kilted menservants were circulating with dessert—plum duff—

Fritzie's minions wheeled a VCR and an outsized television set to the center of the lounge. Ned stood up from Cardigan's table and cleared his throat.

"Ladies and gentlemen, could I have your attention, please?" His trick eye was blipping in and out like a message in Morse code. "I am afraid I have some rather grave and upsetting news to announce. If you would please direct your attention to the video monitor on the dance floor for a moment, all will soon come clear."

The TV screen snapped on. The image blurred, wavered, then focused. There we all were—Cora and Wanda, Ben and I, and Tony trailing behind with his gamebag. Jake quartered in front of the guns. Two birds flushed. Ben raised his AyA and fired. The birds dropped. Jake picked them up, one after the other, and trotted back to his master . . .

The camera zoomed in on the kills. They were, of course, *Scolopax rusticola*—Ben's nifty double on those woodcock.

"Since you're all hunters," Ned said, "I'm sure you recognize these birds as woodcock. Unfortunately the Wisconsin woodcock season has not yet open. Today is September 22. Woodcock aren't fair game until tomorrow. We also found three dozen of these birds in the kitchen freezer, dressed and plucked and ready for the oven, so obviously this illegal harvest has been going on for quite a while. These so-called 'sportsmen' are in clear violation of both state and Federal law, as are those who killed the earlier birds. Thus I can only assume that everyone associated with this establishment, owner, staff and guests alike, is also in violation as aiders and abettors of the offense, if not indeed perpetrators." He looked over at Cora and withdrew a slip of paper from his shirt pocket. "Mrs. Bellefont," he said, "I have here a warrant for your arrest. You are charged with violation of the Migratory Bird Treaty of 1916, a Federal crime, and of the applicable Wisconsin statutes as well, as are all your guests and employees, on charges of complicity in this act. Except for Mr. Cardigan, of course," he added. "And his, uh, entourage."

"Bwavo, Officer Ned!" Cardigan cried. He rose to his full imperious height and brushed breadcrumbs from his vest. "It's about time someone put an end to this twavesty."

The baby game cop nodded, blushed, then continued: "Since we do not yet know who killed the other woodcock, the ones we found in the freezer, it's my duty under the law to confiscate all firearms on the premises."

After a long stunned silence, the room erupted in an outraged chorus.

"He can't take our guns, can he?" someone yelled.

"Oh yes I can," Ned said. He held up a copy of the Wisconsin game regulations. "Not only your guns, but your cars and trucks as well. Anyone who is aware of a state game violation and does not immediately report it to an enforcement officer is considered equally guilty, until proved innocent."

"We had nothing to do with this bird hunting!" screamed the Spudnuts. "We're big game hunters!"

"Woodcock can be killed by rifles as well as shotguns," Ned said. "Since the birds in the freezer have been decapitated, we don't know if some sniper among you didn't shoot their heads off."

"Those are European woodcock," hollered Carlo Sears, "imported birds! Exotics! The statutes you cite don't apply!"

Dorsey Diffendaffer, fumbling for his cell phone, fixed Ned with a stern senatorial gaze and said, "The governor will hear about this, right now!"

Fritz Cardigan smirked. "Don't waste your valuable phone time," he said. "I'm playing golf with the governor tomorrow— it's our usual date—and I'll relay your protest to him in person."

Django Quagga: "I'm only here to ride horseback." His film crew was busy with their minicams, working the room for reaction shots.

"This will set the pharmaceutical industry back to the days of leeches and mugwort," Chester Cheatweed predicted, envisioning tomorrow's headlines in the *New York Times* Business section and the consequent collapse of C&B stock.

"That Holland and Holland double rifle of mine is worth a quarter million," Gus Kohlfresser mumbled. He was slumped at our table, pale with shock. "It belonged to the maharajah of Chingapoor. It's chased in gold and studded with emeralds."

Cora folded her napkin. "Mr. Sears is right," she said to me sotto voce. "Those birds are European woodcock, *Scolopax rusticola*, so they don't fall under any U.S. or state laws. They haven't been drawn or plucked yet. They're in the cooling room with the others we shot this afternoon. I'm going to set that self-righteous little twerp right. Once he sees the difference he'll have to drop these absurd charges. Why don't you fellows slip out through the kitchen and go back to the bungalow? I'll meet you there in a while." She turned to her daughter the scientist. "Come along, Molly. I'm going to need your help."

Ben ripped off his tie and threw the monogrammed blazer in a corner. "Goddamit, Hairball, I had it all set to shack up with Wanda tonight," he said. "Nothing works for me anymore." He started repacking his duffel. "I told you we should never have left the river. I don't know about you, but I'm heading back to the water as soon as I can. Fuck this mickey mouse bullshit!"

"Don't you think we should wait to hear what Cora has to say? Otherwise there'll be a posse after us come morning."

"We can be halfway to Gitche Gumee by then."

"And then what do we do? Listen, Fritz Cardigan is behind all this. He's got Baby Ned in his pocket. He wants to drive Cora out of business and lock up this whole river system for his own private playground. But maybe we can turn the tables on him."

"How do you mean?"

"He must have had all those big brook trout netted out of the spring holes, maybe sold them on the black market, then planted the bull newt up at the headwaters to cover his ass so he could gain control of that property. Now if he bankrupts Cora and buys her out, he's got most of the river clear down to the estuary. Maybe he still has a stock of bull newts somewhere on his estate downriver, or files to show where he got them. If we can prove that, he'll be in deep shit. What I'd like to do is infiltrate his place tonight and check it out. If we can't find anything, we'll just continue downriver as fast as we can and split for the Canadian line. From there we can go anywhere, Tahiti to Timbucktoo—my treat. I've got money to burn. What say?"

"Can we take the girls with us?"

"If they're game, sure."

"Let's do it. Anything to get out of this place."

Cora and Wanda came in a few minutes later. Baby Ned had refused to take Molly's professional word for it that the woodcock in question were of a different, "exotic" species. After all, he said, Molly was Cora's daughter as well as a state biologist—clear conflict of interest. He would send the birds to the state's crime lab in Madison for DNA tests, which could take weeks. Meanwhile, his arrest and confiscation order stood.

"The little rat turd," Cora said. "I'd like to do a DNA test on him—say, on a core from his measly, weaselly heart!"

We put the proposition to them. The raid on Cardigan's castle. They were more than willing. They'd round up Molly and bring her along. She'd be an unimpeachable witness before a fair-minded tribunal if we found what we were looking for.

"Get out of those party dresses," Ben told them. "Wear pants and boots, something dark."

When the women slipped out the back door of the bungalow, Ben smiled. His eyes were bright—at the prospect of action?

"Not really," he admitted. "I've just got to blow this popstand. I haven't wanted out of a place this bad since Hagaru."

"Where's that?" I asked.

He stared at me and shook his head.

"You don't want to know."

THE SOLID-GOLD CADILLAC

Wᵉ walked down to the river. The moon was just sinking behind the spruce spires to the west. Jake, delighted to be out of the bungalow, sniffed, cocked a leg, pissed. Did *I* have to drain the weasel as well?

No. I'd been taking my Micturatrol religiously.

Tony Mezzoni was with us. "Cardigan and his guys are still in the dining room," he said, "celebrating their triumph, I guess. That snotnose game cop's making the rounds, collecting hardware from the customers. He told me to turn yours over to him, but don't you guys worry. I gave him a couple of Ariettas. We keep 'em on tap for the johns without guns."

Mezzoni's men had dropped a tree across the only road leading out of Shikaree. That would further delay Cardigan's return to his estate.

Our canoe was already in the water. One of Tony's guys had loaded the gear. An Avon raft was pulled up on the beach. Weapons glinted in the starlight. Tony handed Ben a BAR—"You're good with it, I'm told"—and me a wicked-looking little machine pistol. "A Bushmaster," he said, "5.56mm. Just in case you need it."

"Let's hold the gunplay to a minimum this time," Cora said. "Shoot only if you have to, and then please be sure to fire high, just enough to keep their heads down. I don't want any dead men on my conscience."

We looked at her.

"Whatever you say, dear," I said. She turned away. I winked at Ben and Tony.

"He's got guards on watch—twenty-four/seven," Tony told us. "Surveillance cameras everywhere. Sound sensors. I've scouted the place, though, and I know how to deactivate them. There's also guys that walk the perimeter. They have to check in every half hour. We can deactivate them too—I'm bringing a couple of my boys. But time is going to be tight."

"Were you by any chance a Marine?" Ben asked.

"Yeah. Fifth of the First. Vietnam and Grenada. You?"

"Same outfit, but the Seventh BN. Korea."

"Frozen Chosin?"

Ben nodded.

"Oh shit," Tony said. He nodded his head. "Right, then. We'll take the ladies and lead the way in the Avon. Let's saddle up and move out."

On the way downriver in the canoe Ben told me that on the MLR in Korea, after the breakout from Chosin and his stay in the Yokosuka Naval Hospital for frostbite, the Marines had conducted nightly forays into the Chinese positions. There were four different kinds of incursions, each with a separate mission and code name. A four-man body-snatching probe, aimed at retrieving either Chinese or Marine dead, was called a "Rolls Royce." A combat patrol, usually squad strength but sometimes numbering thirty men or more armed with satchel charges and bangalore torpedoes, was a "Diesel." An ambush party was a "Mercury," and a recon patrol a "Cadillac."

"This little mission of ours is a Cadillac," Ben said. "We've got to keep dead quiet, move slow, and think ahead. So I've been thinking."

"Yeah?"

"Tony says there's a big pond behind Cardigan's place. One night when he was in there having one of his routine look-sees—Cora's orders, Know Your Enemy—he noticed some long dark things swimming around on the bottom. He thought maybe they were sharks or muskies, but they could be our bull newts."

It made sense.

Or at least it was worth the gamble.

I said, "Maybe I'll rig up that 9-foot 8-weight."

"Not a bad idea. If you can get one of them to take, we'll have the proof we need."

I pondered a minute. What fly should I use?

These salamanders were piscivorous—the old C.K., of course!

"Did you bring along the Cannibal-Killer?"

"Damn straight I did."

"Hand it over."

He fumbled in the duffel and tossed his flybox up to me, where I knelt paddling bow as usual. "The streamers are on the bottom in those long compartments."

There it was. I held it up in the last of the moonlight. White and red marabou saddle hackles for the wings, a touch of green peacock herl, black chenille body with silver ribbing, and an orange-dyed hank of bucktail for a beard—all tied on a needlesharp longshank 3/0 hook. I hooked it solidly in my hat brim. We were locked and loaded.

After clearing Cora's lower guard post, Tony shut down the outboard on the Avon and we paddled the rest of the way downstream, another ten minutes. The current was strong and fast but there was no whitewater. Then Tony flashed a hand signal and pulled in to the east bank. It was dark as a bat's armpit by now but once we'd pulled the boats up into the woods my eyes adjusted to the gloom and I saw a faint, narrow trail leading inland. Ben told Jake to stay and guard the canoe. The dog eyed the guns with a melancholy look, sighed once, then obeyed.

Mezzoni led the way. Ben was right behind him, then me with the rod case and the Bushmaster, the girls on my heels. Molly Bellefont, still woozy on her pins and kind of pale even in that dim light, wore a camera around her neck. Two of Tony's young toughs brought up the rear. Their faces were smeared with matte black camouflage paint. They carried matte black Uzis to match. You've got to be properly accessorized for a quick criminal action. This was starting to feel like a war movie. A commando raid. I hadn't had that sensation since I was a kid playing war.

Then I placed it. Of course . . . the escape from Doc and Curly's cellar.

Only this time we're breaking in, not out.

We came to the edge of a clearing. Cardigan's mansion loomed in the near distance. It was a tall stone structure, rather Gothic, with gabled towers rearing at either end. Lights gleamed from some of the casement windows downstairs but the rest were dark. There were stables out back, and what looked like a carriage house.

Tony motioned with his hand—lie down.

He crawled out through the brush and looked around. His eyes froze to the right and his head sunk slowly into the weeds. We heard footsteps, someone yawning, and a figure appeared. The guy was taking his time. The sweet smell of marijuana drifted with him. He had a headset on and I could hear the faint beat of taco rock on the still midnight air. A stubby little machine pistol dangled on a sling from his shoulder.

Tony signaled one of his boys to crawl forward. The kid waited until the guard was past, then moved like a nighthawk. Something thudded. The kid pulled a cell phone from the night guard's pocket. Tony, right behind him, threw the machine pistol into the woods.

"Wait till they call you from the house," he whispered. He glanced at his watch. "That'll be in about ten minutes. Then say 'Nada'—like N-A-D-A—and make fuckin' sure to mumble it."

The kid looked up at him, trembling.

Mezzoni caught the reaction. Nerves. He smiled. He laid a hand on the kid's shoulder. "But what the fuck, Aldo? You know the drill."

He turned to us. "What's next?"

"You mentioned a pond behind the house," Ben said. "We want to go fishing."

Tony stared at him for a moment, disbelieving. Then he shrugged. "Okay, yeah . . . Korea," he said. He pointed the way. Then he looked toward the house.

"I gotta make sure those guys in there stay busy. See ya in a few minutes."

Bending low, Tony ran through the shadows toward the back of the house, headed for a junction box located between the first floor windows. Bent on deactivation no doubt.

I jointed the rod and tied on the Cannibal-Killer, cinched it in the keeper ring. We ran toward the pond with Cora, Wanda, and Molly right behind us. Molly's camera clinked against the buttons of her coat. Ben turned and told her to hold the damn thing still. Beyond the pond I could see an airstrip with a Lear parked and tied down. There was a helipad too, with a sand-colored Huey Cobra squatting on it. The decal on the hull read "Cardigan Enterprises."

The pond was dead calm. No frogs, no rises. Not even the ripple of moving fish cruising deep. Did bull newts generate wakes? I looked into the depths. No shadows moved across the bottom. I could see the dim shapes of rocks down there, big pale glaciated slabs. Tony must have been here when the moon was out. With the others crouched low behind me, safely to my left, I knelt on both knees and stripped out line, gauging the distance. The pond was about a hundred feet across. I worked out flyline with short high backcasts, low sweeping throws to the front— time after all was of the essence. The fly was a bit too heavy for my 8-weight Trident salmon rod and the C.K. had a tendency to lag on the foreward cast. I beefed up my strokes. Quick into a double haul . . . graphite works wonders . . . and shot the C.K. across the surface. It plopped down ten feet from the far bank.

Ben crawled up and whispered, "Take your time, Hairball. Let it sink . . ."

"Yeah, I know."

The first retrieve drew nothing. Not even weeds.

"You're not deep enough," Ben said. "Let it tick the bottom."

I threw ten yards to the left and let the fly sink until I felt it touch muck, then twitched the rod tip high and started stripping. Two pulls, then a stop, then three faster strips. I let it fall again, and picked up with a series of spastic, stuttering twitches. Stops, starts, stutters, adding a semblance of life and motion to the marabou hackles, all the way in.

Nothing.

Four more throws.

Nichts.

Zilch.

Niente.

Zip.

"That's six," Ben said.

I handed him the rod. He rolled the line, picked it up smoothly, and reached the far side of the pond after only one backcast. He stripped slow, very slow, hand-twisting the line, crawling the fly up and over the rocks. Twice it hung, and when I saw the rod tip bow, I thought he might have had a touch, but he threw some slack into the leader and twitched it clear.

On his third cast, the line stopped halfway back and the rod bowed again, throbbing this time. "Gotcha!"

But it was too small, no bull newt. When Ben stripped it in, it proved to be—of all things!—an outsized goldfish. About fourteen inches of long-finned, decorative carp.

"Well, fuck me," he said. "I thought these things dined only on glass shrimp and fish flakes."

"Carp will eat almost anything," Molly whispered. "But the important thing to realize here is that both *Andrias davidianus* and *A. japonicus* feed on goldfish. Maybe Mr. Cardigan stocks the pond with goldfish to feed his pets."

I looked at Ben. "Want to try live bait?"

"I haven't fished bait since I was ten," he said, "and I'm not about to start again now."

"Then let me try. I'm not fastidious."

"Three more casts and it's all yours," he said.

Maybe it was the turmoil raised by the carp, maybe it was emanations from its lateral line, maybe it was the sweet taste of blood in the water—on his next cast Ben hooked something solid. Something big, and alive. The drag screamed, the leader hissed through the water. Like the first run of a huge northern pike. Whatever it was thrashed to the surface and rolled. In the dim starlight I saw mottled warty skin. And as it rolled again, short, stubby legs.

"That's him," I said.

"Molly, get your camera ready."

"Fuckin' reel makes too much noise," Ben said, glancing toward Cardigan's house.

"Well, subdue him then," I told him. "That's a Mirage fluorocarbon tarpon leader, abrasion resistant and good for anything up to eighty pounds."

He tried. For ten minutes he tried.

"I can't move him."

"Pump and reel."

"I'm trying. Maybe he's under a rock."

"Tap on the butt of the rod."

"I tried that."

"Try it again."

He tapped. Nothing doing.

"Did you see him when he was on top?" I asked Molly.

"Yes."

"Did you see legs?"

"Indeed I did."

"Is it *Andrias*?"

She hesitated, a true scientist. "I can't say for sure until we have him up close."

"All right," I said. "I'll have to go down there and fetch him out for you."

"But Doctor Taggart . . ."

I stripped to my skivvy shorts and waded into the pond. Ben smirked at the scene—a skinny, wrinkled, potbellied old man in his undies. Well, fuck dignity. Somebody had to flush the monster from his lair. The water was slimy but warmer than the air. I swam out to where Ben's line disappeared into the water. Then took some deep breaths and dove, following it down into darkness.

Night diving without a light and a face mask is unnerving under the best of circumstances. I felt my way down the line to a huge granite slab. Clouds of marl were settling around it. The line bent under the ledge with about six inches of shock tippet just showing. I pulled on it and something at the far end shook its head. I peered under the ledge but saw only murk.

I had maybe a minute of air left in my lungs. Okay—now or never. Placing my feet against the side of the slab, I grabbed the shock tippet with both hands and heaved. A moment's hesitation, and then the bull newt came boiling out straight at my face, jaws snapping. I dodged aside. Warts scraped the hide from my forearms and left side. My hand was wrapped in the shock tippet. He shot for the surface with me trailing behind him, flapping like the tail of some godawful Chinese kite. Why hadn't I thought to borrow Ben's K-Bar?

I hit the surface and gulped air.

But then the line slackened for an instant, the stiff Mirage fluorocarbon unbent, and the bull newt barreled straight back in my direction. I ducked to the side again, he brushed past me, and the leader unwrapped itself from my mangled paw. I sprinted for the shore. Cora reached down and helped me from the water. "Are you hurt?" she asked.

"Nothing a hand transplant won't cure," I told her.

Other creatures were roiling the surface now, attracted no doubt by the struggle. Were they all bull newts? It looked that way from the warts. Ben was cranking hard, pumping and reeling. He was gaining line. The bull newt's struggles grew weaker, he rolled again like a big lake trout, trying to wrap the line around his body and with his sheer weight break it.

"Get the gaff, Hairball."

"What gaff?"

"Oh fuck, I didn't bring it."

"Where's your trusty K-Bar?"

"On my left ankle," he said, "in the sheath. What are you going to do?"

"Remember the old Tarzan movies, Johnny Weissmuller stabbing crocodiles to death with the blade of his father?"

"Too much Hollywood," he said. "Maybe that's why you stayed in California, to break into the movies."

I waded back into the pond, K-Bar in hand. "Get ready," I told Molly. "I hope your flash works."

"Oops! I forgot to bring it from the lodge."

Oh hell, I'd have to kill it. Which I did, with one surgically perfect stroke to the base of the bull newt's skull. It shuddered and died. You don't slice eyeballs for a living without learning something about precision.

Just as I hauled it up on the bank, though, a door opened at the back of Cardigan's castle. Light flooded the backyard. An armed figure stared for a moment and then started shooting—single, hurried pistol shots that threw up dirt ten yards short of us.

A machine pistol ripped nearby. The Bushmaster. It was Cora, who had picked it up and was firing back—but high. I heard her 5.56mm bullets spanging off the stonework. Chips flew everywhere. A second-story window blew in. "Run for it, guys," she yelled. "I'll cover ya."

I slung the dead bull newt over my shoulder like a bag of birdfeed—no, a sack of gold—and hightailed it for the woods. The others were hard at my heels. Tony and his men were waiting.

Jake growled low in his throat as we neared the canoe. Ben spoke to him, "Good boy," and the dog relaxed. All was well. But he'd heard the gunfire and seemed disappointed that all we brought back was an outsized skink.

Tony and his boys had lingered on the trail to watch for pursuit.

"Does anyone have a flashlight?" Molly asked. "I've got to get some pictures before this animal starts drying out. The few frames I snapped when that searchlight came on weren't close to definitive."

Ben fetched the underwater spotlight from the canoe. Molly set to work.

"It's *Andrias*, isn't it?" I asked.

"Nothing else," she said. Her motor drive clattered. "And judging by its size, it's the Chinese species—*davidianus*."

"Hurray," Ben said beside me. His tone was flat. "Now can we bid you ladies adieu and shove off downriver?"

"What?" Cora said. "You're leaving?"

Wanda clutched at Ben's arm, crest-fallen.

"Well," I said, "we made a vow to ourselves—and to Jake—that we'd reach Gitche Gumee before the snow flies. We're old guys, all of us. If we go back with you now to Shikaree, we may never get away. There are trout and salmon to catch, game birds still to fly."

"*Wild* birds," Ben added.

"But who knows?" I said. "When we've fulfilled our quest, found our grail or whatever you want to call it, we may be back."

Tony appeared. "They're coming," he said. "Six of 'em with heavy artillery. We better be taking off, ma'am."

"Say goodbye to Florinda for us," Ben said. "Tell her the roast beast was terrific."

Molly wrapped up her photo op. Tony Mezzoni slung the carcass of the bull newt into the Avon. It thumped limp on the floorboards. They boarded the raft and shoved away from the shore. The 40-horse Johnson lit off on the first pull.

By that time Ben and I were already deep into the main current, hellbent for Gitche Gumee.

TRÈS RICHES HEURES

J ust below Cardigan's castle we hit a run of whitewater, but
when we'd cleared it, the river broadened and ran strong
and fast into the starbright north. Ben remembered this
long sweet stretch. No dangerous water ahead until dawn. We
were already below the spot where Stony Creek drained
Twodoggone Lake into the Firesteel, and we agreed that it
would be unwise in these circumstances to detour back up there.
That muskie would just have to wait. Maybe forever.

I reached for the horn and blew us some getaway music . . .

"Keep playing as long as you like," Ben said. "With this
kind of a current all I have to do is steer."

What the hell, I thought, we weren't tied to any schedule.
We'd left behind the world of nine to five, along with Cora and
Wanda. The only hours that concerned us now were dawn,
high noon, and sunset. *Prime*, *nones*, and *vespers*, to put it in
canonical terms. In the God-fearing world of long ago, prayers
were chanted to mark these hours. We'd observe them in our
own neo-pagan fashion— psalms of fin and feather, the sacred
rites of trout fly and birdshot.

There were ducks on the water, mallards, mergansers, a
few early teal, but their season wouldn't open for a week. Geese
were legal, though, and we saw a few rafts of Canadas sculling
for cover along the brushy shore. Jake perked his ears at their
alarm calls. "Later, boy," Ben assured him. "Come daylight."

An owl swooped out of the darkness to check on us, then
hooted once and swept off on silent wings. I picked up on that
note and blew a long random series of interlocked chords that
grew into a number I thought of as "Night Bird Boogie."

We ran past Crusoe's Island in the dark, no sign of the Airstream or that '49 Hudson. Maybe Peter Martin and his druggie pals had gotten off the island, or maybe their bones were mouldering in the leaf duff of half a century, along with the frames of their car and trailer. Not a bad life they'd drifted into, though, cruising America for kicks. The four bees: boo, bennies, bourbon, and bebop. Work only when you need money for gas, or better yet panhandle, then move on down the road to a fresh new scene of scruff and nonsense. Wandering mendicants. Try anything once. What were they seeking? Enlightenment, I guess. Whatever that means. The trouble was they hadn't a clue to how the world really works. Or anything in it for that matter. They couldn't even build a campfire.

We passed Marlow's Leap—a footbridge now crossed the gorge here. A user-friendly place these days. Daylight was coming on. By full dawn we were nearing Chemango, the spot where we'd saved the Stoat entourage with our daring incendiary raid on the old Mobilgas station. Nothing remained of the town, not even the dock. We pulled over to the bank and tied off to a snag. "Let's take the shotguns," Ben said. He pointed to a stand of aspens where the old general store once stood. "Jake needs a workout before breakfast and I'll bet we find woodcock in there—real ones, in touch with the soil, not those phony European birds with their fake standards and perverted values."

As we skirted the alder brake I could hear the throaty rumble of Heartbreak Rapids just downstream. Jake was raring to go. Ben told him to sit and clipped a sheep bell to his collar, then calmed him down with dog talk. "Get around behind 'em boy and flush 'em out to the guns," he said. "And go easy—walk soft. There may be broken glass in there." The dog rolled his eyes back up to Ben's as if to say, "You think I'd forget?"

The big Lab sinuated his way into the alders, treading lightly, head high to catch the first whiff of woodcock musk on the light dawn breeze. I looked down. The ground was blotched white with woodcock "chalk."

"Get ready," Ben said. "He's birdy as hell."

I looked into the thicket and saw Jake's tail upright as the plume on a knight's helmet. The ruff was up all along his spine. He circled to his left, then came back in toward us and froze.

"Put 'em up, boy."

Two woodcock tweetled out from under his nose, straight toward us.

"Take 'em going away," Ben said.

We spun around as the birds passed over our heads and dodged out into the open, their wings impossibly long for the size of their stubby russet bodies.

We fired.

They fell.

"Okay, Jake, fetch dead."

When he'd brought them to hand, Ben held one by a wing and spread its feathers in the dawn light. One of the primaries was half an inch longer than the others. "A male," he said. "And yours is a hen by the size of her."

Jake sat waiting for orders.

"With all this chalk underfoot there's bound to be more birds in there," I said.

Ben looked at me. "But they're so easy, Harry. Too easy. Goofy little bastards. And besides I've come to love them for themselves, more than I love to shoot them."

"Two woodcock make mighty thin soup," I said.

He broke his gun and hooked it over his forearm. "I've got nothing against you shooting. The limit is three a day. But lately I've counted one enough. There's alway tomorrow."

Not necessarily, I thought.

Ben perched himself on a deadfall and lit a cigar, blowing lop-sided smoke rings while Jake and I hunted the covert. In the old days it was fun pushing through alders like Superman, batting them down with a forearm, slogging through the black muck, waiting for the next flush. Now it was damned hard work. I looked back at Ben. An old man in a dry season. Well, that description fit both of us. When I came back with a pair of birds in hand, he smiled.

"Nice shoooting," he said. "It's fun to see someone else fold 'em, and even better to watch the dog work from a distance. He's good, isn't he? Better even than Gayelord in a way."

"Steadier. More biddable. He's a very savvy dog."

"He should be. He's eleven years old, older than us in dog years. But he remembers what he's learned. Hell, Hairball, I'm no savvier now than I was back then, in Gayelord's day. Look how I fucked up my life." He blew a smoke ring and stared off after it, toward the river. "Lorraine."

"Maybe something happened along the way," I said.

"You mean Korea?"

"Yeah, you know—shell shock, combat fatigue, post-traumatic stress syndrome, that kind of thing."

He frowned. "Marines don't get that kind of stuff. If they're prone to it, they never make it through boot camp."

"Still, it might help you to talk about it."

"You're an eye doctor, not a shrink," he said.

He stood up and went back to the canoe, hauled out a cooler. Then he set to work building a fire ring. "Get some firewood for us, hey? My stomach's yowling for sustenance and we've still got Heartbreak to face before we get into the steelhead water."

Florinda had loaded the cooler with eggs, bacon, butter, home-baked sourdough bread, and a waxed carton of heavy cream to go with our coffee. The All-American thrombosis. Well, we've come this far at least.

Better to die on a full belly than an empty one.

Heartbreak Rapids lived up to its name, but with unintended irony. There'd been no rain for close to a month and the water was bony. Ribs of granite reared around every corner, interspersed now and then with a grinning, glacier-scrubbed skull—new fields of hazard opening up at each swing of the Mad River's bow. We worked our minds and arms numb finding dodges to avoid them, scraping off lots of Kevlar in the process. In many places we had to get out and drag the canoe, waist and armpit deep in rushing water. Water travel had never been this tough in the old days, but then the human memory has splendid shock absorbers. It smooths out the ruts and frost heaves of the past so that, a year later, all you remember is the scenery. When we finally reached the bottom of the run, we were dead beat.

"We're five miles from Gitche Gumee as the crow flies," Ben said. "Maybe ten or twelve as the river twists and turns. And we've got a week until ducks are legal. Lots of time on our hands."

I studied the woods on both banks. It all looked like prime grouse and woodcock cover—popple, larch, alder, spruce. No posted signs.

"What say we find a good spot to make camp and just explore this country? Fish or hunt whenever and whichever the mood that strikes us, or just lie around and relax."

"Sounds good to me," he said. "This weather can't hold much longer and we could use a spate of rain to bring the salmon and steelhead into the estuary. Meanwhile, there's plenty of brown trout to keep us busy."

Half a mile downriver we spotted a clearing on the west bank, backed by an endless covert of quaking aspen. After we'd pitched the tent and collected an ample supply of firewood, we took a well-earned snooze. We'd been on the go for twenty-four hours straight, pretty good for a couple of geezers.

When I opened my eyes, the sun was clocking fast toward the western horizon. Ben was out in the river, working the far shore in the low sloping sunlight. His flyline traced long looping words against a yellow-green vellum of spruce and popple. I couldn't quite read them, but they had the grace of those Gothic scripts you see in medieval psalters. Illuminated manuscripts.

Kate had a thing for miniatures. We'd traveled to Italy, Belgium, France, and even New York City to see them. *The Book of Hours* of Catherine of Cleves. The *Très Riches Heures* of Jean, Duc de Berry. The works of the Franco-Flemish Limbourg brothers, Pol, Jan, and Herman.

And Pieter Brueghel the Elder, Kate's favorite, whose art drew from the Limbourgs' only a century later. She loved Brueghel's squat, thick-legged, red-cheeked peasants, the physicality of their lives, fishing boats foundering in the windspiked harbors, hunters in the snow returning with their quarry through gabled hamlets where magpies soar past welcoming pillars of woodsmoke. The Inn of the Stag.

"This is the real world," she'd say. "Those were *real* lives. You can almost anticipate the evening ahead, the songs and prayers and laughter, and smell the wild boar turning on a spit."

"Real lives," I snorted, but only once. "The Middle Ages, like the people who lived then, were short, brutal, and ugly."

She looked at me with pity.

Of course, I thought, all lives are that way, even today. Nobody lives forever, though some may hope so. As my well-traveled daughter once said, "Europeans accept the inevitability of death. Americans think it's an option." Ah yes, death—it's patently undemocratic. But why does time have to accelerate with age? Why, when I was a kid, did the school year seem to last a decade, while I crept toward adulthood like a snail across a bathroom floor? Now you blink and . . . you're old.

Dear God, I prayed now, here on the bank of the Firesteel. Can't you put on the brakes, at least for this one last week? *Please???*

He must have heard me. The days that followed were full of slow riches. The weather held clear, hot during high daylight, the grass furred with hoarfrost at dawn. In the early mornings while the dew was drying we fished the river, upstream and down for miles, casting streamers to cruising browns. They were big fish just in from the lake and charged with the angry hormones of their spawning season, quick to strike at anything that dared to drift past them.

During the afternoons we pounded the endless covert for ruffed grouse. It was a vast stretch of aspen that had been cut progressively for pulp over the past half century or more, so that every stage of growth was represented. Thick stands of doghair popple to provide grouse with safe cover in which to raise their broods. Long reaches of half-grown trees so close to one another that predatory goshawks could not interrupt grouse mating rituals. And tall islands of fully mature aspens with their craggy bark, branches drooping with the burden of catkins on which these birds relied for sustenance. Mixed in with the aspens were stands of hardhack and occasional volunteer apple trees. Partridges picked the seeds from the rotting windfallen fruit. It was ruffed grouse heaven. We hunted it hard, Jake sometimes flushing twenty birds in an afternoon. We'd pause every hour or so to let the dog cool off. Maybe eat an apple from one of the old-time trees or drink from an icy spring. Our legs grew strong, our eyes quick, and we returned to camp each evening full of hunger and that wonderful sense of lassitude that results from a day spent on nothing but what pleased us most. At night we ate what we'd killed, never a whole lot, and played music to the starlit river.

On our forays into the woods we found old cellar holes, family graveyards, an Indian mound, an ancient steam tractor from Paul Bunyan days flaking its hull into red dust, a nest built by golden eagles that contained the sunbleached skull of a coyote. *Change and decay in all around I see*. Deer bounced away from us but Jake never chased them. Once we encountered a bull moose, his neck beginning to thicken with the oncoming urges of rut, but he did not see us and we slipped away without incident. We found a giant white pine log full of carpenter ants. The blowdown had been ripped apart by a bear. Ants scurried around, trying to repair the damage to no avail. At the edge of a clearing one late afternoon we spotted a red fox stalking mice in the tall grass. Ben had Jake sit, and we watched for half an hour. The fox leaped high, tail plumed and black tipped, forepaws spread like a cat's, and never missed. He glowed in the sunset light. Then he caught our scent and *poof* . . . he was gone.

On the seventh morning we woke to the sound of rain on the roof. Drops splatted hissing on the coals of the fire. Ben peered outside. "At last," he said. "It's here for a while, and about time. This'll bring the big fish in from the lake."

"Ducks too."

"According to the regs you can't start shooting at migratory fowl until noon on opening day. That's not a duck hunt to me. Let's skip it today, let 'em move in and get used to the area. Then hit 'em tomorrow at the crack of dawn."

The rain was pelting down now, the Firesteel rising by the minute. The wind picked up from the northwest, the temperature dropped, and we rigged a reflector for the fire with a sheet of corrugated iron Ben dragged up from the brush near the riverbank. We spent the day sorting through flies and shell boxes.

Toward evening I said, "How's about some *chai*?"

"Sure."

We boiled water and steeped a pot of Lapsang Souchong. Florinda's sourdough had gone stiff and stale but we toasted a few thick slabs of it over the fire. Ben spread the toast with the last of our butter and honey.

"Just like Winnie the Pooh," I said.

Ben looked at me, empty-eyed, then shifted his gaze. Glum weather always took him this way. Nowadays they call it Seasonal Affective Disorder. SAD. They've got a new acronym for every quirk or foible of the human condition nowadays, as if by merely renaming our woes they can cure them. Fat chance . . .

Or maybe it was the tea, with its Chinese name, had turned Ben's memories back to Korea. He stared at the racing river for a long while, then squared his shoulders.

"You want to hear about Chosin?" he asked.

"If you're ready."

As we ate and drank our tea, Ben told me about Chosin.

The teapot was down to cold dregs by the time he'd finished. We fed Jake a few leftover crusts of toast. Ben stared off into the rain.

"That tiger was really something," he said.

"Whatever happened to Sergeant Stingley?"

"I heard he died in Vietnam, during the siege of Hué in '68. It was all house-to-house fighting, not his style." He clammed up then, busied himself with a Rey del Mundo, the last of them. He lit up and took a deep toke. Then he coughed for a minute or two.

"Florinda packed a quart of bourbon in her care package," I said. "I think you could use a toddy about now."

He thought for a moment. "Naw. I'm through with that poison. Funny, just being out on the river again seems to have taken away my taste for it. Maybe I'll stay here forever."

We hit the rack early. Tomorrow promised action.

My dreams that night were of Gitche Gumee. The Shining Big Sea Water. But this was an inland sea gone weird and tropical. The Apostle Islands had become the Isles of the Blest. Coral atolls came and went over the horizon, waving the fronds of their coco palms to the beat of southeast trades. I was cruising this sea in a *pahi*, one of those elegant double-hulled sailing canoes carved from pandanus logs in which the ancient Polynesians made their stupendous voyages of discovery. Whales broached and blew and sang in the distance and I sat crosslegged on the deck between the hulls, playing my horn. I was riffing changes around the songs of the whales. We were approaching a high island with a lopsided volcanic cone rising above verdant slopes that were cut with quick rushing streams. The sound of distant waterfalls came to us over the billows. Shoals of wahoo and tuna quickened the surface, and dolphins sported alongside. The volcano puffed smoke rings that wafted out to us across the water. The smoke smelled like Ben's Rey del Mundos. Then as we neared the high island, I saw that the volcano *was* Ben, with a fat cigar clenched in his teeth. He was grinning at me and his arms were draped around the shoulders of two lava maidens. Kate and Lorraine.

We had to run the gap in the reef to reach Ben's island. The current raced through coralline jaws, twisting, eddying, surging, and I could see fangs of bright coral waiting to rip our canoe. Across the lagoon a pair of young dogs frisked on the beach, awaiting our arrival . . .

CODA

It was still raining at 4 A.M. when Ben woke Harry. The rain was a steady thrum with the taste of sleet in it. Full dark, and a north wind rattling the tent walls. He handed Harry a cup of hot tea, black and bitter as the weather. Two hours until sunrise. "There's that little inlet downstream aways," he said. "Good spot to set out the blocks. I heard ducks moving awhile back, high on the wind, a big flock of 'em."

"What flavor?"

He shook his head. "Too dark to see, but from their talk I'd swear they were bluebills."

"Scaup? But it's way too early for them, isn't it?"

"Yeah, they usually don't show till November, when there's skim ice on the water. But with this freaky weather we've been having lately, who knows?"

"Global warming," Harry said. "It's fucked everything, even the seasons."

They ate another thrombotic breakfast—fried eggs, fatty bacon, toast slathered with butter and hunks of rattrap cheese to top it off, delicious—then broke camp, loaded the canoe, and set off downriver. Jake could hear the ducks pass overhead. Silk slashed by a knifing wind. He looked up into the rain and shivered. He whined and mumbled to himself. Waiting.

Short of the cove they pulled ashore. Ben tied the canoe to an ice-sheathed popple trunk and they pulled out the bag of decoys. They waded down the bank to the inlet, skidding on shallow rocks. The water was cold through their waders. A small knot of ducks held against the northwest bank, heads tucked snug beneath the random wind. Redheads or canvas-backs by the way they swam, blocky and low slung, tails down in the water. It was still too dark to distinguish color.

"We'll have to move them out of here," Ben whispered. "That's where I want to put the spread." He sent Jake around the inlet with instructions to spook the ducks. When they'd flown, the men moved. They waded out into the lee and placed the decoys, unwinding anchor lines stiff with frozen sleet. "Leave a nice-sized hole in the middle of the spread to draw new arrivals," Ben said.

"Yeah, Benjamin, this isn't the first time I've ever been duck hunting."

"Sorry, Doc."

Back on the bank they cobbled together a makeshift blind of juniper branches. Ben hacked them with his K-Bar and Harry stuck their butts in the mud, interwove the tough, soft-needled branches. Then they sat behind their dark green wall and shivered, waiting for first light. From time to time, eyes cocked skyward under the brim of his cap, Ben gave a come-hither purr on his call, alternating it with a low throaty whistle or a loud, impatient *scaup! scaup! scaup!*

The sky overhead was shading from black to charcoal gray and then they could see streamers of low black ragged cloud wavering across it from the northwest. Fine weather for ducks. Shifting clots of them blew through, yammering at each other, too high and determined just yet to respond to the call's seductions. Then a band of pale light appeared above the eastern horizon.

They crouched lower in the blind. Ben called, two loud blats. Jake shuddered. Harry put his hand on the nape of the dog's neck and felt its warmth melt the sleet. "Easy boy." Ben's upturned eyes were fixed on something now, they circled, the call purred again, soft and happy. He nodded his head. They were coming. Harry kept his head down and listened, heard a rip overhead, the soft quick flap of slowing wings. The birds circled once, twice, then on the instant they were committed.

"Take 'em."

The old men stood and there they were, a dozen bluebills cupped and dropping toward the water, black chests and glossy dark green heads, white breasts and wings, scrubbing off speed, tilting from side to side, webbed feet the color of cold slate sprawled out before them like dive brakes. A perfect toll.

They fired and fired again.

Four birds hit the water.

Ben threw a hand signal. "Fetch dead, boy."

Jake was over the top of the blind and gone in a long, low racing dive, murmuring low in his chest. He'd marked the birds as they fell and surged toward them, ignoring the decoys.

The men broke their guns and pocketed the hot, still smoking hulls.

"Six ducks each is the limit" Ben said. "But I call this a day."

Harry agreed. "We can't eat more than two apiece."

By the time Jake had the ducks ashore they had torn down the blind, recovered the decoys, and were ready to go.

"What's next?"

Ben looked out into the mainstream, the racing whitewater. "Gitche Gumee."

A fast hard run with the power of the Firesteel fueling their arms and backs. Wind and rain slashed their faces. The salmon were running too, but against the current. The men could see them working along the bottom, dark bronze with the mating urge that would end in a tattered, misshapen death. Brighter fish too, bigger and stronger than the kings and cohoes—steelhead. But a madness was in the men now, the fury of the river, and they could not pause for the cerebration required: fly selection, casting angles, knots and mends and retrieves. You move when the mood is upon you. All urgencies end in death. Upstream or down.

The river sweeps left, then right. In the distance the men can see the highway bridge and beyond it the combers of Gitche Gumee whitecapped and booming as they emerge from an endless fog-bank. The canoe is moving fast on the strength of the Firesteel, closer, closer—a quarter mile to go now, two hundred yards . . .

Parked at the bridge is Ben's rust-scabbed Ford F-250. Men in camouflage slickers stand in its lee, huddled low against the rain. They carry rifles. Squatting on its skids beside the highway, Cardigan's helicopter, the color and shape of a wet sand dune. Its rotors are idling. Someone spots the canoe and points. His words are carried away by the wind. A figure emerges from the truck. Cardigan, dressed in a Barbour coat. He trots over to the chopper and climbs aboard. Little Ned reaches out from the cockpit to give him a hand up. The men with the rifles fan out, sprawl prone behind the riprap in shoot-ing positions. The Huey lifts off, tilts sideways against the wind, and whupwhups its way toward the canoe.

"You men are under arrest." Baby Ned on the bullhorn. "You are fugitives from the law. You killed game out of season. You trespassed on posted property. You murdered a helpless and valuable research animal. You discharged a firearm within 100 feet of an occupied dwelling. Throw your weapons over the side and pull in to the bank immediately. Or we will commence firing."

The Huey hovers overhead now, the downdraft from its rotors further roiling the water. Gun muzzles protrude from the side hatch. Cardigan kneels in there, haughty and tri-umphant. The chopper veers off to achieve a better firing angle.

Ben flips Fritz the finger and the guns open fire. A gust from the lake whirls fog around the chopper and tilts it off bal-ance. Harry grabs his shotgun and fires a load of goose shot at the blurring rotors. One of the blades sheers off near the rotor cap and the helicopter veers landward. The rifles from the shore pop shots at the bouncing canoe but the bullets fly wide or rico-chet off the water—they score not a single hit.

The debate is over. They've reached the twisted, rain-swollen stretch of raging rapids that nearly killed them fifty years ago.

The Haystack looms out of the fog. They can still opt for an easy way out, leave the river and surrender, or hit for the far bank, split into the woods, elude Cardigan and his thugs, and hike to the highway, hire someone in town to drive them to Canada.

But they cannot do that. Boys will be boys.

They see Gitche Gumee glimmering cold and black as steel beneath the mist. It draws them on as it always has.

Beyond the fog bank, far far away, lies Canada. Or possibly death.

One last shot of adrenaline before they go.

"Fuck it," Ben says. "Don't mean nothin'. Drive on."

Jake thumps his tail in agreement.

The paddles dig for darkness.

It never ends in comfort.